About Last
CHRISTMAS

RACHEL SCOTT MCDANIEL

To my readers who stick with me even when I jump genres. I'm grateful.
To every past, present, and future caregiver.
I see you.

CHAPTER 1

IT'S BEGINNING to look a lot like a crime scene. Well, a future one. While elfnapping is not on my itinerary for this evening, nothing about this night has gone as planned. All my hopes were pinned on surviving the chaos of the community Christmas parade, checking on Gran's light display at the adjoining park, then returning home in time to give Gran her meds and hibernate on the sofa while consuming my body weight in overpriced fudge.

I've earned every calorie.

The 207th Silver Creek Christmas parade may be a tradition brimming with holiday cheer and yada yada yada, but so far, I've taken a Tootsie Roll to the forehead (thanks to the Sunrise Senior Center residents) and heard enough creepy renditions of "Santa Baby" to haunt my waking moments (again, thanks to the Sunrise Senior Center residents). I'm a huge supporter of our local elderly, and several of Gran and Pap's friends live in the state-of-the-art facility, but whoever's grand idea it was to glow up the "Ageless Angels" float with a karaoke machine and strobe light did *not* take into consideration the rest of Silver Creek's population. Does *family-friendly environment* mean nothing anymore? To make it worse, the giant nutcracker on my "Santa's Antique Toys" float kept toppling over in the wind and almost brained the mayor as the float passed the judging station. Nearly giving the leader of our fine town a concussion did nothing for my eligibility for the Most Festive Float Award.

Now this.

I never thought an elf would provoke me to a life of crime, but here we are.

Every season, Gran sponsors a turtledove light display. She pays extra to secure the area beside the street clock where Pap had proposed over sixty years ago. This year, the reservation rate spiked an additional two hundred dollars. I didn't have the heart to tell Gran, so I forked over the extra Benjamins to make it happen. Moreover, a few weeks back, I broke a thumbnail and got my hair snagged on one of the birds' beaks while pulling the display out of storage. But instead of a pair of turtledoves with my DNA all over it gracing this snowy patch of earth … it's an elf on a surfboard. I assess the six-foot-tall light display and declare war.

The elf isn't to be blamed, per se, but its sponsor—Josie Dubois. She moved Gran's turtledoves.

I'm generally not two heartbeats away from feral mode, but this happened last year too on account of Josie hating my guts. Her loathing must be a three-for-one package because it obviously extends to Gran and Pap. A year ago, I was the bigger person and went through the proper channels to resolve the issue. Tonight though—I adjust my Mrs. Claus hat—it's on.

Josie put her display and adjacent sign advertising her tanning salon here out of spite. All because her ex-boyfriend took me on a handful of dates, and then tossed me aside like used wrapping paper. Oh, and these infractions occurred in high school. Nearly a decade ago. Josie's grudges last longer than her spray tans. So in petty revenge, she swiped my dear grandmother's spot and placed the turtledoves—I twirl in a slow circle—by the …

I see red. And it has nothing to do with the blinking Santa sleigh to my left.

Josie placed the turtledoves by the porta-john. It's a good hundred feet away, but I could recognize my grandparents' display anywhere. My fingers twitch at my sides, even as a fire builds within me hot enough to counteract the thirty-degree temp.

I've never claimed to possess main character energy. My introvert soul reads side character, at best. You know, the quirky ones in rom-coms with fun fashion sense and witty one-liners. The supporting roles never get the guy though. Such is my life. So yeah, I may not be heroine material, but at this moment, I will happily be the villain. I glare at the surfing elf, and my heart shrinks two sizes. The Greta who stole Christmas ... lights. Not exactly original, but I can roll with it. I cast furtive looks to my left and right to ensure the coast is clear. It's not. At least several hundred people are milling about, enjoying Light-Up Night.

Most days I feel invisible—today is not that day. I'm freaking dressed like Mrs. Claus. The Christmas parade always precedes the Light-Up Night ceremony. My family's antique shop makes a float every year. Translation: *I* make the float every year. I usually enjoy being crafty, but with running the store during the day and being Gran's caregiver at night (and often into the early hours of the morning), my Christmas spirit isn't just weak—it's on life support. So here I stand—in a dark green velvet creation trimmed in white fur, that I whipped up over the past week—contemplating how to effectively remove an elf carcass without attracting attention.

Determination igniting my veins, I bend low and toggle the power switch. The bright lights outlining the metal frame go dark.

Once any risk of electrocution is removed, I plant my feet on either side of the hulking display. My boots may be appropriate for ushering small children toward Santa's lap, but they're a sorry match against the frozen ground. I work the two spikes from the ground, but the last one proves to be the most challenging. With a savage grunt, I tug on the elf's torso.

Nothing.

Did Josie cement this thing to the earth's core? I roll my shoulders and tilt my head from side to side, cracking my neck as if I'm entering a WWE ring instead of wrestling an inanimate object. But my hype trick works because on my next pull, the earth releases its icy hold, and the festive imp is in my clutches.

A throat clears. "Do you—"

I swivel toward the masculine voice. My left ankle balks at the ridiculous amount of physical activity it's been subjected to and decides to collapse like a diva. I pitch to the side and ... stab a random stranger with an elf.

The man's reflexes are impressive, but even his panther-like grace can't compete with my undefeated clumsiness. I find myself on the damp ground, and the mystery man has an elf hanging from his broad chest like an appendage.

"Oh my gosh!" I stagger to my feet. "Are you hurt? Bleeding?" My criminal activity has escalated from property theft to possible man slaughter in less than five minutes. As far as PRs go, it's impressive. But twenty-to-life is not on my Christmas list. "Medic!" I yell and the guy chuckles.

I blink. "Is shock setting in?" I almost stutter on the last word because I've allowed my gaze to take in my unintended victim. His tall, dark, and handsome contrasts with my petite, ghostly, and somewhat mediocre. Should I expect anything less on a day like today? Other women have meet-cutes. Me? Meet-kills. I've hit a new low.

"I'm okay." The man's husky voice carries remnants of amusement. "It's caught on my jacket." With one smooth move, he disentangles his massive body from the stupid elf. The guy's lopsided grin matches well with the gleam in his eyes. "See? No harm done."

I'm about to exhale relief, but then gasp. The confusion in my airways results in my croaky voice. "Your coat. It's gashed." I flutter my hand at the gaping hole.

He glimpses the damage and shrugs. "No big deal." His gaze roams over my outfit, then to the abandoned light display. "Is everything okay, Mrs. Claus?"

No, I'm trying to avoid a nuero-meltdown. "It's a long story." It's actually not. But I don't want to explain myself—or my actions—to a random person, but then again, I just nearly impaled him. I guess he's entitled to an explanation. "I'm in the process of staking my ground." I offer a dramatic lift of my chin as if I'm some pioneer in a land run rather than a small-town antique store owner with seasonal run-ins with a high school nemesis with questionably orange skin.

"So you're from …" He reads the small sign I forgot to kick over. "Josie's Tan-tasy Island."

I'm paler than eggnog. "Uh … no." At his raised brow, I adopt a new strategy. "It's just a little mix-up. My gran's display is supposed to be here. On this spot." I gesture toward the prostrate elf, its head near the toe of my boot as if it's groveling. "Not that."

"So where's your gran's?"

"I think Josie placed it over there. The turtledoves." I wave in the general direction of the porta-john. Fire burns my face, but I'm unsure if it's because of my fuming anger toward Josie or because I'm avoiding discussing mobile toilets with a stranger. I should know him longer than a handful of minutes to reach this level in a relationship.

He follows my line of sight, and I swear his lips twitch. "I see."

"It wouldn't be a huge deal, except we paid to reserve this spot. This is exactly where Pap proposed to Gran. It's special to her." An unexpected blip of emotion coats my tone. "I'm bringing her here tomorrow night." If she's up to it, that is. "I'm just not too sure how many Christmases she has left. Which is why turtledove placement is my top priority."

His face visibly softens, all tease and humor gone. "Let me help you switch them."

I shouldn't take on an accomplice. Even though we've rightfully claimed this spot, I'm still unsure what I'm going to do with Josie's elf. "Thank you, but I got it." I cringe again at the hole in his coat. "Can I give you money for a new coat?" I ask casually while I inwardly freak out. Thirty dollars and a card good for ten car washes from the local Clean & Cruise are all that's in my wallet.

"That's not necessary." He offers a kind smile.

"Then would you let me mend it?" I slip a hand into one of my pockets and withdraw the tools of my trade. Some women are armed with lipsticks. I'm armed with stabby metal sticks of the sewing variety.

His head tilts to the side. "Do you always carry a needle and thread?"

I'm the first to claim I was born in the wrong era. "Wardrobe malfunctions can bring the best of us down. I'm always at the ready." My favorite hobby is restoring and wearing vintage clothing. My little quirk makes me seem seventy-five rather than twenty-five, but I make no apology. I move closer to inspect his coat. "The tear is close to the pocket seam. Easy fix." Only … I can't see well. The surrounding lights provide enough illumination that I can clearly note how the man's dark hair has a flirty curl to it beneath his black beanie. But there's not enough light to thread a needle and stitch a straight line. While this is the kind of mending I can probably do with my eyes closed, I've already revealed enough of my general incompetence, I shouldn't risk this. "We need to go where there's more light."

I tug my phone from my other pocket and check the time. "It's nearly seven. We have to hurry." I hustle as fast as my boots let me.

"Where to, exactly?" His long legs effortlessly keep pace with me.

I sigh, wishing this night to be over. "To the North Pole." I lead him to the back door of the enclosed pavilion. "Santa's on a smoke break." Ned Gilieski is our resident St. Nick. While most Santas subsist on cookies and milk, ours survives on Marlboros. "It's in his yearly contract." Santa Ned is not to be confused with the legendary Silver Creek Secret Santa, our resident philanthropist who helps local families. Only a select few know his identity, me included.

Intent on my current mission, I open the back door to the pavilion, which is kept unlocked during this event. I breeze into the winter wonderland. Well, the pretend winter wonderland. Also, let it be known I'm not an idiot. I wouldn't trap myself in an enclosed space with a man I've known for less than twenty minutes. The pavilion is surrounded by windows which give a clear view to passersby with hot chocolate, kids with sticky faces and fingers from the free candy canes provided by the Lions Club, and, somewhere in the vicinity, a smoking Santa. After nodding toward the fluorescent lights as an explanation, I click open my kit, opting for the needle best for wool. "Give me your coat." I sound bossy and hate it. I get like this when flustered. "I'm sorry. I should probably ask your name before demanding you to remove your clothes." Um. No. Try again. "I mean, I shouldn't tell you to take anything off ..." I groan, and he rubs a hand over his mouth, but not before I catch a glimpse of his smile. "I had a rough day. Clearly, the English language is against me." I stick out my hand, the one not currently holding a needle. "I'm Greta."

His gloved fingers engulf mine. "Leo."

I can't control the wrinkling of my nose. "Sorry. That one's taken. Pick another."

"Name, you mean?" He huffs a laugh. "You want me to pick another name?"

"My Leo quota is full." It's like how mothers reject baby names because they know someone who's already ruined it. My brain won't allow the distinction between the Leo of this evening with the other I've known since forever.

1

Both dark brows rise, disappearing beneath his beanie. "Ah, an ex-boyfriend?"

I snort. "Not even close. He's one of the Mavericks."

"The basketball team?"

"Ha! No, the card players of Silver Creek. He's pushing eighty-five, and let's just say, if ear hair is a mark of intelligence, Leonard Faulk would rule the world." Someone as attractive as the man before me can't share the same name as the one who smells like Menthol and introduces himself to strangers by handing them a copy of his obituary, which he's constantly amending. Leonard refuses to die until he has the legendary account of his life perfected. His words. Though I confess, Leonard is probably my fifth favorite person in existence.

His hands halt on the last button as he glances up at me. "My name's not short for Leonard."

"Leopold?"

"No." He shrugs out of his coat but hesitates. "You really don't have to fix this. I have other coats."

"It's the least I can do." I gently tug the coat from his grasp. "This should only take a minute or two." It's Saturday night. He probably has somewhere to be. I angle toward the light and work swiftly as if Leo the Luring—that's how he's known in my head now—is holding a stopwatch.

"Are you from around here?" He casually asks as he inspects the row of gingerbread houses on display from the local elementary school.

"I grew up here." That's all the information I offer. I deliberately don't reveal my last name in case Leo the Luring is actually Leo the Lurker. I don't feel I'm interesting enough to attract a stalker, but one can never be too careful. "You?"

"In a way." I hear his voice behind me. He's no doubt checking out the selfie station. Those too old to sit on Santa's lap can pose behind a massive plastic orb, giving the appearance that they're inside a snow globe. "I've lived in Silver Creek off and on until recently." His voice fades, and I glance over my shoulder to find him emerging from the storage closet. Hmm, I wouldn't have pegged him as the nosy kind.

After the final stitch, I knot the thread and break it off. "Here you go, Leo," I say, including his name, which makes his lips curve in an attractive smile. "You are presentable for society once again."

He retrieves the coat and examines my work with a nod of approval. "Can barely tell it was ever torn. Thank you." He smoothly puts the coat back on, even as I move toward the exit. "Next time I get pummeled by Christmas lights, I'm coming to you."

I laugh. "I hope we can meet again on less violent terms." I was joining in on his joke, but then realize how forward I sound. Before I can sputter out something that would probably make me sound more awkward, movement outside snags my focus. "Oh no."

"What?" He follows me out the exit, and I quietly shut the door.

"Look. There's Josie. She found her dead elf." I'm not in the mood for confrontation. A half hour ago? Yes. Why didn't Josie stumble upon me when I was full of righteous fury?

Josie's stomping her feet like she's three. "Greta!"

A sigh pushes through my lips. "Might as well hash it out with her."

He places a hand on my elbow. "Let me."

"Uh, I'm not sure—"

But he's already striding toward a fuming Josie.

I slyly get closer, ducking behind one of the pine trees for some covert eavesdropping.

"Are you Josie from Tan-tasy Island?" His masculine voice silences Josie's banshee yell—something about me and my imminent demise.

"Yes." Her tone is suspiciously hesitant.

"I'm sorry about your display," Leo says. "I noticed a light was broken and intended to repair it for you."

What? I peek between the branches, and sure enough, he holds out a bulb. I remember he wandered into the storage closet in the pavilion, but had no idea he swiped a replacement light. How did he know where to find those? Also is the elf really broken? Did I do that in my accidental stabbing?

Josie seems just as baffled. "So, this"—she points at her elf—"has nothing to do with Greta?" Then, before he can answer, she says, "Oh, do you work for the city?"

"You can say that."

I nearly slap a hand to my forehead. He works for the city. He no doubt approached me to begin with to question my actions. I feel super dumb. By this time, Josie realizes the caliber of man standing before her, and her lips shift from scowling to impressively pouty.

"I appreciate you coming to my rescue." Her mouth slowly spreads into a coy smile while her gaze holds intense eye contact. It's impressive, really. As much as I hate to admit it, I should be taking notes. Despite her teeth nearly glowing from her skin being so orange, she has a strong flirt game.

I watch like some weird creeper as Leo fixes a bulb on the elf's foot. The exact spot I hit him with earlier.

"There." He dusts his hands together. "Can I offer you a suggestion?"

She dips her chin and peers up at him. "You can offer me anything."

I snort, then realize it was loud enough to nearly shake the pine boughs and duck.

Both heads whip in my direction, but somewhere in the distance, a man shouts a slew of obscene words, drawing their focus off me. It sounded suspiciously like Santa Ned, but I can't be certain.

Leo claims Josie's attention. "I see that your elf's on a surfboard."

"Uh huh. It gives a beachy feel that matches my tanning salon."

"Right. So what if you place this guy"—he hoists up the elf—"over by the fountain? There's an open spot right behind it. When the water shoots up, it will give the illusion that he's riding a wave to those who pass the fountain. I think it will be a crowd favorite."

I'm now so low to the ground I can smell the wet earth, but I can see Josie teetering. Like there's a war between her grudgy soul and her sound logic. She loves to be the center of attention, and the elf's placement there certainly makes sense.

He leans in and seals the deal. "It'll match your beach vibe."

Oh he's good. He just threw back her words and made her sound brilliant.

Josie beams at him. Really her teeth are super white. It's kinda freaky. "That's a good idea. I don't know why I haven't thought of it before."

Gee I wonder …

"Can I move it for you?" Leo is already holding the elf like some festively-shaped football under his arm.

"That would be amazing!" Josie practically glues herself to his free arm.

Leo glances over his shoulder, knowing exactly where I'm hiding, and gives a subtle nod. Like we're in on some covert operation. But I immediately understand his signal and move toward the turtledoves. It's not as large as Josie's, so hauling it back to the park bench is simple. Once secured into the ground, I plug it in and flick the "On" switch.

I pat one of the lighted birds. Everything's set for Gran's visit tomorrow. I glance at my watch and then the direction Leo went, only to find him approaching. Gran needs her nightly meds in a little over an hour, but maybe I don't have to return home so quickly.

CHAPTER 2

I'M DEFYING SCIENCE. My current mood is contradicting every atom in my physiological makeup. Look at me. I'm being outgoing, and I'm not hyperventilating or breaking out in hives.

Once when I had to address the entire high school student body, my skin was so blotchy with welts that mass panic ensued. The general consensus was that I had an allergic reaction to one of the spices in the mushy meatloaf and was dying. I just let the paramedics haul me off in the ambulance. It was easier to say I was hypersensitive to suspicious cafeteria food than admit I'm allergic to people.

So I'm baffled about how eager—and comfortable—I am to wait for Leo. I don't count the initial moments of our encounter as a sign I'm finally shedding my introverted shell. Because then, I was fueled by an adrenaline rush. It's that epinephrine spike that empowers people to do crazy, amazing things—like pull cars out of ditches, walk across fiery coals, or, in my case, form full sentences that prove I've actually got a brain in my skull. Now that things have settled, it's usually my cue to scramble for an exit, but instead, I'm lingering next to the turtledoves, watching Leo's form stride toward me.

He adjusts his beanie and jerks his head toward the fountain.

"Josie said she wants to claim that spot by the water every year from now on."

"You saved my sanity." I give a slow clap of appreciation. "Such chivalry deserves a hot chocolate. My treat."

He tosses a glance at the concession stand. "Are those good?"

In the name of all things Christmas, is this man being serious? I open my mouth. Close it. But then the question flies from my lips. "You've never had hot chocolate before?"

He chuckles. "You've got this horrified look on your face like I just confessed to kicking puppies or tripping old ladies."

"Uh, that was oddly specific. Do you do that?"

Another smile. "No. Pets and people are completely safe with me." His voice hints of assurance that goes beyond teasing, as if he wants me to know he's genuinely a good guy. "And no. I've never had one."

"Not even when you were a kid?"

He shakes his head. "We never had that kind of stuff where I lived. Then by the time I was on my own, I guess I'd outgrown it."

His phrasing stands out to me. *Where I lived*. He didn't say *home*. I'll let the first part of his remark slide because it's none of my business, but the chocoholic in me won't allow the second to go unchallenged. Seriously, I want someone to look at me the way I do chocolate. "This is not like middle school acne." Or my crush on Big Time Rush. "You don't outgrow hot chocolate." Before I can think better of it, I grab his elbow and tug him toward the nearest concession stand. "I need you to keep an open mind. This one will no doubt be watered down," I say, even as I witness Barbara behind the counter preparing the drinks using one packet for two cups. "But you have to at least try it. Some of my greatest memories are linked to this."

"Such as?" He watches me as if everything I say is important.

"Like when I was a kid. After I spent the day sledding, Gran always had hot choc ..." I realize the line is moving forward, but my legs won't budge. "You're looking like that again. Seriously?"

"What?"

"When I mentioned sledding, you had that same blank expression—like with the hot chocolate. Don't tell me—"

"That I've never been sledding?" His eyes brighten with amusement. "Not sure I should confess since you already pity me."

I gasp. "I don't pity you. Okay, I kinda do. What did you do when you were a kid?"

"I lived a lot of winters in the South."

"But you mentioned earlier that you lived here off and on."

He nods. "That's true too."

He's purposely being vague, but—as much as it kinda annoys me not to have all the inside information—I've only known this man for less than an hour. I shouldn't expect a Netflix documentary, while I should be settling for an Instagram reel. But I can pull some guesses from what he told me. He said he lived in Silver Creek off and on. He also never mentioned home or family. Should I assume he hasn't had either? What if he was in foster care and was shuffled around a lot? But would that account for living in the South? Maybe he lived with distant relatives? A military one? I have no idea. Except, I can't shake the compassion stirring me. "Wait here. I'll be, like, two minutes."

He offers a smile, unfazed by my sporadic behavior. "I'll be here, Greta."

Wow, I love my name on his lips. Never mind. I have a Good Samaritan act to perform, and I won't be distracted. I hustle to the parking lot off Main Street, connecting the park and the town's major thoroughfare.

"Bruce!" I wave down my parade wingman.

He sees me just as he's entering his truck. By the time I reach his Ford Maverick—because *of course* he has this model vehicle—he's eyeing me beneath his Bass Pro Shops hat. "You need a lift?"

"Nope, but I'm glad I caught you." Every year, Bruce

Struthers pulls the store's parade float. He is kind enough to return the trailer to my grandparents' storage unit. Like Leonard and Pap, he's one of the Mavericks. "I need to grab something off the float."

He steps aside and makes a sweeping "be my guest" motion. "Did you see they put that surfing elf by the fountain this year?"

I pause my climbing onto the trailer. "Yeah, I, uh, heard about that. Smart move."

He gives a slow nod. "Oh, and Ned almost set himself on fire."

I crane my neck to look back at him. "Santa Ned?"

"Yep. Fumbled his cigarette, and it got caught on his boot. That stupid fur trim went up in a blaze."

Was that the yelling I heard? "Poor Ned."

"The board will probably retract the smoke break from his contract." Ever since Bruce's grandson passed the Ohio bar exam, the Maverick has been obsessed with legal terms. "Good thing the ground is covered in snow. Ned rolled until the fire was out. Kids thought he was making snow angels."

"At least he's not hurt. I'll offer to fix the suit," I say as I find what I'm looking for and hop down. "Thank you, Brucie." I grin at his eye roll.

I return to where I left Leo, and his brows spike at the large item in my hand.

"Are you serious?" He gives an incredulous shake of the head. "A sled?"

I pat the large wooden contraption. "It's a rite of passage, Leo."

"Are you dressed for it, though?" His gaze skims over my Mrs. Claus costume.

"I'll have you know, I made this thing. And its thermal inter-lining is doing its job. I can be comfortable in the North Pole right now."

He offers a warm smile, and I can confirm the man has dimples. "You seem to have everything I need. First the needle and thread, and now a sled." His dark brown eyes lock on mine. "I'm wondering if you're even real right now."

Instead of explaining the sewing kit is because I'm often wearing vintage clothing that tends to be delicate and the sled was part of my "Santa's Antique Toys" display for my float, I only beam at him. "I'm Mrs. Claus. Isn't it my specialty to grant wishes? And I bet you wished to go sledding at one point in your life. Am I right?"

He examines the sled, and then his gaze meets mine. The meaning in his expression is as hidden as the stars in the cloud-covered sky.

I realize my error too late. This is always my issue. I dive headfirst, or maybe heartfirst, into things without giving full consideration. I just met him, and I'm already wrangling him into drinks and sledding. I can't even claim he's my friend. Oh my gosh. What if he's in a relationship? What if he's married? I can't tell if he's wearing a wedding band on account of his gloves. I should've thought this through. The *only* handsome young guys in this town are family men. The single ones live an hour away in the city, where the action is. I'm a horrible person. This guy is no doubt married with littles, and not only do I look ridiculous, but I'm also pathetic. He's probably looking for a way to let me down gently because he thinks I'm a crazy person.

"Never mind." I look at the 1970s wooden contraption in my hands as if it's crawling with termites. "It was a stupid idea, and you don't—"

"That wasn't what I was thinking," he offers with a shake of his head. "It's just—"

"I know." I finish for him. "You're right. We really aren't dressed for it." *And you have a wife, two kids, and a vacation reserved in Hilton Head, where everyone wears white and poses for pictures on the beach.* Meanwhile, I'll be beachless. Still here. Same day in and day out. I don't even own a white shirt because I spill stuff on myself.

"Actually, I was trying to get a step ahead of you and recommend a hill." He scratches the side of his face. "But I don't know the area that well. I only moved here not too long ago."

He said *I*, not we. Relief floods through me. "I overheard you telling Josie you work for the town?"

He takes the sled from my hands and props an arm over it. "In a way, yeah."

"Is that how you knew about the lightbulb in the storage room?"

"No, I happened to see it. I don't work for the borough but a different division. Just started."

He's being evasive. But I haven't shared much information about myself. I didn't even tell him I owned the antique shop. I don't know why. Maybe I enjoy being the mystery woman. Living in a small town where everyone knows all your business, it's refreshing to stumble across someone who doesn't know my mother had me when she was fifteen and takes more ownership of her schnauzer than she does of me. Someone who doesn't pity me for being left behind to run my grandparents' shop while all my friends went to college. For a few years, I felt like George Bailey from *It's a Wonderful Life*, wanting to travel and see the world but stuck running the family business because a relative's health started failing. I finally realized that taking care of the antique shop is bringing the world to me. Bringing history to me. It's a privilege, not a chore. If it hadn't been for caregiving, I would've never realized the gift before me. I smile at Leo. "The perfect hill is right over there." I point to the edge of the park. "Follow me."

We pass several displays and weave through to the back region, where it's roped off. I see a familiar face and grin. "Mitchell." I wave over Silver Creek's deputy. We only have two, and Mitchell is my favorite. He's the older brother of my best friend, Tilly, and has a stache that can rival any actor from an '80s soap opera.

Mitchell's gaze swings to the sled in Leo's hands and then to me. "You seeking permission to go down Killer Hill?"

Leo coughs.

I prop a hand on my hip. "That depends if you're granting it." It's really not a big deal. This part of the park is only roped off because of the Light-Up festival. The Christmas program runs on donations, and the chamber of commerce wants all visitors to enter and exit through the main areas. But Mitchell likes to act like he carries all the authority that can be scraped up in a town with no Walmart and even fewer delinquents.

He sucks air through his teeth and rocks back on his heels as if he's in great deliberation. After a second or two of this charade, he nods. "I suppose it'll be okay." He pauses. "Only if you tell me what Tilly is getting me for Christmas."

I gasp. "Mitchell! A man in uniform blackmailing me?"

He laughs. "Or suppose I could tell this guy about that sleep-over party your freshman year."

Fear strikes me. "You wouldn't."

Mitchell shrugs, but there's a teasing glint in his eye.

"My faith in your civic integrity is fragile."

"You're so easy to toy with. Go have fun." He unhooks one of the sides of the ropes and lets us through, but halts me with a hand to my elbow. "You know this guy?" he whispers.

"Just met him tonight."

He frowns. "Be careful."

"We're not wandering far." Seriously, the edge of the park will remain in view. But the brotherly look in his eyes slows my steps. "If I'm not back in twenty minutes, assume I've been murdered and avenge my death."

He rolls his eyes. "I'll be right here in calling distance. Yell if you need me."

"Thank you." I pat his shoulder.

He chuckles and shoos me off.

I rejoin Leo as he shifts the sled to his other arm. "I have so many questions."

I wince, thinking he might have overheard Mitchell's remarks. "I bet you do."

"My main one is why you're taking me to a place called Killer Hill."

"It's relatively tame." I usher him to the tree line. "Except for one rough spot. Maybe four." I never went sledding at night, and it's kinda thrilling. A soft glow emits from the park, but I don't need it. Not really. The snow is so white, we don't need a light. I can easily navigate to the edge of the tree line where our destination is. "Behold." I sweep a hand.

He steps next to me and studies the slope. It does look a bit intimidating. It has two ridges that, if you hit them at the right angle, can send you airborne.

I feel his gaze on me. "What are the odds of me coming out of this fairly unbruised?"

I wave him off. "If you do as I say, you'll be fine." I smile. "You might even love it a little." The noise from the park is like a steady hum, but there's a stillness here that I soak in. When Leo doesn't respond, I glance at him.

"Are you sending me down by myself?" He crouches by the sled and places a hand on it as if testing its sturdiness.

"Of course. You're the one who's never been before."

He stands at full height, and I'm once again reminded of how tall he is. He blends in nicely among the snow-dotted pines. The shadow of his stubble gives him a lumberjack feel. That jawline though? I've never understood the appeal of chiseled jaws, but now I can approve such artistry ... and functionality. He could slice through icicles with that thing.

He moves closer. "I'm beginning to think your elf assault earlier wasn't an accident."

It takes me a full second before I catch his meaning. I laugh. "I'm not trying to kill you."

"Prove it," he challenges, but his tone brims with amusement. He taps the sled with his foot. "There's room for both of us."

All of a sudden, the huge sled that had made my left arm sore from lugging it around looks small. A child's toy. "I ..."

"You two okay over there?" Mitchell's voice booms from behind, and his flashlight gauges my vision.

Seriously? Calm down, Mitchell. It's only been two minutes.

But before I can answer, Leo says, "I'm trying to convince Greta to sled down the hill with me."

"You sure about that?" Mitchell's tone has me glaring at him. "Sorry, Greta, but I feel honor-bound to share about—"

"No," I interject. "That was years ago. Go away," I call. "If anyone is to be murdered tonight, it's you."

Mitchell chuckles and resumes his post defending Silver Creek Park from crime.

I turn my attention to Leo and almost groan at the arrested look on his face.

"Is there something I should know, Greta?"

"Yeah, that men can't be trusted with secrets," I say loud enough so Mitchell can hear. I glance back at Leo. "I may or may not ... sometimes struggle with ..." So much for being the mystery woman. My most glaring fault (well, maybe not my MOST glaring but definitely in the top ten) is about to be revealed. "Differentiating between my left and right." There. My dignity is now forfeited.

To my surprise, Leo isn't laughing at me. He just shrugs. "I couldn't tie my shoes until I was eight. I rocked Velcro like a champ."

I tilt my head. He didn't have to trade an embarrassing moment, but he did. I somehow feel warmer. "So there's this story that Mitchell knows. In sixth grade, Nick Gerrick fractured a bone going down Killer Hill. Thing is, it was my fault. I mixed my left and right and directed him wrong." The guilt weighed heavily on my little soul for a while, until he was partnered with me for the science fair and left me to do the project by myself.

"Yet you say this hill is tame." He sweeps a hand toward the slope.

"Fine. I'll join you." I glance at my phone. I still have a half hour. "But I'm steering. I know the spots to avoid. Which means you have the important job of pushing the sled from behind." I position myself on the sled. "Are you ready to become a true Silver Creek resident?" I smile and put my boots on the wooden cross-piece that controls the runners. "And fulfill your childhood dreams?"

"I like that you're so concerned about fulfilling my dreams."

Before I can respond, he's pushing the sled like we're qualifying for the Olympic bobsled team.

CHAPTER 3

WE ZIP FORWARD, and I leave my breath at the top of the hill. At the last moment, muscle memory takes over, and I angle us away from a hazard area. Though with Leo's thighs wrapping mine and his arms braced on either side of me, I'm in a different danger zone altogether. So yeah, I'm distracted, but I manage to control the wooden beast.

The speed at which we're moving is thrilling, and a laugh rips from my lips. We catch a little air, and Leo gives a whoop. But then ... the left metal rail beneath us snaps from the frame. Tossing us off kilter, the sled shooting out from beneath us. We're a tangle of limbs amidst flying powder.

When all the snow settles, I'm on top of Leo.

"Are you okay?" Alarm threads his tone.

"I think." I take bodily inventory. Nothing hurts. Not at present, at least. "You?"

"I'm good." His warmth seeps into me, and I realize I am still, in fact, atop the man, my blond hair pooling against the curve of his neck.

Worse, I ruined this experience for him. "I'm sorry. Your first ever sled run, and it's a disaster." Meanwhile, I try to think of the most graceful way to remove my body from his.

Before I can move, he brushes the snow from my cheek. "Don't apologize. It was memorable." His leather glove, soft against my skin, trails down my jaw. "Thank you."

My attention-starved heart is holding up a cardboard sign saying, "Free to a Good Home." Ridiculous. I quickly swat away the absurd thought. Aside from his touch, which is enough for me to click repeat on my memory's playlist, the man smells amazing. It's some woodsy spice cologne that has my senses screaming for more. "Of course." My voice pitches an octave higher. "I'm just … uh … gonna …" And I roll off him like a log. My boot gets caught under his leg, and I hit the snow again with a thud. "This is not my night." I am staring into the sky. At least the clouds have cleared. The glistening stars blink an "all is calm, all is bright" kinda thing. A pretty view, but I currently have snow dripping into my ear.

Leo, in a much more athletic way, climbs to his feet and helps me stand.

I turn and glare at the sled. "You had one job," I say to its mangled form, and Leo chuckles beside me. I found it at an estate sale for super cheap. I only intended to use it as a prop for my float, and now I see it should've remained in that role. "Well, we made it to the bottom." I state the obvious because my intelligence clearly shines in these moments. "We probably tumbled about a fourth of it, but we still made it."

"If you wanted to roll in the snow with me, you should've asked."

I gasp. "That was not my fault. I—"

"I know." Shadows flit across his face, but I catch his teasing grin as he raises both hands. "Sorry, it was too good an opportunity to pass up."

He's flirting with me. I've never really been good at this kind of stuff. Actually, I'm not good at all. I'm currently caught in this whimsical evening, powered by dancing snowflakes, multi-colored lights in the distance, and a handsome guy who seems like some Christmas mirage. Everything is surreal until I realize snow has leaked into my boot. Nothing zaps a girl to reality like the threat of pruney toes.

I glance at Leo, then down my snow-crusted body. "I think we're wearing half the slope on our persons." We begin dusting ourselves off and help each other with any missed spots. Leo is very respectful in his hand placement, keeping to my shoulders and back.

He ties the rope of the sled to the broken metal rail, securing it to the seat.

I wrinkle my nose at the hill. One thing about sledding, it takes ten seconds to get down and roughly a hundred years to climb up. However, I don't have that much time. I check my phone.

Fifteen minutes to get to my car and drive home. "I'm sorry to cut this"—whatever this is—"short, but I have to go." So I don't sound like some teen with a curfew, I explain, "I'm my Gran's caregiver. It's nearly time for her meds."

"Is your grandfather—"

"He's very much alive, and very much clueless on anything but playing cards and making inappropriate jokes to Gran. He loves her, but he can't be in control of her medications." The man can remember a hand he was dealt in a 1980s cribbage tournament but can't recall if he put on clean underwear. He's clearly not fit for the task of measuring her sleeping doses and administering the correct thyroid pill.

"I bet they're thankful for you." He grabs the sled, and we make the slow journey up the hill. "Though I can see how it can get overwhelming."

"Yeah, but when I think about what I'm doing, it's rewarding." It probably sounds like I'm trying to convince myself, but I honestly believe my words. "It's something of value. I mean, what's more valuable than a human life?"

He slows his steps. "I wish more people felt like you." There is something in his gaze that makes my heart stretch toward him a little. I don't know his background, but while I'm gabbing on about family, he hasn't mentioned his once. I'm excused from answering because my feet slip like Bambi on ice.

Leo reaches out and saves me from faceplanting into the snow.

"Thanks," I mutter. Another strike against my "mystery girl" persona. Instead of exuding an air of intrigue, I'm showing off my awkwardness.

He offers his arm. "I'd volunteer to give you a piggyback, but Mitchell might come after me." He nods to the top of the hill where the Silver Creek deputy is indeed standing guard.

I laugh. "He's a bit protective of me."

"I'd be too," he says casually as if it doesn't make my pulse stutter.

We safely reach the top of the hill. Mitchell gives me a nod and wanders off to the apple dumpling food truck. Oh, that reminds me. I grab my wallet and fish out a five. "Here."

He eyes my wadded, probably mildly damp, bill. "And this is for?"

"Have you learned nothing?" I would shake his shoulders, but I've touched the man enough for one evening. "Your hot chocolate. It's what you do after sledding. I have to run, but don't let that keep you from experiencing the full effect."

He takes my hand and gently curls my fingers around the money. "I've a better idea. How about we both go for hot chocolate when you have more time?"

"But—"

"It'll technically still be *after* sledding."

"It's more than that." A group of teens is moving like an amoeba down the walkway, so I step closer to Leo, letting them pass. "It's that jolt of warmth after being in the cold."

"I can't have my first hot chocolate experience without you."

"Looks like we're at an impasse."

His mouth arcs into a flirty smile that I'm not prepared for. "Not if you agree to meet me again."

We haven't even exchanged numbers or last names. The

romantic part of my brain is on its knees begging me to say yes. The practical side has its arms folded with an upturned sniff because I don't even have time to paint my toenails, let alone date anybody. I barely get time to shower and cram food in before duty calls me away. But a man, a very handsome man, is interested in me. Although … he hasn't yet seen me in the light of day. Once the ambiance of this night fades, his interest might as well. Tonight I've been spontaneous and fun, but the every-day-life Greta Carlton gets a dopamine hit from changing the bed with freshly dried sheets. "I … don't know."

"How about this …" He holds the sled in front of him and crosses his arms over it. If it were anyone else, I'd totally call them a poser, but Leo looks so natural and attractive that my resistance is weakening. "I'm going out of town, but I'll be back a couple of weeks before Christmas."

I nod, but my mind's like some freakish snow globe—thoughts swirl about, but as soon as one almost settles, my rattled nerves decide to give my brain another shake. It's been forever since I've been on a date. The last time was because Leonard, the ear-haired Maverick, set me up with his great-nephew. As far as dates went, it was about as delightful as a case of food poisoning. The guy smelled like McDonald's onions and claimed to use the restroom and never returned, leaving me with the steakhouse bill.

Leo is completely unaware of my inner struggle. "I'll be by the bench near the turtledoves display with two hot chocolates on December fifteenth. Say, around seven."

"No." I sigh. "I can tell now that I'm no good for you."

He raises a brow. "Because?"

"You just named a date off the top of your head. This makes me assume you're one of those organized people who can visu-alize calendars and commit to schedules. Thing is, I usually can't remember what day it is." I'm all over the place, organizationally speaking. "Wait. Are you a spreadsheet person?"

"Not really." He smiles. "But if you're trying to pull some

weird confession out of me, I use Google Tasks several times a day."

"See? That's what I'm talking about. You use digital task managers, and I write on receipt backs that I end up losing. I'm dangerous to your kind of efficiency, Leo." I pat his shoulder with a slow shake of my head. "I'll ruin you."

"I like your kind of danger." His low-pitched voice smooths over me, pricking my body with chills.

Okay, time to go.

"The fifteenth is a Sunday, if you're wondering."

I nod again because, apparently, that's the only movement my brain allows at present. I could probably do that day and time. It'd be simple to get Gran and Pap their dinners and head here.

"But no pressure. If you don't show, I'll take that you're not interested."

Oh but I am. Though I'm not sure I can commit. Thankfully, I have two and a half weeks to decide. I love how he doesn't push for my number or even my name. Just leaves the ball in my court. "Thank you." I smile at him. "I better get going."

I don't know if I should do one of those side-hug things or shake his hand. What is the protocol for this kind of situation? A fist bump?

Leo decides for me by motioning to the sled still in his possession. "Are you sure you don't want me to haul this to your car?"

Ugh. I forgot about that. I reluctantly take ownership of the distorted contraption. I scan the general vicinity. "Think there's a garbage bin big enough for it?"

He gently clamps his hand over mine on the sled as if he's afraid I'm going to launch it into the dumpster from here. "You want to toss it?"

"It's worthless."

He scoffs good-naturedly. "This thing carried me on my

maiden sledding adventure. I'm wounded you think so little of it."

"Carried is an iffy word choice."

His dimples deepen with his wide grin. "I was trying to be somewhat poetic to persuade you to keep it." His gloved thumb absently runs over the side of my hand, and I'm trying to act casual as if the movement isn't messing with me.

"You can have it then."

"Really?" His face softens as if I've just given him something of worth rather than a mangled sled.

"Of course." The bell chimes from the church down the street. It's like some weird version of Cinderella, but instead of running to a pumpkin carriage, I've got a beat-up Highlander awaiting me. However, Leo still has my hands captive on the sled. Not that I mind, but … "I really have to leave."

He squeezes my fingers and nods. "Thank you for tonight, Greta."

I really want to say, "See you soon!" but I haven't dedicated enough time to overthinking this. I settle on a smile and try to look graceful as I hustle down the walk. I can still feel the heat from his gaze on me.

All my anxieties are present and accounted for.

I am here.

It's Sunday night, December 15, at exactly 6:59, and I'm perched by the turtledoves as Leo suggested. Since Light-Up Night, I was in a constant battle with myself. This morning, I woke up and was eighty percent uncertain of my certainty. What good could come from going? But then the "what if" scenarios taunted.

What if you don't get another chance like this?

What if he really is into you?

What if you regret not going?

What if he is The One?

What if he shows up and says he's been counting the days, the hours, the minutes, until he was able to see you again?

Okay, the last one is a result of my recent rom-com binge, but still, I need to explore the possibility of this rendezvous. Also, I've never rendezvoused before, and I find the word fun to throw about. What says intrigue and possible romance better than a fancy ten-letter word with a silent 'Z' AND 'S'?

Gran took an early nap after dinner, and Pap turned on some war documentary. Everything was under control. I wasn't needed. So I didn't see the harm in coming. I nestle my chin in the thick wool collar of my coat. It's cold out. The chill from the park bench is numbing my backside. Snow swirls around me, as if uncertain where to land.

I glance down the walk. With only two Sundays before Christmas, the park is buzzing with activity. Carolers are strolling along the walk singing "God Rest Ye Merry Gentlemen." Families are meandering about, gawking at the displays. Thankfully, Josie's surfing elf has remained stationed by the fountain.

I glance at my phone. It's five after seven. No sign of Leo yet. But it's busy here. Finding parking nearby is practically impossible. I left my car behind my antique shop on Main Street and walked over. My only sustenance today was a PBJ five hours ago, and my stomach is calling me out on my neglect.

My gaze drifts in the direction of the concession stand. Nachos sound divine right now. I never consider myself a foodie, but I'm definitely one who scopes out the food options at an event before deciding if I attend or not. Oh, that wedding shower will have a donut wall? I'm RSVPing. That recital will have a catered reception from Chick-fil-A? I'll wear my stretchy sweater dress. And so on. I'm a sucker when it comes to food that I don't have to prepare myself. Sadly, those opportunities don't arise too often.

And even more sadly, I can't venture toward the concession

stand without losing sight of the park bench. With the crowd tonight, I could be in line for several minutes. No, I'll wait for Leo and subtly persuade him that nachos go great with hot chocolate. He's never had the drink before, so I think my convincing him is pretty high.

If only he'd get here.

7:10.

7:15.

7:20.

My butt is officially frozen to the park bench. I'm slowly turning into stone. People walk by me in a blur. My phone buzzes. It's a text from Tilly, my best friend. She's the only person I told about tonight.

TILLY

Do NOT forget to get his number this time. Or at LEAST his last name! I can't stalk his socials without such crucial info. Don't fail me!

I bend my fingers to get blood back into them and text ...

GRETA

He's not here yet

TILLY

I thought he told you 7???

GRETA

He did

Didn't he? What if he said eight? My gut sinks. See? I should've written it down. My neuro tendency to forget the second I hear stuff is my worst enemy.

GRETA

He might have said 8

TILLY

Keep me posted!

I "thumbs up" her comment and stand. I swear I can feel my frozen bones snapping into place. I grab a rogue sticky note from my purse. I tear off the edge where I blotted my lipstick earlier. The paper still has enough stickiness, so I write:

Leo, find me at the concession stand.

At least I won't be hangry when he finally shows up. I was right. The concession stand is crowded. It takes me forever to go through the line. Once I get my cheesy fried tortilla fix, I return to the park bench.

It's already after 8. No sign of him. I sigh and look at the turtledoves. "I don't think he's coming," I say to the unassuming display. Either the cold is making me delirious or I'm just pathetic. Because the same spot where my grandparents sealed their love for each other is the exact place I got stood up.

CHAPTER 4

ELEVEN MONTHS LATER

ON A CHILLY NOVEMBER DAY, Adelaide Springfield bursts through the door of my antique shop, The Memory Bank, holding something wrapped in her gloved hands. "This is your lucky day! Such a treat for you, dear Greta."

My definition of *treat* involves sweatpants and sugar. Both of which are not in my near future. "Good afternoon, Adelaide."

"It's going to be a good one for you," she singsongs the last word, and my toes curl in my Chelsea boots. She gently places the swaddled item on my counter. She peels back some protective lining, followed by bubble wrap, and lastly tissue. Each layer is removed painstakingly slow, as if she's building suspense. "Ta da!"

I must have missed something. "It's a bowl."

"Not just any bowl, mind you. It's from the Ming Dynasty. These babies go for five hundred thousand." She grins at it fondly, like it's her firstborn. "I found it at my weekly browsing of the flea market. And what a find it is!"

I reach deep, deep within me to scrape up a morsel of patience. "It's a beautiful dish." Most likely from Target. Movement passes my front window. It's just Mitzy and her legendary baby carriage. Mitzy Clemens is nearing eighty and takes daily walks, pushing a stroller holding a doll from her vast collection. My gaze bounces between Adelaide and Mitzy. And the town council wonders why Silver Creek isn't attracting new families. Mitzy is eccentric but harmless. Adelaide, on the other hand? I look at the bowl. "However, this is not a fourteenth-century piece. Or from any century of that imperial reign." Usually, Adelaide's visits are somewhat amusing, but they've been occurring more frequently. Last week she'd attempted to pawn off a copy of *Pride and Prejudice,* saying it was a first edition. I had to inform her that the binding was too modern to be an early nineteenth-century text. Poor Adelaide. She tries so hard to be a con artist but is very much lacking the con factor. And perhaps the artist part too.

She gently runs a finger over the bowl. "I'm almost certain this is a high-quality heirloom."

"There's a 'Made in China' sticker on the bottom."

"Right! The Chinese claim this piece as their own. Certainly, you can't disagree now."

I pick up the bowl and refrain from frowning when Adelaide tells me to "Be careful!" I give a good show of examining it, but, really, I'm thinking that I only have fifteen minutes until I can flip the CLOSED sign on the door. "Ming pieces are top-tier porcelain. During the Ming empire, no other country had the ability or technology to produce porcelain. So basically, the pieces were the first of their kind. Which is why the china is so rare and valuable."

She blinks at me.

I sigh. "This, here, is cheap ceramic. The famed dynasty pieces are also known for their curved rim. This one has an oblong ridge." There's also the aspect that Ming pieces have a certain color palette, usually an under-glazing of cobalt blue. It's not remotely close. I'm kind of disappointed in Adelaide. It's like she's not even trying. "I can't accept this."

Her shoulders lower with a heavy exhale. Next, she'll pout her lips in 3, 2, ... ah, there it is. At least she's consistent in her acting. "You can't?"

"Sorry, no." Because I like Adelaide, despite her endeavors to cheat me out of half a million, I say, "But I can spring five bucks for it." I need a good cereal bowl for my apartment. I moved into the space above the store a few months back.

The first part of the year after Gran passed was grief-filled misery. But if any good came from her passing, it is my wayward mom's return to Silver Creek. It's weird. All my life, April Carlton only made appearances at big events—Christmas, birthdays, graduation. Things like that. Now she's living with Pap while also trying to shove two decades of neglected mothering into a span of a few months.

Speaking of which ...

The bells jingle over the door as Mom breezes into the shop. "Hi, honey." She waves exuberantly as if I'm five and she's trying to catch my attention while I'm jumping rope with school friends. Which she never actually did during those formative years. I remember watching with longing as other moms would collect their kids from the playground. I had either Gran, Pap, or one of the Mavericks.

"Hey, Mom." I offer a smile and return to Adelaide. "What do you say?"

She arches a brow. "How about ten fifty?"

Some people assume that an antique store is like a pawn shop's rich aunt, as in, it's customary to negotiate the price tag. I'm usually okay with a small amount of bargaining, but I'm starving and feel the onset of a headache. "I'll help you wrap it back up to take home."

She holds out both hands. "Five, and that's my final offer."

"Okay." I forego all the paperwork because the bowl isn't going anywhere near my antiques. It's new home is by my plastic Walmart plates in my cupboard upstairs. I hand her the money. She smiles as if she pulled one over on me. But she doesn't realize I would fork over the money just to get her to leave.

With a hasty wave, Adelaide nearly bounds out the door as if nervous I'll change my mind. I watch the door swing closed with a relieved exhale. "The Silver Creek Swindler needs a more vivid imagination. Ming Dynasty? Pfft." I place the bowl under the counter to take upstairs later.

Mom laughs. "You want her to give you more of a challenge?"

"Is it too much to ask?" I don't hold claim to many talents. Sewing and my knowledge of antiques. That's it. I've been taking on more difficult sewing projects to keep my skills sharpened. Regarding my vintage prowess, my mind feels kind of dulled. I have two types of customers—those who want to browse the inventory and those who are looking for specific pieces. While I'm all about any interest in the store, I actually prefer the second. It's like an antique scavenger hunt to find those items for my clients. If I don't have that particular piece, I have a network of connections that can help me locate it. The thrill of the challenge is in the search, and that's where my heart is.

"Are you hungry?" Mom's voice cuts through my thoughts.

I almost forgot she's here. Which is kind of a habit. I've seen more of my mom in the last several months than I have in my entire life. "I'm starving actually. I have some leftovers—"

"No need!" Mom pulls a Chick-fil-A bag from the giant tote slung over her shoulder. "I brought this."

Another meal. She's been doing this too. Feeding me every time she gets a chance, as if trying to make up for all the missed meals over the years. I'm not sure if this is healthy, emotionally speaking. Should I assuage her guilt? Call her on it? I don't have the energy, and honestly, I don't have the willpower to turn down waffle fries. So like the adult I am, I'll ignore this issue and postpone any impending drama until further notice. "Thank you." I accept the savory offering.

She gives me a quick hug. "Love you, sweetie. I have to go make sure Pap hasn't burned down the house." As much as Mom's sudden reappearance in my life has confused me, I'm grateful for her taking over Pap's care. Those years as Gran's primary caregiver seemed both a blur and an eternity. "Oh and I bought the turkey for Thanksgiving. Thought I'd beat the rush."

This year, Thanksgiving is later in the month. This means Light-Up Night is the week before the fall holiday. I have lots to do and zero enthusiasm for it. My mind drifts to last year's event. The turtledoves fiasco. Meeting Leo. Sledding and carefree smiles. He flirted like he meant it, then ghosted like he didn't. I haven't seen or heard from him since. Which is probably for the best because that night waiting for him in the cold haunts me. For so many reasons. "That's great." I muster all the enthusiasm I can.

"Maybe we can go Black Friday shopping." Her eyebrows raise, her voice hesitant.

"I have to work." I won't get the foot traffic that department stores will, but every year I have my faithful customers. I glance around at my very Christmas-less store. I need to get all my decorations out of storage for the shop. Those need to be up by Friday too. Plus, I have to decorate the float. I haven't decided on the theme yet. If I think too long, I get overwhelmed.

I'm behind.

It's that time of year when people measure your festiveness by your efficiency. Do you have your tree up? Got all your presents bought? Wrapped? Me? I shaved my legs last night. My leg hairs no longer hold up my socks. How's that for productivity? Next time I'll hum "Jingle Bells" so I can claim it as a festive activity. It's not that I don't like Christmas. I love it. I'm just tired. Caregiving these past few years required so much of me. Like I lived through a thousand lifetimes yet never actually *lived* a single one. But I don't regret a second that I cared for Gran. I sacrificed, sure, but I had her. Memories I wouldn't have if I'd gone off to college like I planned, if I hadn't stayed to care for her. Now this is my first full holiday season without her.

That's the heart of it all. She's gone, and I'm missing her. This is her favorite time of the year, and the ache seems to grow as I look around at all she loved.

"Okay, sweetie." Mom smiles. "Just don't work too hard this season. Leave time for yourself and what you want." Motherly wisdom at its finest. Where was the sage advice when I was fifteen and cut my own bangs? I shrug off the negativity.

"Will do." I give an awkward thumbs up.

"I have some business of Gran's to finish up then back to Pap."

I blink. "What kind of business?" I handled everything after she passed, the insurance, the finances, down to the little stuff like canceling her *Woman's World* magazine subscription.

Mom waves me off. "Just some stuff I ran across while cleaning out a drawer or two. It's nothing big."

This is another feature of April 2.0. If she sees something of Gran's that I hadn't already done, she snaps it up. I'm unsure if it's a bit of daughter remorse because she hardly had much contact over the years, or if this is mom guilt because I had to sacrifice so much to take care of her parents. Probably both. But again, I let it slide. I know I took care of the major aspects of Gran's affairs. If Mom found some trifle to appease her conscience, I'll let her run with it. Plus, I have only a few minutes till closing and my pajamas are summoning me.

I say goodbye and savor the quiet settling around me. My antique shop is my haven. I stand among hundreds of stories. Treasures from the hands of the past. I never feel alone here. With another appreciative sweeping gaze of the floor room, I head back to my office to put the food there. I only have a few things left before closing, but one of my rules is never to have food out on the counter. I wouldn't want my customers walking around with food because I have some furniture that costs thousands. So I keep my own back in my office. Though that doesn't mean I don't stuff a couple of waffle fries in my mouth. I hear the bells jingle from the door, signifying Mom's exit.

I'm in the process of squeezing some ketchup into my mouth when my phone buzzes in my pocket.

It's Tilly.

TILLY

SCSS Sighting!!!!!

SCSS is code for Silver Creek Secret Santa. I wipe my fingers on a napkin and text back.

GRETA

Where? When?

My stomach yells at me for teasing it with two fries, so I shove as many as possible in my mouth before moving to the front of the store. Tilly works at the café, four shops down. I'm uncertain if this sighting is recent or if she's saying the man is walking down Main Street. Either way, I'm scurrying toward the picture window. My best friend brags that she could sniff a rich man from a mile away. I must be nose-blind to such a scent because the Silver Creek Secret Santa is standing only a few feet away from me.

Just in time for a dollop of ketchup to drip from my chin.

CHAPTER 5

VERY FEW IN this town are aware of the Silver Creek Secret Santa's identity, but everyone, I repeat everyone, knows that Fletcher Thomas is the area's most eligible single. If Silver Creek ever hosted their own small-town version of *The Bachelor*, the line for contestants would stretch into the next county. Of course, the man shows up at The Memory Bank when I look my absolute worst. I grab the napkin I stuffed in my pocket earlier and angle away to wipe my chin as I chew like a mad woman. In my panic, I bite my tongue and my eyes water.

The world is against me. However, Fletcher is accustomed to my awkwardness. So today's just a new episode of the latest season regarding my socially weird self in public settings.

I clear my throat. "Hey there, Fletcher. I didn't hear the bells." I motion toward the door.

"I came in when another customer left."

My mom. She could've given me a warning text that the town's hottest single was here.

Speaking of texts, my phone buzzes.

Tilly again.

TILLY

He's in YOUR STORE!!!!

Not exactly helpful, but I appreciate her excessive use of punctuation. Because this is a four-exclamation-points situation.

On top of Fletcher being wealthy and handsome, he's genuinely a nice guy. His family owns a large law firm, and his ancestors helped establish Silver Creek. For being a man of means, he does the whole nine-to-five workday thing.

"Sorry about my"—I wave at my mouth, drawing his attention to my lips. Not my intention, but it's better than the ketchup smear on my wrist—"little mishap. I totally thought I was alone. I usually don't eat like a crazed beast in front of customers. I keep that secret between me and my waffle fries." As usual, oversharing does not curb my embarrassment.

He laughs, and I notice how his bright blue eyes pair well with his sandy blond hair. "I love a girl who attacks her food with no mercy. My only complaint is you didn't offer to share. Waffle fries are my weakness."

I smile at his remark because our shared love of cholesterol-inducing food is the *only* area in which we're compatible. Thanks to many exchanges where my social ineptness was on full display in his immediate presence, I have zero chance with him. Still, I can't help but become a tad swoony-eyed in his presence.

He glances around, most likely to ensure we're alone. "Just wanted to verbally confirm you're still good with having a Silver Creek Secret Santa mailbox."

"Um, yeah. I'll place it on the counter like always."

"Great. I'll have the box sent over tomorrow morning." Those who want to nominate an individual or family to the community's own Secret Santa can send their letters to a P.O. Box or send an email. I love the many options allowing anyone to participate. And if people don't have access to email or a stamp, they can place a letter here at The Memory Bank or Brewtiful Grounds, the local café. "Is our agreement still okay with you?"

"You mean, I still can't auction off your identity to the highest bidder? I'm not sure, Fletcher, I've been getting some pretty interesting offers. Adelaide Springfield offered me the knife she said was used in the Lincoln assassination if I leak the name."

His brow lowers. "But Lincoln was shot."

"Yeah, I didn't say it was the *actual* weapon. It just happened to be her con of the week. So now you see what I have to deal with to keep this secret."

This pulls a laugh from him. "I appreciate your sacrifice."

Sacrifice? I wasn't the one giving out thousands to the community. Last year, he granted the wish of a military family whose basement flooded while the dad was deployed. Not only did Fletcher pay for the cleanup, restoration, and the glow-up of the space, he somehow managed to bring the dad home so the family could be together for Christmas. "What you're doing is really generous."

He gives another smile, but this one lacks … something. I bet he gets tired of people complimenting him left and right. "I'll have the box collected the day before Thanksgiving. That will give residents about three weeks to submit their nominations."

"That works."

"Great. Are you, by any chance, running in the Turkey Trot this Sunday?" His family's law firm sponsors the yearly event, and all the proceeds go toward charity. Because, of course, it does. Fletcher Thomas can do no wrong. Well, except for his tie choice. It's synthetic material and really lacks drape. Since it's him, I can easily believe a loved one gave him that tie, and he knows it's cheap, yet wears it anyway.

As for the marathon. "Uh, no. I don't run unless someone's chasing me. Even then, it's debatable. I'm in charge of snack distribution at the aid station. That's more my skillset." I glance over, and he's watching me. I must still have ketchup on my face. I subtly swipe at my chin again. Which reminds me. "I promise I don't have the same vigor for granola bars as I do fries. Those marathon snacks are safe around me."

"I'm counting on you, Greta," he says in a mock seriousness that amps up his charm. He leans in, his voice dropping to a whisper. "Just be sure to hold back the one with chocolate chips for me."

And if there isn't one of that flavor, I'll be sure to swing by the store and grab it for him. "You have my word. The only thing that makes granola bearable is chocolate."

"Agreed." He dips his chin. "By the way, I never said I was the Silver Creek Secret Santa."

"You never denied it, either."

Another full smile and he was gone.

Whoever coined the term "Turkey Trot" must've been hurling spitballs at the whiteboard during life science class. "A trot is technically a pattern of limb movement reserved for four-legged animals. Like a horse," I explain to Tilly who doesn't seem interested in my monologue. "Turkeys have two legs. Only two. They are not equipped to trot."

She adjusts her marathon number and rolls her eyes. "But trot sounds better."

"So alliteration goes before anatomical accuracy?" I realize the irony of using alliteration to prove my point, but I digress.

"I don't understand why you're in such a weird mood over the marathon name." She looks to the left, and her dark ponytail swishes over her shoulder. "Ah, now I know."

I point to the turtledoves display that is backward, mind you, and fold my arms. "That has nothing to do with it."

Tilly's not buying what I'm feebly selling. "So the fact that this aid station is literally beside the place you got ghosted last year has nothing to do with you picking apart a yearly tradition you haven't objected to before now?"

"I feel that the name can give children the wrong ideas about turkeys. I'm passionate about education."

"Yeah. Okay."

Ugh. Why does she have to nitpick my psyche? "All right. Fine. I'm not happy about staring at the spot that was such an ugly memory." For so many reasons.

She links her arm through mine in sisterly solidarity. "Think you'll see him again?"

I shrug. "Probably not. I'm not even sure he exists." Silver Creek has about 6500 residents, which is a decent number for being considered a small town. I've never once run into him over this past year. Though I don't go very many places, so that could be on me. The major point in my argument is that no one has heard of him. I asked around if anyone knew a Leo who worked for the town, and the resounding answer was no. "I wish I never went that night." I start pulling the bottled water from the packaging and lining them up on the table.

"Maybe he had a good reason." This isn't the first time she has offered this counter.

"Yeah. But it's more than that."

She nods in understanding, then flicks a glance at the turtle-doves. "Twenty bucks says you'll fix it by the time the race is over."

I blow out a breath. "Mom did that. She didn't know which way to face it apparently." She offered to arrange everything regarding Light-Up Night and Gran's display. This was one area where I held zero resistance. "I'm gonna leave it."

Her brows spike. "Really?" But then her face morphs into shock. "Fletcher. *The* Fletcher is approaching. Don't look," she panic-whispers. "Code Fourth Runner-Up."

"Ugh, no."

She puts her hands together in a begging pose. "Come on, please?" Code Fourth Runner-Up is her signal for me to reference her pageant era. Tilly was titled fourth runner-up in the Miss Ohio contest three years ago. I'm her designated hype girl.

Silver Creek Secret Santa, aka Fletcher Thomas, approaches. He's wearing weather-appropriate running gear and looks like he could be on some kind of protein supplement ad. He smiles at me. "Hey, Greta. Got any waffle fries for me?" He says this like we have our own inside joke.

"Sadly, I do not. But it's cute that you think I would share such a treasure with you."

He laughs. Tilly nearly chokes. As I said, zero chance with this man. So he gets my full snark. "But as promised." I pick up a chocolate chip granola bar and wrinkle my nose at it. "There's probably one morsel of chocolate per gazillion granola flakes, but it's all I got."

He nods in approval. "Just keep it back for me, if you don't mind. I'll swing by after the race."

Tilly nudges me but hits a rib, and I almost squeak. "You remember, Matilda Davies, from Brewtiful Grounds?"

He shifts his focus to my pretty bestie, and she is in full pageant mode—perfect posture, wide grin. If she spouts off something about world peace, I'm out. He extends his hand. "I met you the other day, right?"

She dips her chin in this demure expression. She really is brilliant. "I made your peppermint macchiato."

I pat her shoulder. "She has a knack for remembering people's coffee orders and for placing fourth runner-up in the Miss Ohio pageant." Not my most brilliant of transitions, evidenced by Fletcher's rapid blinking.

He quickly recovers and offers a friendly smile. "I see, uh, congratulations."

Tilly's grin widens. "Oh, it's nothing. Greta just likes to brag on me."

"Yep!" I'm gonna throttle her.

"Sounds like Greta is a great person to have as a friend." His warm tone is sweet. "Well, I better sprint." Then he realizes what he says. "That wasn't supposed to be a pun about the race, but—"

I laugh. "Just *run* with it."

"Nice follow-up." He winks at me. "See you later."

Tilly turns to me after he leaves. "Uh, I think the rich Santa is into you."

"No." I nod at one of the Mavericks who is heading up the Silver Striders age division. "I'm not Fletcher's type."

"And you know this …?"

I'm not going into the humiliating incidents that marked me as a weirdo forever in Fletcher's estimation. "I'm just not." I glance at the street clock, ignoring the familiar pang. "Besides, I'm not going to fall for that again. The last time I thought someone was into me, it turned into a disaster."

I left it at that.

That evening found me at my design table in my apartment, trying to put together ideas for the Light-Up Night parade, but my brain doesn't want to focus. The marathon was counted a success, raising thousands of dollars for charity. Fletcher did return to my station for his granola bar, but everyone seemed to be vying for his attention. Our conversation lasted about two minutes before the mayor claimed him. And that was all. I didn't detect anything beyond a friendly demeanor.

I glance down at my blank drawing tablet. This year's theme for the parade is Classic Christmas Movies, and each float is to represent an iconic film. This is right up my alley, but my heart's not in it. I should claim *Home Alone* and just stay home … alone. I flick a glance at the picture frames above my table. I set them beside my designing pad for inspiration. They're photos of places I've visited, like when we went to Germany when I was a kid. And also pictures of people I love. Tilly and me at our high school graduation. Gran and Pap. My eyes glue to the picture of Gran and me. It was the last selfie of us I found on my phone. I took it when we put up our tree while watching her favorite movie.

And just like that, I have my float.

In honor of Gran this year, The Memory Bank float will be decked out like *White Christmas*.

CHAPTER 6

THERE IS NOT enough caffeine in existence that would enable me to be prepared for Tuesday morning. The shop is closed Mondays, and so I spent most of the day drawing plans for the float, gathering supplies, and altering my costume. At least I didn't have to start from scratch on my wardrobe. Still, I am behind and have no one to blame but myself. It's not like the annual parade is a surprise. I've had plenty of time to prepare. If procrastination was an art form, I'm the Van Gogh of shirking responsibilities. I flip my sign to OPEN and pray no one wants to browse antiques for at least another hour.

"My baby!" A woman's squeal from outside yanks me from my drowsiness.

My gaze darts to the window in time to see a blur rolling onto Main Street.

The woman screams, "Please, someone!"

Oh my gosh! I race to the door, but everything happens in slow motion. A man darts onto the road. A screeching of brakes.

I gasp. My hand flies to my lurching heart.

The car stops just shy of the man cradling a small bundle.

I burst onto the sidewalk, and the situation becomes clear. All too clear. My breath seeps slowly from my lungs.

Mitzy Clemens is frozen on the sidewalk, pale hands slapped against her horrified face. Beside her, the antique stroller is tipped on its side. The man climbs to his feet. His face is bleeding, but I recognize him.

Leo.

The guy who stood me up last December.

Confusion darkening his face, he swipes at the blood with the back of his left hand. "Lady, this is a doll." He holds out Mitzy's treasured plastic newborn. The baby doll has a scuff mark on its face but doesn't seem broken.

Mitzy throws her hands in the air, a mixture of relief and pure joy overcoming her wrinkled face. "You saved her! I got Frieda on my seventeenth birthday!" She takes the doll from Leo and hugs it to her chest, making shushing noises as if the doll were crying uncontrollably.

Leo jolts as if more alarmed by an old lady talking to a plastic figure than rolling in front of a Buick. With a shake of his head, he reaches down with one arm and rights the stroller.

Mitzy gently places the doll inside, and she fixes her rheumy stare on Frieda's rescuer. "That's so good of you, young man." She yanks on Leo's jacket collar, pulling him lower, and plants a kiss on his cheek, her other hand wandering curiously over his chest. "You're a hero."

He stiffens at being manhandled, amongst other things, by an eighty-year-old woman, but he soon softens and says, "Be safe." After Mitzy's slow retreat, he jogs to the stopped car and addresses the driver. Mitzy is a well-known character around here, so I doubt Leo will have to explain much. I'm right. The guy behind the wheel shrugs and pulls away.

Leo hasn't seen me yet. I can make a getaway. I *should* make a getaway. I want to avoid seeing Leo the Let Down, but also, there's a gash on his head because he's also Leo the Lifesaver (of creepy dolls). My stupid caregiving soul cements my feet to the walk. It's during this moment of awkward indecision that he glances over, and our gazes collide.

Oh.

That one whimsical meeting in the park happened at nighttime. Because I hadn't glimpsed the man in the light of day, I allowed my imagination to run wild with Leo's looks, dethroning whatever image I had of him on Light-Up Night. For many months, the Leo in my brain could rival a gremlin. I'm talking monstrous nose, beady eyes, and crooked teeth.

Now, however, no shadows cling to him. In the glow of winter sunshine, the man nowhere near resembles a fictional creature from an '80s horror film. Wait, is *Gremlins* a horror? A freaky comedy? I don't think anyone knows the answer. What I do know is that Pap claims it as a Christmas movie, right up there with *Frosty the Snowman.*

"Greta?" Leo swipes again at the cut. The left side of his face is a mixture of grime and blood, while the right side boasts a bright pink lip print, courtesy of Mitzy.

"You're bleeding." I point out the obvious, somewhat distracted by his dark locks. Last year, I had no idea that stuffed under that beanie was wavy brown hair. He styles it shorter on the sides and longer on top, just enough length to make a woman's fingers itch to tunnel through.

He's staring at me like I materialized out of thin air, and not as if this particular dot on the map is where I spend ninety percent of my life.

"I can't believe it's you," he finally says, the dripping blood runs over his lip, and he gives a quick shake of the head, as if remembering he'd just had a near-death experience. "Did you witness that?" He jerks a thumb at Mitzy's retreating form.

"Your heroics? Yes."

"All for a doll."

It's not difficult to grasp his frustration. He could've been seriously injured, killed even. It does prove that he's not the villain I painted him for all those months. "Well, think on the bright side. Mitzy called you a hero. You'll be named heir to her vast doll collection. I hope you don't find a hundred unblinking eyes deeply unsettling."

He chuckles lightly, which brings out his dimples. "Was it me or did she get handsy?"

"Trauma response. Probably." She really does love those dolls. And apparently, she loves a fine, masculine physique. Leo seems to have a way with the ladies from Silver Creek. Not me, though. Absolutely not me. I take in the gash on his face. "You should probably get cleaned up." My conscience pinches my stubbornness. "Come on." I wave at him to follow me into the store.

He does. I turn back at him, and he seems more confused now than when lying in the street holding Frieda. "You work here? At The Memory Bank?"

I nod. "I own this place." I watch as he glances around, and my breath thins. This is my fifteen-hundred square feet of safe space. I have every aisleway, nook, and corner memorized to the point that I could skip around with my eyes closed. But having him here feels like I'm exposed somehow, like that reoccurring dream where I'm standing on the fifty-yard line on the high school football field wearing only a towel. Though I have to say that dream's far better than those in which I'm losing all my teeth. I shudder and return to the moment—the one where Leo's in my store, bleeding, and I'm trying to remember when I dusted last. I offer him a wad of paper towels from the roll behind the counter. "Give me just a sec to grab the first-aid kit."

He pats the makeshift bandage on his face but completely misses the source of the wound. Without thinking, I take the towels from his hand and press it to the cut near his hairline. "Hold firm. Like this."

He clasps his hand over my own. "I didn't know you owned this place."

And we're back to this again. His palm is warm and calloused and doing things to my brain, though I'm more concerned about his right now, namely if it's swelling. "Do you have a concussion?" I lift on my toes and peer into his eyes. Attractive, yes, but something else lingers in those dark depths. While I can't determine the mystery swirling among the gold flecks in deep brown irises, I can see that his pupils aren't dilated. "How many faces do I have?"

"One." A flirty smile touches his lips, then quietly fades. Just as I had examined his features, scanning every spot, he's now studying mine. Except I don't have a bloody gash on my head. His inspection is different, an excruciatingly slow perusal. "An unforgettable one."

Before I sway under his charm, I realize he didn't say anything romantic about my face. Not pretty. Not beautiful. Only unforgettable. Some could say my tenth-grade science teacher had an unforgettable face, but it was the absolute opposite of dreamy. I tug my hand from beneath his, ignoring the tingling sensation racing to my toes, and he resumes the task of putting pressure on the wound. "Are you turning delirious? Head wounds can do that to you."

"No, it's just … your store was where I was headed before all of this happened." He gestures with his other hand toward his bleeding face. "I didn't know you'd be here."

I retreat a step. "So if you'd known, you wouldn't have come?"

He blows out a breath. "No. Not that at all. I'm glad you're here." The taut line between his brows gentle. "I was hoping to see you again."

Okay. This is interesting. "You could've asked around. I'm not that hard to find."

"I had. But I guess I asked the wrong people. I even talked to Mitchell, you know, the deputy. I've bumped into him several times, but he refused to tell me anything."

That tracks. Growing up with Tilly as my best friend, Mitchell thinks of me like a little sister. He's both protective and annoying. Though he at least could've mentioned Leo asked about me. Knowing Leo was searching for me would've chiseled down the spikes of my irritation.

"About last Christmas," he begins. "I owe you an apology. Something came up." And that *something* must've been an interesting event because his jaw hardens and his gaze drops to his boots. He shifts from one foot to the other, as if weighing what he wants to reveal. After a few seconds, his lashes lift, and whatever emotion he was working to hide is gone. "I couldn't get in touch with you to let you know I couldn't make it."

"I see." His excuse is believable. I'll give him that. It's hard to contact someone without their full name or number.

"I was planning on going." His voice lowers. "But work needed me, and I couldn't get out of it."

I tilt my head. His work. Right. He told me he's employed by the town of Silver Creek, and yet no one knew of him. I'm not sure I feel like calling him on it. What would it accomplish? It's not like we can go back in time. Oh, but if that were possible, I wouldn't have gone to that icy park bench, and I wouldn't have missed so much that night.

"I'm really sorry."

"It's fine." I shrug like it's no big deal. "I'm not heartbroken or anything." And I wasn't. I was more annoyed at the situation and what resulted from it. I glance at the paper towel, now stained red. "You need something on your head. I'll be right back." I hustle to my office and grab the first-aid kit.

I return to find him bending over the glass case, surveying the assortment of vintage tools. He finds me approaching and stands to full height. I don't recall him being that tall. He's got about a foot on me, making me wish I would've worn higher heels to narrow (at least slightly) the difference between us.

I drag my stool out from behind the counter and point. "Sit." I don't always treat my customers like German Shepherds but nothing about this is normal.

He obeys with a slight twist to his mouth.

I crack open the kit and grab a cleaning agent. Sunshine from the storefront window streams across the space, washing Leo's profile with light. Dots of grime sprinkle his brow ridge, and his hair is dusted with dirt. Ugh, I should probably scan his scalp for injury too.

After setting down the cleaning wipe, I approach my patient and am hit with that same woodsy scent I recall from last year. Those warm, cozy notes remind me of moonlit sled rides, dancing snowflakes, and two carefree souls. This … this is a result of my biology. The olfactory nerve—the one responsible for the sense of smell—has a direct pathway to the emotional and memory parts of the brain. Which is why certain scents trigger visceral memories more than any of the other senses. So my reaction is purely scientific, not emotional.

He looks at me, expectantly.

"I … uh … should check the rest of your head to be sure there aren't any knots."

"Sure." Still holding the towels to his forehead, he dips his chin to his chest, and I tentatively run my hands through his hair. My fingertips tingle as I sift through the silky strands while dozens of questions filter through my brain. How is this happening? Why do men get beautiful, wavy hair and long lashes? Speaking of hair, how many women have tousled these locks? *Stay clinical here.* I straighten my spine and finish my examination. Once I'm certain of no more bumps or scrapes, I force myself to step back.

My purpose is to get this man patched up and out of my store. I snatch the cleansing wipe from the counter and clear the area of the cut. "The gash isn't deep," I say as I apply a butterfly bandage. Now to clean the rest of his face. A few scrapes stretch across his upper cheekbone but thankfully aren't bleeding.

Leo's gaze wanders to something behind me. "Is that a vault?"

"It is." I grab more cleansing packets. "This building used to be Silver Creek's first bank. Hence our name." I open the packaging and remove the pads.

"Does the vault close?"

"It used to. But when I was little, I accidentally got trapped inside. Gran immediately had it welded open."

"I bet that was terrifying."

I shrug. "I don't remember being scared. Somehow I knew Gran would find me." Gran and I had a special bond. If she was near, I knew everything would be okay. Perhaps that's why I struggled so much after her passing. I'd never known a time without her, never been solely on my own. I shake off the pressing sadness and ease closer to Leo. "Just going to clean off the excess blood and dirt."

I stand in the opening between his knees, awareness of our close proximity burning through me. I hate the quiver in my fingers as I cup his chin and tilt his head up. The stubble on his jaw grazes the soft flesh of my palm. Breath shaky, I gently swipe his upper cheekbone, sliding the pad downward. I fold the pad, searching for a clean spot.

I slide my thumb under his chin again and tentatively place my other hand on his large shoulder to steady myself. Maybe it's the antiseptic making me woozy. Let's go with that. Because it's easier to blame the pungent cleansing agent for this current wave of headiness than to acknowledge it might be a visceral reaction to touching Leo. Never mind my feeling the coiled strength of his solid form beneath my fingertips. Or the way my body has been brushing his inner thigh. This interaction feels too personal, too intimate, and the quicker it's done, the sooner my heart rate can return to a non-alarming level. I dip closer and scrub at the crusted blood at the edge of his mouth. The side of my thumb brushes over his lush lower lip. I don't realize how near my face is to his until he turns and our noses brush. I jolt back, nearly bumping a display of vintage frames.

Clinical. I can be clinical.

Pulse pounding, I return to the task at hand and spot tiny pebbles embedded in his skin. "You, uh, have Main Street stuck in your face."

"I don't even feel it." His gaze clamps mine, and a bolt of warmth surges through me.

Needing a second, I angle away and grab another cleansing swab. With a gentle swipe, I clear away the last of the offending stones. "Do you want to keep Mitzy's lip print as a souvenir?"

He snorts. "I'm good."

I wipe the bright pink hue from his right cheek and step back. "All done."

"How's it look?"

Stupidly beautiful. I know, I know. He's talking specifics, the cut, and not generalities, his face, but I'm not too proud to admit Leo's features are attractively arranged. "I think you'll live."

"That's reassuring."

"But, hmm." I inch closer and study his forehead. "It hasn't entirely stopped bleeding."

"Head wounds do that."

"I realize this." I grab a few more butterfly bandages and press them into his palm. "These should help. But if the bleeding doesn't quit, you might need stitches."

"I'm sure it'll be fine."

"Do you want any aspirin?"

"No, I'm really okay."

I crumple the wrappers, and he places his hand atop mine. "Thank you, Greta," he says in the same reverent tone he'd used last year after sledding. His gaze melts into mine with an intensity that cinches my chest.

"No problem." My voice is shaky, and I hate it. "Just glad you didn't die saving Frieda the Fake."

His brow raises. "Frieda the Fake?"

Oof, I didn't mean to confess my neuro tic. "Yeah, because it was a fake baby ... never mind. I kinda do that. Tack on descriptors to names."

"Did you do that to mine?"

Several times over, but I'm not going to admit it. Instead, I adopt a professional air. "What brings you to The Memory Bank?"

He catches my avoidance of his question, and his eyes gleam with amusement. "I need help finding something." He tugs a piece of paper from his pocket. "Would you happen to have these items?" He hands me the note.

I read it over and let out a whistle. "Atlantic Mold Company ceramic tree 1965, and Vallerton nativity set." Wow. I'm not even sure Santa himself can fulfill this wish list. "May I ask what this is for?" Leo doesn't strike me as a guy who's into vintage Christmas decorations.

His gaze drops to his folded hands. "It's for someone else."

Cryptic much? I open my phone and google "Atlantic Mold." Most people would recognize these items. Atlantic Mold Company spearheaded the ceramic trees trend. The countertop-sized trees have holes in the boughs to place multi-colored plastic pieces. A single light is placed at the inside tree's base, so when turned on, all the little plastic colors are brightly lit. "These are fairly popular, but the year might trip you up. The stamp on the bottom of the tree doesn't mean the year that particular tree was created, just the year that the mold was. A certain tree can be made later but have an earlier date on it because of the mold type."

"Okay."

"Do you have a picture of what color the tree was? Green or White? Snow on the boughs?" The options are endless.

"Yeah." He stands to pull his phone from his jeans pocket, and after a couple seconds, angles his phone screen toward me, showing me the tree.

"That helps. I have something similar in storage, but it's not that mold. Hold on." I move behind my counter and scribble down Jared's name on a scrap of paper, so I remember to call him later. "I've got a friend who specializes in antique Christmas décor. He might be able to help you."

"I appreciate it."

"As for the other piece, that's an extremely rare find. Just to make sure, are you certain you need a Vallerton and not a Garrick set? People often confuse the two." Mostly because both sets were made around the same time. They are pretty much equal in value, but the styles are completely different. Gran has a Garrick, which she always promised I'd inherit. My heart squeezes at the thought. There are many meaningful memories attached to that nativity set.

"It's Vallerton. I'm sure of it."

"That nativity set is ridiculously hard to track down. And if one happens to get listed, it's usually snapped up by an inside buyer." I personally saw one of those nativity sets years ago. The detail on those pieces is impeccable. Sadly, it's so rare, just like the Garrick brand, I wouldn't know where to start. "If I find one —and that's a big if—it'll have at least three zeros in the price tag."

He grimaces. "So you're saying it's impossible?"

"I wouldn't say impossible, but challenging for sure." I admit the lure of the hunt appeals to me, but I've got to be realistic. Plus I don't have time to be chasing a unicorn piece like a Vallerton. "It'll probably lead to a dead end. You might need to scratch that off your list." I hand him back the paper.

A crooked grin splits his face, and he steps closer. "I used to have an in with Mrs. Claus. She once told me she likes to grant wishes."

"You're *so* out of wishes, pal." I point at him, nearly skimming his chest. "You'll be lucky if you escape my naughty list."

He raises both hands, gaze on mine. "I suppose I deserve that."

Yeah and much more.

"I really am sorry, Greta. That day was … out of my control."

"For me too."

He gives a questioning look.

I glance away. Those details will not be delved into. "At least it all went down at Silver Creek Park and not at the top of the

Empire State Building." Maybe that's why we didn't work out. Those women were meeting their soulmates at one of the world's tallest buildings, and I was meeting Leo at an iron bench with a small plaque reading, "Sponsored by Debbie's Donuts." Though Debbie's maple cremes *are* fire.

His face is blank, and I gape at him. "Have you not seen *Love Affair? An Affair to Remember? Sleepless in Seattle?*" I count on my fingers for emphasis. He doesn't exactly strike me as someone who likes those kinds of movies, but still, the plots are iconic. "The Empire State Building was the meeting place in those films." A far, far cry from that humble park bench.

"Ah, got it." His lips bend into a smile, but his eyes don't share a similar brightness. He seems different. Jaded. Or maybe that's me. I'm not the same woman who darted down Killer Hill at night.

"I understand if you hate me. I never meant for that to happen, but it's no excuse."

"Let's just forget it, okay?"

He presses his lips together as if wanting to say something more, but in the end, he only nods.

"I'll make some calls and see what I can find."

"Should I leave my number?"

I shake my head a little too rapidly. "Just come back some-time next week."

He catches my meaning with a softened smile. I don't want his contact info. It's for the best. The less I know about him, the easier I can put everything behind me.

Now if only I can close the door on my guilt.

I had the rest of the morning to recover from Leo's unexpected appearance. Thankfully, the foot traffic had been slow. I contacted Jared, and he's going to check his inventory for the Atlantic Mold ceramic tree and get back to me.

As for the nativity set, I've called several places with no luck. Like me, they don't have any more clue where to find one. Leo might need to abandon the idea or pray for a Christmas miracle. I glance at the silver mailbox on the counter that Fletcher sent over. Maybe I should've encouraged Leo to write to the Silver Creek Secret Santa. Though I'm not sure Fletcher could grant that wish. Vallerton pieces are scarce and elusive, kind of like my Christmas spirit. My attention drifts outside, and my gaze snags on the strings of lights swooping between the streetlamps. When did those go up? The shop across from mine already has its windows decorated. All these festive details have escaped my notice. Or I've been subconsciously blinded to them. Sometime between last year and now, I've developed Christmas cataracts.

It's nearing lunchtime. I always get philosophical on an empty stomach. I move to lock the front door for my thirty-minute break, but Fletcher's already entering.

He strides right toward me. "Hey, Greta. How's it going?"

I'm starving and have to pee. "Good. What brings you—"

"Would you like to go with me to the Firefighters' Charity Gala? I'm the keynote speaker, and my date just backed out."

It takes me a second to register his rushed invitation. "Oh, Fletcher." I shoo him away. "Come back through that door and try again."

"Why? What did I do?"

"You don't ask a girl on a date by saying she's replacing another girl. You should know this. No woman likes to know she's the second option." Unless she's Tilly. Tilly's pretty proud of her fourth runner-up status.

He winces. "That was a pretty bad approach."

"Not exactly awful but kinda close."

"Okay. How about this?" He stands taller. "Greta Carlton, I came here today with the sole intention of asking you to be my date to the gala. I promise you no marathon running is involved and, while I doubt there will be waffle fries, you can stuff your face with overpriced hors d'oeuvres."

I huff a laugh. "Better." Though I should do a solid for my best friend and urge him to ask her. Tilly would look better on Fletcher's arm than I would. Oh wait. She can't. She's working the event. Brewtiful Grounds is in charge of drinks and desserts.

He flashes a smile that would weaken the knees of most women. "It's next Wednesday, and I'd be honored if you'd go with me."

That's two days before Light-Up Night, and I haven't gotten my float done. At all. But if I go with Fletcher, I score free dinner and get to wear a fancy dress. Since Gran passed, I've managed to have two looks. One, slightly disheveled enough to remain invisible to society. Two, overly disheveled to where people would drop coins in my coffee cup. I used to have confidence and put in more of an effort. If only just for me and my under-nourished morale. I lost that piece of me and want it back.

Moreover, I need out of this mental rut I've been stuck in. My gaze roams the shop, so familiar, so … safe. Yes, this place has been my haven, but it's also become my hideout. The world is spinning around me, and I'm huddled behind my counter, too nervous to step outside. Maybe Fletcher's invitation is my sign to join the land of the living again. "I accept."

He grins. "Good. I'll pick you up at seven."

CHAPTER 7

MOM MIGHT STUBBORNLY ADHERE to her newly adopted catchphrase, "Leave it to me. I have it all taken care of," but I'm not cruel enough to abandon her on the Mavericks' card night. It's a fixture here at the Carlton house, like the drippy kitchen faucet and the midnight-blue shag carpet Pap swears will come back in style. Pap adored Gran, but even she couldn't nudge him out of his stubborn ways. Much to Gran's grief, their house never boasted a three-leaf table in their dining room, but four strategically placed card tables surrounded by plush seating.

The very tableau now before me.

"Why'd you throw that ace, partner?" Leonard slaps a hand over his chest as if the sight of an ace of diamonds gives him instant heartburn. Maybe it does.

"Because I had to," Pap answers with a growl.

"No table talk." Bruce's severe gaze toggles between Leonard and Pap. "If you two can't handle your tricks, then bow out."

Such is an evening with the Mavericks. They may be grumpy, loud, and sport an embarrassing amount of Western wear, but I love them dearly. Growing up, I always had a built-in cheering section. Like the time Leonard brought a foghorn to the children's church Christmas pageant. I hated being in front of crowds, even then. I was the Star of Bethlehem with zero lines or solos, but I felt on top of the world when I stood through all four verses of "Joy to the World" without puking. Mom missed the program, but at the time of my bow, the Mavericks gave me a standing ovation, punctuated with the unloading of Leonard's entire foghorn can. Such devotion followed me throughout the years, and so I will forever tolerate the ever-present smell of menthol cream and tubs of Metamucil in the cabinet.

Most think their name is because of poker, but they barely play the game. No, they call themselves the Mavericks because that's the only brand of cards they accept. Once, I went to the state capitol for a school field trip and brought home a deck made by Bicycle. Pap didn't speak to me for a week.

So yeah, the men take their cards seriously. Right now, they're playing Spades at two tables, and the pair that wins from each battles it out for the trophy—the winning hand. Which is actually … a hand. Gran had an old mannequin from the shop that cracked down the center after tumbling down the stairs. Pap had dismembered it and took the hand. So the champ receives the "winning hand" along with murmured old-people puns like "Gotta *hand* it to you." It's been passed among themselves for two decades now. The Mavericks see the trophy as a token of cardsharp supremacy, but I see it as something that needs to be disinfected.

"Who wants snacks?" I wasn't joking when I told Fletcher that snack dealing is my skill set. It's been my lifelong role to be the DD—designated distributor.

All the men raise their hands like first graders. I smile and pass out the goodie bags I made earlier.

"Leonard." I purposely withhold his. "Did you bring me what I asked?"

"Give me my snacks, woman." He lightly slaps the table. "That's bribery."

I cluck my tongue and step back. "No, it was our agreement."

After a lengthy sigh, he jerks a thumb toward the foyer. "It's in the box by the door." He motions me closer. "But if anyone asks, I had nothing to do with it."

"Deal." I hand him the two bags he requested last week, and he grins wide. "You better not have been shy with the chocolate chips in the brownies."

"You insult me," I say and turn toward Bruce. "And you? Are you ready for next week?" This time next Friday, we'll be gracing Silver Creek's Main Street.

Bruce chomps on a pretzel stick, his lips smacking loudly. "Have I ever let you down?"

"Never, but your role is bigger this year."

He scoffs, disturbing the salt crystals that crumbled onto his gray whiskers. "I was born for it."

It seems like everything is falling into place for my *White Christmas* float. I may not be great at papier-mâché or painting décor, but I am skilled at one thing—wardrobe. This year, the people are going to be the props.

Mom breezes into the room, her schnauzer, Oggy, following close behind. "How does it look?" She spins around, her voluminous skirt flaring out in waves of red satin.

I examine my stitchwork like an artist scrutinizes their brushstrokes. The A-line silhouette gown was a slippery beast to sew, but worth it. The faux fur on the collar, cuffs, and hem offers the perfect contrast to the shimmering crimson.

Once satisfied, I smile at Mom. "You look like Judy Haynes." And she did. Mom's hair is a lighter shade of blond than mine, and her frame's thinner. While I prefer Judy's dress to Betty's in the final scene of *White Christmas*, I will swallow my pride for the good of the prize. If The Memory Bank doesn't win the Most Festive Float Award, it won't be for lack of effort. If we do win, it's in Gran's honor.

She and I began making these costumes a few years ago to wear to a caroling event. Gran initially helped me cut the fabric but turned the entire project over to me because she didn't trust the steadiness of her hands. I loved the challenge of recreating the timeless pieces, but it means even more to know she had a part in all of this.

Earlier in the week, I recovered the pieces from the attic to alter sizes. While both the men in the actual movie were several years younger than the ones for our float, I can't complain about that either. I have to work with what I've got. Plus, the Mavericks are easily bribed with baked goods.

Speaking of baked goods, Mom offers me a plate of raisin cookies. "They're fresh from Merrit's Bakery." She moves them closer to my face, and I try not to gag. I struggle with raisins, the grainy texture, the shriveled look. Blech.

I politely decline.

"A little birdie told me," Jonesy, the oldest Maverick, speaks up from the other table, "Fletcher Thomas is taking you on a date."

Mom's brows waggle, and Pap grunts his disapproval. If it were up to him, I wouldn't date until forty.

I shrug off the attention. "It's just for the Firefighters' Charity Gala because his date bailed on him. We're only friends."

"The richest family in Silver Creek, eh? Not bad, not bad." Leonard swigs his milk as if it were spiked eggnog.

"He's not from the richest family." Professor pipes up from across the room. He's playing the second game, along with Jonesy, but keeps his ears perked in every conversation, mainly to correct his fellow card players' verbal mistakes. He taught at the local university for decades, hence the nickname *Professor*. As to his actual name? I've no idea. "The Mathises are the richest."

Pap sniffs. "Mathis." He spews out the name as if the family were responsible for world tragedies, like global hunger.

"Just because Archie Mathis turned down your invitation to be a Maverick doesn't make him a bad person." This from Bruce, a former minister who never fails to uplift a fellow human, except when playing gin rummy, then it's every man for himself.

I mock gasp at this new information. "You mean the

legendary, exclusive club once extended an elite welcome to its hallowed doors?"

"I note that sarcasm, young lady," Pap grumbles. "Not to speak ill of the dead, but Archie was too dignified to accept. Too busy with his nose in the stock market."

I shake my head. "Cardinal sin, indeed."

The Mavericks mumble at my sassiness, and a piece of caramel popcorn hits my cheek. "Hey!" I scoop it from the ground. "I used the name-brand ingredients for this. Show some respect."

Pap shuffles the deck. "I'm good as long as this Thomas boy shows *you* respect. Let us know if he needs roughing up," says the man with a double hip replacement.

Mom links her arm through mine like Tilly often does. "Those events are fancy. Do you need a dress? Because we can go shopping." She brightens. "I know I missed my chances to get your prom gowns, but I'm here now."

She's missed more than just gown shopping, but I'm not ready for that conversation yet. You know, the one where I ask where she's been the past twenty-some years. She moved out when I was three to pursue her own life. At least that's what Gran claimed. I know Mom traveled a lot for her job as some sort of international tour guide, but I never asked her to explain all the particulars. It was my teenage self's mild version of rebellion, as in, why should I invest in her life when she hardly cared about mine. "I already have a gown." I watch her shoulders lower. Barely into her forties, she's retained a youthful glow I hope I inherited. Yet the dejection on her face makes her appear older. Despite my mountain of mommy issues, I soften. "But I still need shoes."

She nods rapidly with a growing smile. "Then we'll find you the perfect pair. Besides, I need to find a pair of boots for this costume." She runs a hand over the fur trim. "You've outdone yourself with this."

"I enjoy it." And I do. Sewing is one of my creative outlets.

I'm grateful that everything is coming together for the float, but something—no someone—is missing in all of this. I glance at Gran's empty chair. As hurtful as it sounds, my birthmother stands only a few feet from me, but Gran had been my true mom all these years in April's absence. This will be my first Thanksgiving without her, and I'm not sure my heart can take it.

The venue for the Firefighters' Charity Gala is a historic inn at the edge of Silver Creek. This facility is used for everything from benefits to bingo tournaments. But tonight, with the addition of soft twinkle lights and silver chiffon panels sweeping from marble pillars, the space has been transformed into one of elegance. Beyond an archway comprising shimmering Christmas bulbs, numerous tables are arranged around a gleaming dance floor. An orchestra is gathered in the left corner, playing a gentle rendition of "Have Yourself a Merry Little Christmas," and a coffee bar is situated to the right, my favorite barista standing behind a stainless-steel espresso machine.

Tilly glances over and makes an exaggerated motion of fanning her face, followed by an enthusiastic thumbs up. I'm grateful for her support, but man, I wish I had even an ounce of her poise. Seconds ago, I nearly faceplanted into a potted poinsettia while climbing the steps to the building. Fletcher deftly clasped my elbow just in time.

Fletcher follows my gaze. "Ah, your friend." He helps me out of my wrap and hands it to the attendant.

"Tilly's working the drinks and dessert tables, but I'm hoping she gets a break long enough to hit the dance floor. She *loves* dancing." I throw Fletcher an obvious hint he clearly doesn't catch, given that his attention is hyper-focused on his cufflinks.

He cleans up nice. He moves about with the ease of a man who wears tuxedos regularly. Meanwhile, my contouring bra is digging a trench into my skin. Though even shapewear discomfort can't dampen my mood because the ambiance is something straight out of a movie. "Everything looks so beautiful."

His gaze runs over me. "I agree."

I fight a blush. "Thank you." My gown's a 1960s vintage, but no one would know. I found the floor-length evening gown at an estate sale, and it became my first restoration project. It had some fraying along the seam, so I decided it would be the perfect place for a side slit. I'm not usually one for a thigh-high opening, but in this case, it works. The black silk whispers over my form. Nothing flashy. Just a quiet statement that matches my style. I completed the look by sweeping my hair in an updo with a few tendrils framing my face.

His mouth quirks. "I thought you hated exercise."

My brow lowers. Is he talking about the Turkey Trot? "Running? Yeah, it's not my thing."

He looks pointedly at my bare arm. "You don't get that from waffle fries."

Nope. You don't. My muscle tone isn't some indicator that I love working out. Not even close. But I'm not going to explain the motivation to Fletcher. It's too personal. I smile my thanks at his masculine appreciation and leave it at that.

Fletcher introduces me to several people I've seen around town, though never actually spoken with. The banquet room is quickly filling, and the dance floor is attracting more couples. A silent auction lines the side of the space by the coffee bar.

Fletcher nods at the tables brimming with goods that will hopefully bring in support for the fire department. "Did The Memory Bank donate something?"

"Yeah, a vintage basket filled with tea items." I put it together last week after Chief Garrison Todd visited the store, asking for donations. Though I did turn down his request of my stocking their firefighters' yearly calendar. It's for a great cause, but last month Adelaide tried to sell me a cardboard cutout of some guy named Fabio. I suspect he was once popular, considering after I refused, four female customers got into a bidding war over it.

Adelaide raked in a hundred bucks, and I scored a headache. Half-dressed people do *not* belong in my shop.

As if I conjured him up, Chief Todd approaches. "Hey, Greta." He beams. "Did you change your mind about the calendars? I got a box in my truck."

"Goes against my brand. All my merchandise is at least fifty years old."

His dull blue eyes spark with mischief. "Mr. October is fifty-seven."

I snort. "Hard pass, Chief."

"Oh well. Thought I'd try." He takes a sly glance at Fletcher and lowers his voice. "If you need me to introduce you to some single firefighters, let me know."

Fletcher chuckles. "Are you trying to take my date away?"

"Not at all." Chief Todd's innocent expression seems well-practiced. No doubt it's one he uses on Mrs. Todd. "Have you seen Remington yet?" he asks Fletcher.

"No, but he doesn't like this kind of thing."

The chief's jowls shake with a heavy sigh. "He's had a rough year. I guess we can cut him some slack." The two men continue the conversation while I try to keep up. After several nods and some well-placed I-agrees, the chief's gaze drifts over my shoulder. "There's the fire marshal. Excuse me." He gives a parting smile.

Fletcher angles toward me. "Let's put our stuff down, then how about a dance?"

"Certainly."

I follow him toward a prominently placed table at the front of the room. Of course, he'd be seated near the podium since he's the keynote speaker. I leave my clutch on the pristine white tablecloth beside my place setting as Fletcher chats with an older couple. Fletcher sends me an apologetic smile, but I'm fine just glancing about, taking in the general splendor.

My gaze scans the space but freezes on a familiar form striding through the door.

Leo?

My throat goes dry. Dressed in a fitted tuxedo, the man looks like a hundred daydreams followed by a thousand heartbreaks. Those wavy brown locks gleam beneath the chandelier. Sadly, my inspection is cut short by his angling away. Like Fletcher, he seems comfortable in his tux as he moves with athletic grace toward a group of guys by the archway. I try not to observe how Leo's tux is perfectly sculpted to his form, making the other men seem like they scraped pieces of their suits from their grandpa's closet.

Why is he here? A few in his circle are speaking animatedly, but Leo, while engaged, doesn't seem to share their excitement. He turns, his gaze drifting across the room until landing on me.

I know the exact second recognition hits because his head rears slightly back, then he leans forward as if the movement will give him a clearer view. He takes a slow sweep of my figure, and my skin burns at every place his gaze touches.

He says something to his friends and moves toward me, determination marking his steps. That is, until he spots Fletcher, who has just rejoined my side.

Leo slows his stride, his gaze hooking on my date and holding. "Fletcher, good to see you." The tight lines framing his eyes seem to counteract his greeting.

Standing side by side, the two men couldn't be more opposite. Fletcher is polished perfection with his smooth jawline and center-parted hair, while Leo's charm lies in the rebellious tousle of his dark locks and roguish, two-day stubble.

Fletcher's smile is faint. "Ah, Remington. Chief was just looking for you. We weren't sure you'd show up tonight. You've been kind of scarce since the *incident*."

Remington? Who … what? My stomach dips. Why did Fletcher call Leo by another name? And what incident is he talking about?

As questions dance upon my parted lips, Fletcher places his

hand on the small of my back—a move Leo doesn't miss—and says, "Greta Carlton, have you met Remington Mathis?"

Mathis? Didn't I just hear that name somewhere? But my brain has clicked off those mental tabs and is overheating with this new information. I narrow my eyes and tilt my head to the side. "Hmm, I'm not sure." I cross my arms and take my time studying the imposter before me. "He doesn't look like a Remington."

Fletcher laughs as if everything I say is comical. "Well, that's his name. What else should we call him?"

Oh, I can call him some interesting things. No wonder I couldn't find him this past year. He gave me a fake name! What else is phony about him? I'm questioning everything now.

For being caught in a lie, Leo doesn't recoil. If anything, with his confident posture and steady gaze, he seems emboldened. "Greta, I—"

I face Fletcher, cutting Leo the Liar from the conversation with a cold turn of my shoulder. "Are you ready to dance?"

My date flashes a smile. "Absolutely."

CHAPTER 8

FLETCHER LEADS me through a horde of couples and smoothly pulls me toward him, sliding his hand in mine while the other settles on the bare skin of my back. Shouldn't I have some kind of response to this man's touch? Where's a good outbreak of goosebumps when you need it? I'll settle for a heart palpitation or two. Unfortunately for me, nothing. My thoughts are on Leo. Remington. Whatever. My mind's knotted like a hundred strings of Christmas lights that I don't have the energy to untangle. Why did Leo give me an alias? What's the point? Unless he didn't want me to know who he really was. Does that mean he never intended to keep our date? His apology at The Memory Bank seemed so genuine.

Fletcher squeezes my hand. "Thanks for coming with me tonight, Greta."

My smile's wobbly. "I appreciate being your second choice."

He chuckles. "I feel foolish for not asking you first." He twirls me while his words spin in my brain. Events like these call for a certain charm, and he certainly has it.

Come on, internal butterflies. Any second now.

I catch sight of Leo just as his gaze flicks my direction. I adopt a nonchalant expression, as if his lying ways don't bother me.

His mouth curves into a smile that should earn him a lump of coal.

Our silent exchange is cut short by a group of women surrounding him like he's one of the options up for bidding.

I fight an eye roll and look up at Fletcher. "Have you known, uh, Remington long?" I want to ask if Fletcher's sure his friend is not a con artist. Okay, I kind of need to chill and remember I'm an adult. Mostly. I attempt to be anyway. Maybe Leo has an explanation for his multiple personalities.

"I've known him all my life." He nods at an elderly couple beside us and returns his attention to me. "Certainly you've heard of the Mathis family."

That was it. The family Pap mentioned. All I recall is that they're wealthy and the older Mathis refused to join the Mavericks. "I don't really know much."

"You know more than you think." His smirk lingers on the smug side, as if he's the proud keeper of all Silver Creek's secrets. "The Mathises own Ivy Hall."

All breath leaves my body. "*The* Ivy Hall?" The massive estate is situated on the outskirts of town and has been the subject of numerous rumors. The more opulent and absurd, the more likely it's connected to Ivy Hall. Speculation, like the mansion having an Olympic-sized koi pond, or a ballroom that transforms into an ice rink, or—my personal favorite—a gallery lined with sconces salvaged from the Titanic, has swirled in my ears for as long as I can remember. I feel silly for never making the connection. I'm certain the Mathis name has been mentioned around me countless times, but my antique-loving heart must have been more focused on the house than its owners.

"The same," Fletcher confirms. "My family's been connected to his since we were kids. Remington would spend summers at Ivy Hall with his grandparents."

"I see." I'm struggling to wrap my brain around this new development. Ivy Hall aside, I do recall Leo saying he'd lived in Silver Creek off and on. At least he told the truth about *that*. I remember wondering if Leo grew up poor or was shuffled about with foster families. Wow, was I wrong. "So is he a donor?" I'm guessing he writes checks with several zeros for the department.

He shakes his head. "Remington's a firefighter."

And the surprises continue. Yet the weird part is, I can more easily picture him subduing chaotic flames than being interviewed by *Forbes* for a "Forty Millionaires Under Forty" article. Leo has a certain ruggedness about him that pulls my gaze even now, but I resist and concentrate on the man before me. "Are you nervous about the keynote?" I probably should refrain from telling Fletcher about my awful public speaking experiences.

"Not really. You get used to this kind of thing after a while."

"Really? I'm no good at it. Crowds freak me out."

"I can't see you failing at anything."

"Do I need to remind you of what happened when we first met?" A nervous laugh escapes, lending a throatiness that sounds more sensual than skittish. "Besides, I rarely accomplish what I wish to on my first shot. Which is why I avoid skydiving."

He chuckles. "I love your wit."

I smile in return. It's nice to be appreciated.

The song ends, and Fletcher's brows raise. "Care for another?"

However, a stalky man about my age appears at Fletcher's side. "Hey man, I need you for a second."

Fletcher pulls close, his hand pressing the curve of my side, and whispers, "We'll dance again. Promise."

I nod, though I'm unsure about all this touching. "I think I'll go attack the fancy snacks for a bit."

He grins. "Leave some for me."

"I make no promises." And I am off in the direction of expensive food. I snatch a program from a nearby table and almost choke on the admission fee. It's five hundred bucks a ticket. I'm assuming Fletcher is the guest of honor, and me, by default. I cannot imagine paying that much for an event. That's like thirty Chick-fil-A runs.

My traitorous gaze locates Leo. He's on the dance floor. I can't see his partner because another couple's blocking my view. He probably paired up with that leggy blonde I noticed earlier. Not that I care. He can dance with whomever he wants. Just then, someone shifts, and … he *is* dancing with a blonde, but one I least expected.

It's Mitzy Clemens.

The eccentric woman who nearly made Leo roadkill last week is currently grinning like it's Christmas morning. Leo gently sways with her, and my heart thaws a little. Strapped to Mitzy's back is a baby carrier, a doll's head peeking out at the top like a bald meerkat. Leo doesn't seem to mind her quirkiness. He's chatting with her, looking her directly in the eyes, giving her his full attention. It's sweet. This decent act of humanity almost causes me to forget the fake name situation. Almost.

My stomach growls, and I abandon my creepy watching of the millionaire bachelor and the babydoll connoisseur.

I grimace at the small plates and an even smaller selection of hors d'oeuvres. Using my back as a shield, I prepare to load up my dish like it's an all-you-can-eat buffet. The Memory Bank was busy today, and I didn't get a chance to eat. But the food before me is unappetizing at best. Smoked oysters. Pickled mushrooms. You'd think for five hundred bucks a person, they would also cater to those who have the taste buds of a kindergartener. Would it hurt to spring for some cheeseballs and crackers? I glide to the dessert table. Much better. Tilly never lets me down. I grab as many cheesecake bites as possible that wouldn't embarrass me if Fletcher returns. I'm midbite of velvety goodness, when a presence is at my shoulder.

"I can explain," Leo's masculine voice rumbles in my ear.

Goosebumps erupt from the base of my neck to the tops of my toes. I slide my eyes shut. So unfair. I face Leo, or whatever his name is at the moment. Remington? Asher? Blitzen? It's all up in the air now.

His gaze skims over me, his brows knitting together. "You cold?" He runs a calloused hand down my arm as if trying to warm me up, but it has the exact opposite effect because a shiver races down my spine. My body needs to stop being ridiculous. "Want my jacket?"

"No." Though I bet it smells amazing. "I want answers." I step away from his touch. "When we first met, I totally gave you an opportunity to pick a different name. And you stuck with Leo when it's obviously *not* your name."

"But it is." He reaches around me and pops a cheesecake bite in his mouth. "You look beautiful, by the way. Black's your color."

"No."

He quirks a brow. "No, as in you don't think you look beautiful? Because you're—"

"No, as in I can't trust anything you say. So if you call me beautiful, I'm going to assume I look like a cave troll." I'm expecting people to approach me asking for a riddle even as we speak.

"My name's Remington Orileo Mathis."

I guess the more syllables you have, the wealthier you are. I eye his outstretched hand with suspicion. "My name's *still* Greta." I weakly slip my fingers in his, and he engulfs them with a firm shake. I don't understand why he didn't tell me his real name to begin with. I'm about to call him on it when Leo eases closer.

"I see you're here with Fletcher Thomas?"

"Yes."

"Did you two recently meet?"

Weird question. "I've known him for years."

"That so?" Leo rubs the turn of his lightly-stubbled jaw, his sights training on my date, who's now chatting with the mayor. It's like Fletcher is some sort of politician, the way he's shaking hands and working the room. Leo's gaze shifts to the left, and his eyes widen. "Greta?" My name's a whispered plea on his lips.

I follow his line of vision. The women who huddled around him moments ago are approaching fast like a pack of she-wolves in stilettos.

"Will you dance with me?"

My gaze seeks out Fletcher. He's still in deep conversation, and it doesn't look like he'll be free anytime soon. "I don't know." I expel an exaggerated sigh. "I just ate. Isn't there some kind of rule about not dancing thirty minutes after food consumption?"

"That's swimming. And it's a myth." He catches up my hand and presses it to his heart. "Please? I appeal to your mercy side."

Let it be known Leo's jacket is made from high-end Italian wool, and the seamstress in me wants to run my fingers all. over. it. I'm tempted to take him up on his original offer of lending it to me for warmth. I refrain, but I do allow my fingers to remain captive in his. "How do you know I don't have a payback side?"

His mouth arcs in a smile, and, oh great, he brought his dimples along. "You're enjoying this, aren't you?"

"It's not every day I see a grown man squirm." Squirm is an exaggeration. He's not running a finger under his collar or anything, but he does have a flair of apprehension in his eyes. "If I dance with you, you answer all my questions. Those are my terms." Seeing this dance as a transactional agreement will keep my mind rooted in something else besides how my veins are thrumming with heat.

"Deal." He wastes no time leading me to the dance floor.

The band starts playing "The Way You Look Tonight," and I slide my hand into his as he curls his arm around my waist. The slower rhythm of the music is a stark contrast to the rapid tempo of my pulse. I blame Leo. When dancing with Fletcher, I didn't need to remind myself to move or to force my intake of breaths. Just as Fletcher and Leo have opposing looks, they have different auras about them. Fletcher is Christmas night by the fire, steady and cozy with a gentle hum of contentment. Leo is New Year's Eve, the seconds ticking till midnight, and the palpable thrill of something new and unpredictable. Each is alluring, though one has a slightly better edge.

"I prefer Leo." He breaks the silence, forcing me to look into his eyes instead of at his tie. "It's from my middle name."

"Orileo, right?"

He nods. "Remington's too stuffy. Like a politician or bank president. Someone who wears three-piece suits to bed."

"And you don't." The mistake hits the second the words fly from my stupid lips. "I mean, of *course*, you don't. Well, not that I know what you wear to bed. I just mean … ugh." I slide my eyes shut. It was only a matter of time before my awkwardness kicked in. I slowly lift my lashes to a fully grinning Leo. "Is there any way to strike what I said from your memory? Are you by any chance prone to bouts of amnesia?"

He makes a show of trying to think. "Not that I remember." His cheesy teasing restores my conversational equilibrium.

"Leo does seem to fit you more." I agree with his preference. It's more down-to-earth.

His expression softens. "Most people in Silver Creek know me as Remington because that's what I was called when I lived here."

At freaking Ivy Hall! "With your grandparents?"

"Yeah, they're both gone now. But I lived here during the summers or would come for weekends when not in prep school."

His confession takes my mind off Titanic décor and onto something more human and devastating. "I'm sorry for your loss," I say softly. I have no idea if his grandparents passed this year or a decade ago, but, as one whose grief is still fresh, I ache for him, nonetheless.

His throat bobs. "Thank you."

I'm aware of every place he's touching me. The way his

strong fingers clasp around mine. The pressure of his hand on the bare skin of my back. I'm scrambling for what to say next, when my brain snags on something he just told me. "Did you say you went to preparatory school?"

"I did."

"Isn't that like a boarding school?" This man missed out on the brilliance of public education. How is he a functioning adult without ever learning "Hot Cross Buns" on the recorder?

"My parents traveled abroad a lot. So they put me in a school where I could live on campus."

And my stupid heart cracks a bit more. I couldn't imagine living away from family, being separated from everything I knew as home. I feel like I should match his admission with one of my own. "I never knew my dad, and my mom was never around—or just didn't want to be around—when I was growing up. I understand what it feels like to have absent parents."

His thumb skims along the ridges of my spine. "I can't imagine anyone not wanting to be around you."

Good thing I'm in the arms of a man who handles hot things because my internal temperature is concerning. "Fletcher told me you're a firefighter?"

"I am."

"You told me you missed our date because you had to *work*. Am I to assume, Remington Orileo Mathis, that there was a fire the night we were to meet?"

He swallows and looks away. "Yeah."

I lightly swat his shoulder. "Here I was thinking your office copier jammed, and you used that as an excuse. I had no idea you were out battling a fire."

A smile returns to his lips. "A paper jam?"

"Or delayed by a pretty secretary."

The warmth of his laugh surrounds me. "Our secretary is a fifty-year-old man named Mike. He'd throat punch me if I called him pretty."

"I'm sorry I somewhat loathed you when you were out being a hero."

A shadow flickers across his face. "No need to apologize, Greta. I'm no hero." He eases closer. "I wasn't trying to deceive you about my name. But I never get the chance to be just Leo. People know me for my family, my status. Mostly for my—"

"Money?" And probably Ivy Hall. The tight lines framing his pensive gaze are enough to squelch any enthusiastic curiosity I have about his family's estate.

"Yeah." His eyes catch the soft glow of the twinkling lights, and I note the amber flecks among darker shades of brown. "But you knew me just as some dude you nearly skewered with an elf."

I snort. "And being almost stabbed is better than being known as rich?"

"Yes." His tone's dead serious.

"I can see how it would be tough to know who's being genuine or not."

He shrugs. "I can usually tell someone's motives within two seconds of meeting them. It's one of those things you learn when your family has money. You learn to use your gut."

I don't know how to respond. I've never had the burden of being stinking rich. But the feathering niggle in my chest wants to know—what does his gut say about me? Of course I'm too chicken to utter such a thing. So I switch the subject. "I found some information about the ceramic tree."

"Really? That was quick." The pleased surprise in his deep timbre slides over my skin.

I smile. "I should be getting a call back with more details on Thursday."

"I can swing by your store on Friday."

Fletcher did awesome in his keynote address. He discussed the merits of the fire department, approached the topic of renovations for the station, and kept everything under twenty minutes, which my acorn-sized bladder heartily approves of. I text Tilly to meet me at the women's headquarters—aka the bathroom.

She squeals the second she sees me. "I saw you dancing with Fletcher the Fine!"

I press a wad of paper towels against my armpit because sweat and silk are about as compatible as a snowman and a blowtorch. "I never dubbed Fletcher that way."

She gives a skeptical look. "Fletcher the Fetching? Oh I like that. It just rolls off the tongue."

I laugh. "I don't think I gave him a descriptor."

"No way. I won't believe it." She fishes a lip gloss from her purse and runs it over her mouth. "You give everyone a descriptor."

"Not everyone. There is a good deal of the world's population that remains descriptor-less."

She screws the lid onto her gloss, and her voice drops to a conspiratorial whisper, "I thought maybe you heard the rumor."

This is new. "What rumor?"

"That Fletcher Thomas isn't as loaded as we thought. As the community barista, you know I'm like the coffee addict's bartender. Fletcher's personal secretary was complaining about a lot of budget cuts going on. She's nervous she won't get as big a Christmas bonus this year."

"But he's the Silver Creek Secret Santa." Or was he? Fletcher did point out that he never actually *said* he was the community philanthropist. Maybe he works on behalf of the real one? I have no clue. It's none of my business anyway.

Tilly shrugs. "Speaking of the Secret Santa business. I caught someone taking the letters from the mailbox at the café and stuffing them in the trash."

I gasp. "Isn't that a federal offense? Okay, maybe not." Since those letters aren't going through the actual postal system. "But it's still a huge moral violation. Please tell me you threatened to never serve the culprit quality hot beverages again." Tilly may be pageant material, but she's fierce when she needs to be.

"When I yelled, he ran out the door. I had to dig the letters out of the garbage. Some were soggy. Here's hoping they're legible." She gives herself a once-over in the mirror, then looks at me. "Enough about that. Tell me how many firefighters' numbers you raked in. I'm thinking with that slit"—she motions at my dress—"you should at least be in the double digits by now."

"I have three-fourths of the firefighters in my contact list now," I say dryly.

"Sheesh. Leave some for me." She tries to adopt an expression of mock offense, but we both know she's usually the one attracting all the attention. Her vibrant personality, coupled with her pretty features, serves her well in the dating department. Which is why it frustrates me that Fletcher ignored my hints about asking her to dance. "Okay. I think I've waited long enough. Spill it. Who was the TDH you were dancing with before the keynote?"

TDH is code for Tall, Dark, and Hot. "That's Leo."

"*The* Leo?" Her brown eyes widen, then narrow. "What? You danced with the man who stood you up?" Spoken in the same scandalous tone like, *What? You ordered decaf?*

"Well, apparently, he's a firefighter and was facing a fire at the time of our meeting. Saving lives and all. Since he didn't have my number, he couldn't explain."

Her bottle-rocket emotions seem to fizzle with a shrug of acceptance. "Okay, that's valid." She fiddles with her earring back, her mouth tugging into a frown. "Speaking of facing fires … I sent that email."

I pull my gaze off our reflections in the mirror and gawk at my bestie, who just slayed her giant. But just to be sure, I ask, "To the regional campus?" Tilly had a rough go of things in high school, academically speaking, and so, after she graduated, she'd sworn she'd never step foot into another classroom again. Lately, she's been toying with the idea of enrolling at a state college. "It's all online, right?"

She bites her lip and nods. "But that doesn't mean I'm going through with it. I just wanted more info on their communications program. That's it."

I bracket her narrow shoulders. "You can do this."

"We'll see." She musters a smile. "Back to Leo. How am I supposed to act? Am I mad at him at all on your behalf? Is there any toilet-papering his house in the near future? Or do I hype you up? Guide me here."

I know the change in conversation is more for her sake than mine, but I roll with it. "Nothing yet. But he'll be stopping by the store Friday to discuss an antique."

A knowing gleam enters her eyes. "So he's inventing ways to see you again?"

I'm not sure that's it. He'd planned on inquiring about the antiques before he knew I owned the store. Though something in my gut flips, nonetheless.

CHAPTER 9

I STUB my toe on the ornament box. I shouldn't have kicked off my boots in favor of fuzzy socks. Cookie-patterned footwear is not professional, but I worked late last night on the float and this evening is the parade and Light-Up Night. Another day stretches before me of being on my feet.

I only work until noon, since all the shops on Main Street shut down in preparation for the parade. Are my shop's halls decked with boughs of holly? No. But am I full of Christmas spirit to tackle this project? Also, no. Thankfully the float's finished, and this is all I have left to do.

While my pinky toe's in recovery mode, I plop down beside the decorations. If I'm being honest, I've been avoiding decorating the store. My gaze takes in Gran's handwriting on the cardboard box—*Bulbs 1950s*. I trace my finger along each letter, the ache settling in me, hollowing out another portion of my soul. I open the box, and my eyes slide closed.

I can't do this.

It feels so wrong to decorate without Gran. Last year, she sat poised in her wheelchair, directing where she wanted everything. One may think she was bossy, but I encouraged her involvement, since each day had seemed to rob her of another freedom. I lean my head back against the wall. This pity party sucks. The company's dull, the stereo's autoplay switched to the Jackson 5, and there aren't any snacks.

I should've done all this during off hours. Because I clearly don't have it together right now. Why did I think I could power through?

The bells jingle over the entrance, indicating a customer's presence, and I want to curl into a ball behind the tree. Though whining never pays the bills. I swipe at my cheeks, blink away the moisture from my eyes, and climb to my feet.

"Greta?" Leo's voice has me scrambling for my boots, but in my dash, I kick the ornament box. Again! The same freaking toe! Pain shoots through me, and, instead of presenting myself as a chic shop owner, I'm hopping around on one foot, clamping my mouth shut to stifle a yelp. It's crazy how one tiny appendage triggers a full-body reaction.

Leo comes into view. "You okay?"

No. Not even close. "I stubbed … toe … box." Why do people ask questions when you can barely function, let alone carry on a conversation? I squeeze my eyes shut and tears leak out. Shoot. I don't have time to deal with mascara tracks on my face.

Leo's at my side. "Is it broken?" He slings an arm around me and hauls me to his side. While braced against his solid frame, we hobble-walk behind the counter like some weird three-legged race. With his free hand, he tugs the stool closer. "Here."

I sit with a nod of thanks. The throbbing in my toe lessens with each passing moment. The ache in my chest? Not so much. The bare, artificial tree taunts me from its place a few yards away. "I should've known this would be rough."

Leo's in this half-stoop stance, and I'm not sure if he's preparing to bolt from the scene or contemplating giving me a foot massage. I really hope it's the latter.

"How can I help?" he asks. "Does it still hurt?"

"It's better." I wipe my eyes on my sleeve. "I'm a mess because of that." I nod at the array of ornament boxes strewn about my showroom floor. "My gran always looked forward to putting up that tree. She selected each of the vintage bulbs."

His warm hand settles on my shoulder. "I didn't know she passed. I'm really sorry."

I swipe at my eyes again and wonder if he realizes he's skimming his thumb along the slope of my throat. The rhythmic sweeps are soothing, and yet short-circuiting my system. "She always took special care in setting up the store Christmas tree."

"Tell me about it." His soft demand is all I need.

"Everything that goes on the tree is entirely vintage. The yarn mesh star is from the '40s. And the tinsel. Oh that stupidly wonderful tinsel is from the '50s. After each season, my job was to put it away. Imagine being ten years old and hand-picking five hundred foil strips about as delicate as tissue paper."

"Sounds brutal."

"It wasn't something I looked forward to. That's for sure. So Gran drew up a contract." I gingerly stand, happy that my toe is no longer screaming for mercy, and retrieve the precious paper from the top of the ornament box. "For every forty pieces of tinsel collected," I read aloud, taking in her loopy script, "the collector earns one cinnamon bear." I glance over. "That was my favorite candy as a kid. We kept the agreement in place every year until it turned into a tradition." It's all memories now.

Leo joins my side and gently bumps my arm. "She turned the job into something fun."

"She did."

He cracks a smile. "Are you still easily bribed with sugar? Just taking notes here."

I appreciate his effort in making things light. I need this. "Not sure if I should confess my weaknesses." Or that I could see him becoming one of them if he keeps looking at me like this. A switch in conversation is in order. "My contact called, and he does have the ceramic tree from your list."

Leo's lips twitch at my obvious redirection, but he lets it slide. "Really? Same style?"

"Yes." I wave for him to follow me behind the counter and open the lid to my laptop. "It's an Atlantic Mold and from the same year. The color is just a touch lighter than the pic you showed me. But it's pretty close." I angle my computer toward him and show him the image of the tree that Jared sent over.

"You did it. That's the one." The warmth in his voice is like that first sip of hot chocolate on a snowy morning.

"Might want to save the praise because I'm struggling with the nativity set. I called all my contacts but nothing. I put feelers out, so maybe something will come of it."

"So you're saying not to get my hopes up."

I think he'd have more success convincing Santa Ned to kick his nicotine habit than finding this Vallerton set. "'Tis the season for miracles, right? It's also the season for elevated stress, but let's stick with the miracles thing."

He huffs a laugh. "I appreciate your optimism."

"I'm the soul of positivity," I say brightly. "But seriously, if anything comes up. I'll let you know." Guess I'll need his number after all. I hand him a customer contact form and a pen, even as my phone buzzes in my pocket.

It's Bruce.

"Excuse me. I have to take this."

Leo nods and turns his focus on the paper.

I hit accept and lift my cell to my ear. "Hey, Brucie. You ready for tonight? I've been bragging to everyone that I have the best float puller in all of Ohio."

A beat of silence.

"Bruce?"

"Hey Greta," he rasps. "I, uh, got into a little fender bender."

"Oh my gosh. Are you okay?"

Leo glances over at the alarm in my tone.

Bruce coughs. "I hit my shoulder pretty hard off the steering wheel, but the doc says I'll be fine with rest and limited movement."

And now I understand the meaning of his call.

"I'm sorry about tonight." Regret roughens his voice. "I hate letting you down."

"No. Don't apologize. You need to rest."

"I'd offer my truck to pull the float, but it'll be a while in the shop."

My heart sinks as I lower onto the stool. "It's fine. Don't worry about me. I want you to get better." I hang up with Bruce and can't help the sag in my spine. I'll have to back out. Not only was Bruce my driver, but he was the key component of the float. Ugh. It's mandatory for Main Street shops to have a float in the parade, but what else can I do?

"Everything okay?" Leo's voice breaks in.

"My wingman can't make it tonight."

"For the parade?"

"Yeah, Bruce has hauled my float for the past five years. Both he and his truck are out of commission."

Leo sets down the pen and hands me the contact form. "I have a truck."

Temptation is a six-foot man with a backward hat offering to save my Light-Up Night. "Don't you have to drive the firetruck and annoy everyone with the siren?"

"No, the city allows families to ride along. Those with kids get first dibs." He quips a smile. "So I'm all yours tonight, if you want me."

"Your phrasing is questionable."

"I'm under your command."

"Worse."

"Come on. Let me help." He dimples at me as if he knows that a dented smile never fails to get him what he wants. He's not exactly wrong because I feel myself caving.

"I don't know."

"If you're worried I'll ghost you again, I promise to remain by your side until parade time."

Well, that's a danger all its own. "It's more than that. Bruce promised—"

Leo raises his right hand as if swearing a vow. "I'll do anything Bruce was supposed to do."

"You don't realize what you're signing up for."

"Who's this Bruce guy?" Now Leo's acting alpha male as if Bruce is his rival. I hold back a laugh, even as his gaze is hot on mine. "Please?"

"Why do you want to help me?" I could think of a million better things to do with my time than volunteer for a night full of festive chaos. "What's in it for you?"

He steps closer, pinning me with his dark gaze. "A spot on your nice list."

"Mmm." My bored hum doesn't fool anyone. "My nice list might be full."

"Is that a challenge?" He tugs on my hands and brings me to my feet. "Because I promise I can be the nicest of the nice." He dips his head, his voice a gruff whisper across my skin. "So nice you won't be able to handle it."

Of that, I've no doubt. I retreat a step, only to knock my heel against the stool. "Fine. I'll take you up on your offer." My lips tug in a smile, and something in it makes Leo's smug expression turn wary. I shouldn't be enjoying this. "I hope you don't get stage fright."

All amusement drops from his face. "Why?"

"Because tonight, you get to sing."

CHAPTER 10

"IF YOU'RE LOCKED in the parade lineup, it's as serious as a blood oath," I say from beside Leo in his truck, one so monstrous it eats Fiats for breakfast. We spent most of the afternoon decorating the store. Leo helped in more ways than reaching the taller boughs of the tree. He encouraged me to share memories of Gran. So I talked about how she taught me to drive at Silver Creek Park and nearly bailed when I almost veered off the one-lane bridge. How she would make chocolate chip waffles on the mornings of my birthday. I found myself telling him things I never shared with anyone else, not even Tilly. Instead of the past few hours being heartbreaking, they were therapeutic.

Also, not only did Leo listen, but he fed me Chinese food. The DoorDash came as we were finishing up decorating, and now, with a heart full of nostalgia and a stomach full of orange chicken, I'm ready for part two of my day—the parade. First, we need to pick up the float. Thanks to Leo, I won't be getting fined tonight. "Because of the Main Street Revolt, there's no escaping the parade without some sort of consequence."

He backs out of the shop's lot. "Revolt?"

"A few years ago, several Main Street businesses enrolled for the parade and all listed elaborate ideas for their floats."

He flicks on his turn signal and glances at me. "I sense a but."

"Yep, the big but of Mayor Perkins." I shake my head at the memory. "He wanted Silver Creek to be tech friendly. So he requested all businesses use QR scanning only. That didn't go over well." Most of the shop owners haven't even graduated to smartphones yet. Poor Mr. Gunther, the Farmers' Market Manager, was adamant that QR codes are secret government trackers and that he didn't outlast Y2K, AOL dial-up, and a string of forgotten email passwords to be overtaken by a splotchy square. His words. He can be a bit much, but what he lacks in tech-friendly cooperation, he makes up for with quality produce. "In retaliation, the shop owners dropped out of the parade at the last minute to embarrass the mayor."

He chuckles. "Main Street mutiny. I like it." He leans on the center armrest between us, sending notes of his cologne my way. "Did you join the rebellion?"

"Nope. Gran and I went. Her love of Christmas outweighed her thirst for revenge." My elbow bumps his, and I'm kinda flustered by his nearness. Needing something to do, I adjust my scarf. "Though I think Gran really wanted to win the Most Festive Float award. With the majority of the competition out, she knew her chances were high." Pap wasn't the only competitive one in the family.

"Did you win?"

"A last-minute entry knocked us out of the running." Oh, the fury that lit Gran's eyes when the winner was announced. "We lost to Rhonda's Party Palace. Gran claimed it was fixed because Rhonda donated several bouncy castles to the Fourth of July event that year."

He shakes his head in commiseration. "Small-town politics are the worst."

"Gran voted for his opponent last election. All because Mayor Perkins is easily swayed by Rhonda's inflatables."

Leo coughs.

"Anyway, after the Main Street Revolt, if a business backs

out, they get fined. I think it's only fifty bucks, but it's about principle."

He nods in solidarity and pulls onto the storage facility's lot. The sky's dimming by the minute, but I easily direct him to my unit. Once parked, I punch in the code, and Leo helps me with the massive sliding door. I flip on the lights to reveal the Christmas wonderland that is my float.

He does a double-take. "You did this?" He steps inside the unit and pauses in front of the *White Christmas* sign that I patterned after the opening credits of the movie. On the front of the trailer is a red bag filled with wrapped boxes. The karaoke machine Leonard stole from the senior center sits near the back, along with tubs full of candy to toss along the parade route. The rest of the space is taken up by a massive Christmas tree like the one from the final scene of the movie.

Leo slides a finger over the silver garland. "I recognize this tree."

"You've seen the film?" I didn't mean to sound doubtful, but this guy doesn't seem like a song-and-dance movie lover. He looks more like a *Die Hard* person. I bet every Jolly Rancher in those buckets that Leo has the movie memorized.

He points at me with a teasing smile. "Just because I didn't know your romance flicks doesn't mean I'm ignorant of all movies."

"Only the best ones," I counter. "But yeah, I stayed up most of the night finishing this." Which is why my feet and back hate me right now. "Anything for Gran."

His head tilts in question. He ditched the baseball cap in the truck, so that lone curl topples over his forehead.

"Oh, I went all out this year in her honor."

"Everything looks amazing." His reassurance bolsters my hope.

We need to hitch the float to Leo's truck, but first, I grab Bruce's costume from the standing rack in the corner. I skirt around the large dressing screen. Over the past years, this storage unit has also served as my personal changing room for parade night.

I grip the costume, hesitation flooding through me. Because I didn't want to risk the seventy-five-year-old Maverick catching pneumonia, I purposely made the shirt larger to allow for Bruce to dress warmly beneath. My gaze toggles between the shirt and Leo's frame. I'm unsure if it will fit, and I'm not about to break out my measuring tape to gauge his chest. Oh well. It's too late to adjust anyway. "Might be a tad snug." As for the pants, I'm not going to bother. Leo's at least a foot taller than Bruce. Guess Leo's black joggers will have to do.

His gaze roves over the shirt. Most guys wouldn't be thrilled to wear a red button-down with decorative sequins and faux fur trim, but appreciation warms Leo's eyes. "You made this, didn't you?"

"Of course. You, my friend, are Bob Wallace tonight." I plop the Santa hat on his head. "There."

His eyes dart to the rolling rack, which holds my dress. "Are you Betty?"

"I am."

He steps closer. "And we're recreating the final scene of the movie?" His tone takes on a sudden interest. "The *entire* scene?"

"Um, no," I sputter. "We're not making out behind the tree." Awareness pricks like a hundred pine needles across my skin. Nope. I will not acknowledge this ... or even name it. Gran once warned me—when a stray cat took refuge under our porch— *never* to name something, unless I want it to become mine. Because once I named it, my heart would take ownership of it. She knew that about me. And I need to take heed of her words. Leo is not mine. So I will not claim this attraction. I brush away that pesky feeling, refusing to feed it.

He shrugs with an easy grin. "Just want to stand by my promise of full cooperation."

"That's *too* much cooperation."

"Anything for Gran," he tosses back, and I bite my bottom lip to keep from grinning like an idiot.

Instead of noting how the left side of Leo's mouth climbs higher than his right when he smiles, I force my focus on the costume. "Maybe you should try it on." If it doesn't fit, I'll have to improvise.

He nods and tugs off the Santa hat and hands it to me. With smooth finesse, he removes his hoodie, revealing a snug tee beneath. I remember once laughing how women from the Regency era never showed their ankles because it was considered scandalous. Ankles, really? But this is the first time I've seen Leo in short sleeves, and I'm feeling stupidly warm about something so basic. His biceps are certainly worth noting, but I'm oddly drawn to his wrists, which are twice the size of mine. So while ankles were the hot joints two hundred years ago, in modern days, for Greta Carlton, it's wrists, specifically Leo's. Now I'm annoyed at my own weirdness and am super relieved when Leo reaches for the costume, our fingers brushing in the process.

I don't know why I hold my breath as he masculinely slips the shirt over his form. Something about him wearing my creation makes my pulse pound faster. I'm a hundred percent certain I wouldn't have this reaction for Bruce.

I was right. It's a snug fit, but it's not exactly awful. "Maybe just don't, like, flex or anything." The second that's out of my mouth, I regret it.

Leo's roguish grin unleashes.

And of course, because I'm me, I follow up with something even worse. "You know, because the seams could rip. I won't be able to fix it on the parade route."

He reaches for the hat I'm currently strangling. "But it would be like old times." His thumb runs over my knuckles, then he hooks my fingers in his and tugs me a step closer. "You have a habit of demanding I take off my clothes."

A sharp squeak rattles my throat. "What?"

"To mend them."

Oh, that's right. Last year, I fixed the hole in his jacket. But I cannot come up with a witty reply because Leo knocked my brain out of service. I make a show of checking the time on my phone screen. "We should probably hurry." I grab my gown from the rack.

"Got it, Betty." He nods. "Any last-minute instructions?"

"Nope. Well, maybe. You'll be driving along the parade route, but when we get to the judging station, I need you to put the truck in park and join us on the trailer. We have exactly two minutes."

"And that's when—"

"You wow the masses by singing 'White Christmas.'"

He runs a hand over his face. "Okay."

"Are you regretting your offer to help?"

He looks at me with a curious bend to his brow. "Will this make you happy?"

"Very."

"Then no regrets." He tugs his keys from his pocket. "But don't expect a perfect Bing Crosby performance."

"You'll be great," I say before disappearing behind the screen with my gown. Once I slip into it, I grab the silver-plated combs from my purse. I use the selfie mode on my phone to quickly fix my hair. I emerge just as Leo jumps out of the truck.

His gaze sweeps over me. "Red's your color."

I raise a brow. "You told me black was."

"Right." He grins, but his eyes remain fixed on me. "I can't believe you made that."

"Thank you." I'm no Edith Head, but I'm proud of this dress as if I designed it. I wish Gran could see everything. I press my lips together. No sad thoughts tonight.

Because it's nearly go time.

It takes us thirty minutes to crawl across town and get in the parade line. We meet up with Mom and Leonard already in full costume. I make the awkward introductions.

"Mom, this is ..." How am I supposed to introduce him? As Remington? Leo?

He answers for me by sticking out his hand. "I'm Leo."

Mom shoots me a sly smile that makes me want to hide under the trailer. I can't have her making cringy remarks as some sort of weird psychological move for all the times she never embarrassed me during my teens. "I'm glad to meet you," she responds sweetly. "I'm April. But tonight, I'm Judy Haynes. Greta outdid herself." Pride coats her voice as she glances over. "People are always saying we look like sisters, right?"

Always is a stretch. It happened once. And the person who made such a claim, Mrs. Haskell, has had four LASIK surgeries, so I wouldn't count her as a reliable source. Yet Mom does have a youthful glow about her. She can easily pass for early to mid-thirties.

I finish the introductions. "And this is Leonard, one of the founding members of the Mavericks." I smooth out Leonard's collar. "He's our Phil Davis."

Leo shakes his hand. "Greta's talked about you."

The older man tugs a slip of paper from his pocket and shoves it into Leo's palm. "This is all you need to know." The Maverick claps his shoulder, and I wince, knowing full well what he just handed an unsuspecting Leo.

Leo begins reading, and his eyes dart to mine. "Is this ... an obituary?"

"Course it is." Leonard huffs. "Tells you my life story. Saves on small talk."

Mom laughs, but I wonder if I should've prepared Leo better for this encounter.

Leo politely reads the life summary until his head rears back. "This says you dated Marilyn Monroe."

"The butcher's daughter," I insert. "Not the icon."

"She was iconic enough for me." The decrepit Don Jaun gives an exaggerated wink and elbows Leo.

Just as the Maverick is giving Leo a detailed rundown of his time with Marilyn, the butcher's daughter, Tilly approaches wearing a pink bunny costume. This day can't get any weirder.

"Don't laugh." Her bottom lip rolls out. "I drew the short straw. Literally."

"Going out on a limb here, but I'm guessing *A Christmas Story*?"

She adjusts an ear. "I pulled for *It's a Wonderful Life*. I even have a wig set in victory rolls, but no."

"When did you get a wig?"

She scowls. "You're not keeping up with the real issue here. Tell me, on a scale of one to ten, how ridiculous do I look?"

I step back and take her in. From her wired ears to her bunny-slippered feet, her outfit is nearly an exact replica from the movie. I'm impressed, but I don't think Tilly would appreciate my remarks on the craftsmanship. "You look very warm."

"That means ten." She exhales a sigh. "But I *am* actually warm. If someone pulls my tail, I won't be accountable for my actions." She seems to put aside her current rabbit drama and studies my gown. "But you. You look beautiful. Though, where's your red lipstick? Betty Haynes always has red lips." She pulls out a bag from some hidden compartment in her bunny suit. "Come here."

I humor her, mostly because she's dressed in a bunny suit. It's a humble day for the beauty queen. Tilly, who's used to wearing glitz and glam, has googly eyes on her feet. She applies the lipstick and hands me a tissue to blot.

"There." She fixes a lock of my hair. "You look like a movie star and me a giant Peep. Whatever. I'm good. Actually, I'm great." The glow returns to her face. "I didn't get to tell you yet, but Mitchell gave me my Christmas gift early. He's gotta go to NYC for something. Don't ask because I can't remember. But"—she clasps her hands together—"he's taking his baby sis along. Complete with Rockette tickets!"

Along with beauty pageants, Tilly also had dreams of being a Rockette, but she's a quarter inch too short. "Ah, you get to see the kick line in person!"

"Yes, the fifteenth can't come any sooner."

"Oh, the fifteenth?"

Her smile drops. "Oh my gosh. I can't believe I forgot. I won't leave you alone that day. I'm the worst best friend."

I glance at Leo. He's a lot closer than I thought. Needing to end this conversation quickly, I tug Tilly out of his earshot. "I'm fine. Nothing I can't handle." I brush at some pilled fur on her shoulder. "I won't let you throw away this chance."

She gives me a hug. "We'll FaceTime that day."

I nod, even as I hear the parade manager signal we're about to start. "Now head back to your float, Ralphie. And keep clear of Red Ryder BB guns."

She jogs away, her bunny ears flopping.

Mom's already on the float, but Leonard's in deep conversation with Leo, and by the Maverick's mischievous look, he's totally scheming something. Better put a stop to that. I order Leonard to the trailer and say a parting "thank you" to Leo as he jumps behind the wheel. The parade begins, and Leo dutifully pulls us at a snail's pace along Main Street. I'm tossing candy, keeping an eye out for the shy, bashful kids too gentle-tempered to elbow their way to the front. Meanwhile, Leonard's lobbing the treats like he's in the running for the Heisman.

"Leonard, don't hurt small children. Easy on the tossing."

He harumphs, and Mom subtly nudges the candy tub out of his reach. We approach the judges' station, and Leo slows the truck to a stop. He jumps out of the driver's side and rounds back toward the float. I glance over at Leonard who's inserting a CD rather than connecting to my Bluetooth, but before I can question him, the music starts playing. He shoves the micro-phone into Leo's hand with a "Don't mess it up." It's safe to say, the Maverick won't be replacing Fletcher as a keynote motivational speaker.

Leo looks at me as if he's about to utter his final words. "If this doesn't prove how sorry I am for standing you up, I'm out of ideas."

I laugh and it's almost his cue to start singing, but the music switches to some sort of techno version.

I gasp and shoot a glare at the aged delinquent. "Leonard, what did you do?"

"It's one of those remixes." The old man grins. "Snazzy, huh?"

Never trust a man who says snazzy. I *knew* he was up to something! That's what I get for putting him in charge of the music. Maybe this loud style is the only kind of music that can penetrate through all his ear hair. The beat is loud, and people are clapping their hands. Hip-hop "White Christmas" is a thing now, I guess.

Leo lifts the microphone and … raps the lyrics. I snort. This is absolutely not what I pictured, but somehow, it's better. Leo's style matches the hip-hop vibe, and he's actually pretty decent. Then there's old Leonard attempting a beatbox.

Mom and I share a laugh because it's hilarious in an awesome kind of way. Somehow, Leo finds his way to my side. Because of the faster tempo, he finishes the first verse quickly. During the break in the vocals, he offers me the microphone.

I freeze.

In the movie, the second verse is when Betty joins Bob. But I'm Greta—the girl who once passed out at the fifth-grade spelling bee. One minute I'm spelling "architecture," and the next, the gym teacher's blowing a whistle in my ear. All this to say, I should've warned Leo.

I'm not sure if he read the fear on my face or if he's just caught up in the moment because he slides his hand in mine and says, "Anything for Gran."

He couldn't have uttered anything more powerful. For Gran.

I'd do anything for her. Even face my childhood phobia. Plus I'm not by myself, Leo's *singing* with me.

I haul in a deep breath and join in. I'm terrible at rapping, but I keep going, and Leo's grin is encouraging me.

What I thought was going to be a terrible day is turning out to be memorable … in a not horrible way.

Until old Leonard decides it's his turn for his solo debut and takes the mic. I spend the rest of the parade route apologizing to the crowd for his questionable dance moves.

CHAPTER 11

"I CAN'T DRINK THIS. It's cement." Frowning, Pap stirs his milkshake with his straw. It doesn't matter if it's eighty-five or twenty-five degrees out, if we go to McDonald's for lunch, Pap gets a strawberry milkshake.

It's the following Monday after the Christmas parade, and I took Pap to run errands while Mom's at a hair appointment. Since the shop's closed today, I'm able to get some personal stuff done. So far, I've taken Pap to the barber, the bank, lunch, and now ... "Heading home?"

"I have one more stop." He shifts in his seat. "The Thomas building."

I flick him a look. "Uh, why?"

"I like this Mariah lady." He turns up the radio. "She can really belt it out."

"This is Kelly Clarkson." While I think it's weird Kelly needs people stuffed underneath her tree, I find Pap's behavior even more bizarre. So I mute Kelly and turn full-on investigator. "Why the Thomas building?" Then it hits me. "Nope. No way. If you're trying to set me up with Fletcher, storming his place of employment isn't exactly subtle. We're not repeating the junior prom fiasco."

"The kid took you, didn't he?" he grumbles.

My prom date, Dax Joseph, tried to cancel because he—and his parents—couldn't afford the tickets or his tuxedo rental. A legit reason. But Pap and the Mavericks weren't having it. They went to the local pizza joint where Dax worked and left him a five-hundred-dollar tip with the caveat that he had to take me to prom ... and get a haircut. We did end up having a great time. "But this is different. Fletcher isn't some seventeen-year-old kid."

"You like him?"

"Pap, we're going home."

He motions with his hand. "This has got nothing to do with your love life. I've got an appointment and want you to be there."

He totally misses my suspicious side-eye. "About?"

"It's legal stuff that he can explain better than this old man."

I blow out a breath, knowing that's all I will get out of him. I pull down the lane leading to the Thomas building and sigh in relief at the empty guest lot. No other Maverick in sight. At least Pap was telling the truth. We find a spot and exit the car, but not before Pap drops his milkshake. I grab my stash of fast-food napkins from the glovebox and quickly sop it up. We make our way inside. Molly Blevins, the kind secretary, welcomes us and shows us to Fletcher's office.

As far as offices go, it's pretty spacious, with bookshelves lining one side of the room and an espresso machine Tilly would drool over standing in the other. Lots of fancy papers hang on the walls. Diplomas, awards, certificates. Everything screams successful professional. I don't think Thomas Law Incorporated would be impressed with my Most Festive Float award. Yep, despite old Leonard's unintentional attempts to sabotage our chances, our *White Christmas* float emerged as the winner. I may or may not have carried the plaque around all weekend until I nearly dropped grape jelly on it.

Fletcher stands from behind his enormous desk. "Thanks for

coming in." He smiles at me and nods at Pap. "Clifford, I'm assuming you told Greta everything."

"That's what I hire you for," he grouches and lowers onto the seat opposite Fletcher.

"Pap, don't be rude." I aim an apologetic smile at Fletcher. "Ignore him. He dropped his milkshake before he came in."

"That was five dollars. Five!"

"A tragedy," I mutter and turn my focus to the attractive lawyer. "So, what was Pap supposed to tell me?" No doubt about the will's timeline stipulation. I forgot all about it until now. When Gran's will was read, Fletcher mentioned that one item was scheduled to be discussed at a later date in November. I knew then what this was about—Gran's antique ornaments and the Garrick nativity set. She was eccentric when it came to, well, pretty much everything, but Christmas in particular. Gran held firmly that one can NOT gift decorations and ornaments outside of the Christmas season. So Gran decided to waste poor Fletcher's time just to tell me I inherited her decorations that are already sitting at Pap's house waiting for me to pick up.

Fletcher folds his hands in front of him on his desk. "Greta, before we begin, I must apologize for leading you on."

Huh? Leading me on? Not the opening I expected. Especially with Pap sitting beside me. Yeah, maybe Fletcher was on the touchy side at the gala, but I chalked that up to him being an attentive date. This could get weird. "Um, what?"

"I let you believe I'm the Silver Creek Secret Santa."

My brow lowers. "Aren't you?"

He gives a slow shake of the head. "No, I only act on behalf of the true philanthropist."

"Who?" I try to think of any rich people I know. A handsome firefighter flashes in my mind. "Wait. Is it Leo?" I pitch forward. "Is he the Secret Santa?"

"No. Remington Mathis is not. Truth is"—he glances at Pap, who's studying his fingers like hangnails are works of art—"your grandmother was."

"What?" I grip the sides of my chair. "Gran? Like *my* Gran?"

"Yes."

"Iris Carlton? The one who was weirdly thrifty? Who'd regift greeting cards by cutting them up and regluing them?" I once got a card for my seventeenth birthday that read, "Thinking of You During this Time. Congratulations on Your Retirement of Sweet 16!" So yeah, this is beyond anything I can reasonably believe. "Are you telling me she's the one who has donated thousands these past years?"

His smile's too tame to match my crazy. "Yes. She's faithfully served the community."

"I don't understand." I catch Pap shifting again, and I level my gaze on him. "Did you know about this?"

He clears his throat. "Yes, I did."

"But how?" My gaze toggles between the men. "She doesn't have that kind of money."

Fletcher slides a paper toward me. "Actually ..."

I pick up what looks like an account sheet, register all the zeros, and promptly fumble the paper. Trying to catch it, I knock over a wire mesh container of pencils. "Sorry!" I nearly fall out of my chair reaching for the scattered pencils rolling everywhere.

"Perfectly all right." Fletcher comes from around his desk. "I know this is a surprise."

A surprise is learning that your cycle started while you're wearing a white pleated skirt. A surprise is biting into your favorite takeout and finding a hair. No, this is a shock. I help Fletcher pick up the remaining pencils and slide back into my seat.

I look at the paper again. "So this is her—"

"Her assets. Yes." He reclaims his chair, but not before moving the pencils slightly out of my reach. "After her passing, you received the building on Main Street, and everything else went to your grandfather, who is now ..." He looks intently at Pap.

My sneaky grandfather picks up on Fletcher's cue. "I'm

giving everything to you. Your Gran wants you to carry on"—he waves a hand—"the Silver Creek Secret Santa tradition."

Me? Someone needs to pull the brakes on the wacky train. "Hold on. Back up. How did Gran get all this?" I shake the paper with all the zeros. "We never lived extravagantly." Gran reused her tea bags until her morning cup was just brown water. She mended my clothes until I learned how to do so myself. They'd bought me my Highlander, which was super cheap, because it was once totaled and had a reconstructed title. That does not scream wealthy woman!

"Apparently"—Fletcher's voice lowers as if he's about to say something controversial—"your great-grandfather was a shrewd businessman."

Pap scoffs. "He was a dirty swindler. Cheated half of Silver Creek out of their money to stuff his own pockets. Never knew such a crook."

Fletcher looks to me, then to him. "Nothing was proven."

"Because the man knew loopholes. But my Iris had a good heart." He runs his thumb over his wedding band. "She didn't want his money when he passed. She never saw it as hers, so she gave it back to the community he stole from."

I think this is all some weird hoax until I see his glassy eyes. I settle back in my chair. "That's how the Secret Santa thing began?"

Pap clears his throat and folds his hands in his lap, regaining composure. "Yup."

"And I'm to carry on this legacy?" I think back on all the good the Silver Creek Secret Santa had done over the years. Gran was behind it all. How can my heart ache and swell at the same time?

"She trusts you," Pap says as if that explains everything.

"Here." Fletcher meets my gaze and holds out an envelope. "This might help."

It's a letter. I notice my name in Gran's handwriting. My breath catches, and I reach for it slowly, not wanting to bobble this like I had the account sheet. Because this—this!—is a true gift. I'm shaking. I can't help it. But I don't really care. I want to pore over this letter, though not with two men staring at me.

I gently tuck the letter between my hands and move to the door. Only it's a closet. "Fletcher, what did you do with the door?" I turn and realize I moved to the opposite side of the room. "Oh, there it is. You two ..." I point at them. "I'm going to read this letter in private, and maybe I'll return. No guarantees. You both have been hiding this from me, which is uncool. But, Fletcher, one of those frothy drinks from that fancy espresso machine might induce me."

He grins. "You got it. I'll make it extra sweet."

"For your safety, you better." I don't always threaten kind and handsome lawyers, but I feel really stupid that I never knew this. I escape into the hall and search for a secluded spot. I end up sitting on a bench outside another office.

Treating this letter as if it were one of my precious antiques, I gently ease open the envelope and slide the paper out.

Dear Greta,

I address you from the grave. Ha! How's that for a dramatic opening line? Okay, I'll stop with the theatrics, but it's not every day I can communicate a message from the afterlife. There I go again. Truthfully, as I write this, you're making me a salad downstairs— I hope you put pecans in it. I love when you put pecans in my salad. But if you don't, I won't complain because you've been such a dear.

I can't express how grateful I am for all the love you've shown to us. I've seen your selflessness in how you daily cared for me and your Pap. You could've left. But you stayed. You gave of yourself for nothing in return.

This is why you're the perfect fit for this, my sweet Greta. By now you've heard that I am (was) the Silver Creek Secret Santa. (Don't get mad at Fletcher Thomas. I practically made him be the face of this and what a face it is. Do you think he looks like a young Marlon Brando or is that just me?)

It may seem high-handed that I stipulated a timeline for this "reveal" in my will, but you and I love Christmas so much. I know you're ready for this undertaking.

I'm passing this festive mantle on to you. I want you to carry on the tradition. Our souls may be separated, but we share the same heart. I know you, Greta. Your spirit is never soaring unless you're lifting up someone else. Here's your chance to live a little and bless somebody this season.

I ask that, this year, you give someone the best Christmas.

On top of this duty, please remember to keep your Pap in line. If you haven't found it yet, he keeps a stash of York Peppermint Patties in a Pringles can hidden in an old boot. I love you, sweet girl. Just know you always made me proud.

Gran
P.S. Always Believe

I sit frozen, letting her words embed in my soul. I don't know how long I linger in the hall, but I numbly rejoin the men. True to his word, a steaming cup of espresso awaits me on his desk. I reclaim my seat, fully aware of the lone tear rolling down my cheek.

Fletcher offers me a tissue, his eyes holding notes of compassion and expectancy.

I should say something. Anything. "I really hope I put pecans in her salad."

Pap looks at me, the grooves in his forehead deepening.

"Here." I hand him the letter and glance at Fletcher. "I should be angry at you."

The young lawyer places a hand on his chest, his expression one of innocence.

"All this time. I thought it was you." A soft laugh escapes me. "And it was her."

"And now it's you?" Fletcher's tone is hopeful.

"How can I refuse anything she asks?" Something I no doubt believe my crafty grandmother knew. I glance at Pap. He's engrossed in the letter. Probably feeling close to her once again as I had. Reading her words, I could hear the soft lilt of her voice, almost smell her lavender hand cream.

"She knew about the candy," Pap murmurs under his breath in a gruff but affectionate tone. "Of course, she knew." He all but presses the letter to his heart, and I melt a bit. Their marriage was one of devotion built upon friendship.

I want that.

"So what do ya say, Greta?" Pap hands me back the letter, his fingers a little unsteady. "Are you going to carry on your Gran's wishes?"

Twenty minutes ago, I thought I was only inheriting Gran's Christmas decorations. Never would I have believed Gran was bestowing some massive community tradition upon me. I turn to Pap. "I'm shocked you kept the secret for this long. You're the man who always let me guess my birthday presents."

"It was self-preservation," he protests. "She threatened bodily harm if I told anyone."

I shake my head, not believing him. But I'm sure Gran convinced him one way or another to keep silent. She always got her way. It seems she still will. "Fine. I'll do this."

"Fletcher." Pap climbs to his feet and holds out an age-spotted hand. "May I have the Cranial Claus Couture?"

"The *what*?" I watch as Fletcher leaves his post at his desk and retrieves something from a cabinet.

Pap shuffles to stand before me. "On this day—" He stops his speech to glare at Fletcher. "You missed your cue, kid."

"Clifford, I don't think—"

"Hum," he gruffly commands.

After a lengthy sigh, Fletcher starts humming … "Here Comes Santa Claus."

What. Is. Happening?

Pap clears his throat and begins again. "On this day in the year of our Lord, we celebrate a momentous occasion. With this Cranial Claus Couture." He wiggles his fingers, and Fletcher drops into Pap's hands a …

"Santa hat from the dollar store?" The tag's still on it.

"Shh. It's your ordination. Show some respect, child."

I hear Fletcher chuckle behind me, and Pap levels him with a look he only reserves for those cheating at Hearts.

"Today, I crown you, Greta Jane Carlton, the official Silver Creek Secret Santa." He holds the hat just above my head. "Do you so solemnly swear to uphold the integrity of this revered position?"

"Uh, I think so." It's difficult to take this seriously when the plastic tag keeps smacking me in the right eye.

He smooths the hat over my head and, I kid you not, shakes a jingle bell.

"Do I need to, like, recite a Christmas carol or kiss a reindeer or something?" Okay, this is the weirdest and silliest ceremony

I've ever endured, but I don't think this was for me. Pap did this for her. Gran. This quirky "passing on" of the Santa hat would've delighted her, right down to Fletcher's off-key humming.

Speaking of Fletcher, he's currently placing a thick folder in my hands.

"And this is?" I look up at him.

"The letters to Santa. To you." He taps the thick folder, and I swallow. "These are the printed emails, letters from the mail-boxes, and the bundle from the P.O. box."

Now that his role's complete, Pap seems bored and starts sneaking chocolate from the candy bowl on Fletcher's desk.

"Your grandmother would always have the recipient selected by the eighth, but since this is your inaugural run, you can turn in a name anytime up to the twentieth."

I sort of remember that's when the news would cover it. I raise my hand to ask a question as if I'm in junior high science class and not a mature adult. I realize what I'm doing and lower my arm. "Do we have to broadcast this all over the news? I'd rather not make a huge deal. If a family needs help, wouldn't that be exploiting their hard times for the sake of a feel-good, sob story?"

Fletcher reclaims his seat. "I understand what you're saying. But it's good for the spirit of the community. It's to let the resident or residents who are selected know that they are not alone. Besides, those who submit a letter understand the media coverage is part of the process."

I'm not sold, but I'm too overwhelmed to contradict anything right now. Needing a jolt of caffeine, I grab the espresso and resist the urge to down it in one scorching gulp. The folder is burning a hole in my lap. I hesitantly open it and browse the top letters. "How did she narrow this down?" I lean forward, and the stupid dollar store tag smacks me in the eye again. "Can I take off this Cranial Claus ..."

"Couture," Pap corrects. "And, no, you may not."

"I wouldn't want Fletcher's secretary to burst in the door and discover my festive little secret."

"Okay, fine," he mumbles and grabs another candy.

I remove the hat, but the static electricity has strands of my hair standing on end. Wonderful. I try to smooth it out and nearly drop my espresso. With a sigh, I set the cup on the edge of Fletcher's desk and try to act composed.

Fletcher folds his hands atop the desk, appearing very professional. "May I make a suggestion?"

"Yes!" I nearly shout in my seat. "Do you have someone already picked out? That would make this a lot easier."

"Sorry, no." He points at the stack of letters. "I remember your grandmother having to sort out the phony from the real. It's crucial to use discernment when reading those."

My shoulders slump. "You mean people lie?" Of course they do. I wasn't naïve enough to think people wouldn't resort to scamming to get some quick money. "What did Gran do?"

"She vetted them, but she was quick. She had a gift for that sort of thing."

"I don't feel like I have that gift." Sure, I can spot the false in antiques, but people? That's more challenging. How do I tell who's just after money?

"There's one last thing from the will."

I'm almost afraid to look at Fletcher. Can I handle anything else? "If you dare tell me my grandmother willed me a herd of reindeer, I'm out."

"No." Fletcher smiles with warmth in his eyes. Or laughter. I can't tell. "I only wanted to add that she left you her antique ornaments."

Because you can't gift ornaments outside of the Christmas season. Nice one, Gran.

After the shock at Fletcher's office, the first day of my hidden identity as the Silver Creek Secret Santa is relatively uneventful. I drive Pap home, promise my mom I will make the pies and green bean casserole for Thanksgiving dinner, and then go to the grocery store.

When I return to my apartment, I ditch my sweater dress and leggings for an oversized sweatshirt and fuzzy pajama pants. I stare at the empty space that remains Christmas tree-less. With all the decorating for the store and the float, I had zero motivation. I'm a terrible Santa. I have no zeal to deck the halls. Not even tempted to say "Ho Ho Ho." Though I could go for the whole eating a plate of cookies thing. I grab the folder of Secret Santa letters from the counter, the weight of it pressing more upon my heart than my palm. Can't I just go "eeny meeny miny moe" and pick a random letter? Voila. All finished.

Ugh, I can practically hear Gran clicking her tongue. Meanwhile, Pap would remind me that I took some sacred Santa blood pact. As far as weird days go, this one ranks at the top. Well, except for the day I met Leo when I was dressed as Mrs. Claus. I joked that I was granting wishes.

And yet ...

I now have the chance to do something good. No, amazing.

With a new sense of purpose, I move to the sofa and crack open my laptop. Typing "Silver Creek Secret Santa" in the Google search bar pulls up dozens of articles. I tap the first one. It's a news article that lists the community gifts from past Christmases. One year, a family had their car repossessed because they fell behind on payments. Not only did they get their car back fully paid off, but they also received a grocery gift card for five thousand dollars, and their credit card debt eliminated. One woman gave up her trip abroad when her sister got sick and helped nurse her back to health while also caring for her nieces and nephews. She was gifted another trip abroad with all her expenses paid and spending money. An all-abilities playground was built for the local school. The women's center got new laptops and a state-of-the-art security system to protect those fleeing from domestic violence.

I lean back against the sofa cushion, my eyes welling with tears. Gran had been the one to do all of that. She's always been kind and generous, but this? It's like I'm seeing a whole new side of her. A secret she'd kept for so long that I'm now part of.

Grabbing the folder, I skim over the first few letters. Someone nominated their little league baseball coach, asking for a Ford truck because he would always pick up and drop off the kids from underserved neighborhoods to ensure they got to play. Another nominated their high school math teacher, asking for a shopping spree, claiming her wardrobe is embarrassing. Oh, the brutal honesty of teens. As I read through a few more, I realize I need to have some kind of system. But being more organized is like asking me to add leafy greens to my diet. Like, I know it's good for me, but the reality of me doing that is pretty slim.

Suddenly tired, I flip on a Christmas movie, *Miracle on 34th Street*, for inspiration. I'll take any advice I can get, but I fall asleep before the Macy's Thanksgiving Day parade is over.

CHAPTER 12

SOME SAY that Silver Creek has an unspoken bylaw stating that the Christmas season begins in early November and is in full swing by midmonth, regardless of when Thanksgiving falls. This year, Turkey Day lies only a couple of days before December. So even though Frank Sinatra has been crooning "Let it Snow" over Main Street's PA system for the past three weeks, Silver Creek residents properly carve out twenty-four hours to be grateful.

Thanksgiving night at the Carlton house is always chaos. The Mavericks, having celebrated earlier with their families, come over for dessert and cards. No surprise there. Though the holiday looks different this year, I've promised myself I won't be sad about missing Gran, if only for Pap's sake. From my earliest memories, she'd always been here for this day. It's weird without her. I make it through our small family dinner, mostly because of my latest festive distraction. This morning, I found the perfect candidate for my inaugural term as the Silver Creek Secret Santa.

Mr. Henry Sawyer has been caring for his terminally ill father. In his letter, he requested a heated sunroom because his father always wanted one added onto his home. Mr. Sawyer went into great detail about how the sunroom would give his dad something to look forward to. I understood where Mr. Sawyer was coming from. When I was caregiving, I would've done anything to make Gran happy, anything to give her something to live for.

I'm glad I have the candidate selected because I can focus on running the store. Though now, I must concentrate on *not* dropping the pumpkin pies I'm currently holding while Mom's in the kitchen making homemade whipped cream.

I'm arranging the dishes on the buffet table as voices sound from the foyer, marking the entrance of more Mavericks. Except ... one distinct timbre has me abandoning the dessert station.

I peek into the hall to find Leo Mathis wiping his boots off the mat. Beside him, old Leonard is tugging off his trapper hat that has seen one too many winters. Wait. Did Leonard invite him? I don't understand, since the Mavericks never invite outsiders, but the current of heat pulsing through me is as unexpected as Leo's presence.

Leonard spots me first. "This fella decided to join us." He claps Leo's shoulder.

Leo's gaze collides with mine. It takes several heartbeats to adjust to seeing this man in my childhood home. His hunter green sweater paired with nice-fitting jeans really works for him. So glad I put effort into my appearance today, but then I remember I'm currently wearing a faded apron that says, "Hot Stuff Coming Through."

Leonard keeps talking, completely unaware of my wardrobe regret. "After our success at the Christmas parade, the Leo Bros are ready for another gig."

I laugh. "Leo Bros?" I nod at the younger Leo, who seems to take in stride what sounds like being recruited for a geriatric boy band. "And we have plenty of food. We're always happy to have extra company." Especially one under the age of seventy who talks about things other than bowel movements.

Leo turns his beanie in his hand, a shy smile in place. "I

didn't mean to crash your party." He leans closer and whispers, "Leonard told me *you* invited me."

My stomach dips. That's why he came? Because he thought I wanted him here? Before I can respond, Leonard waves him off.

"Greta never turns away a man at her door." Leonard's insinuation has Leo arching a brow.

"Not true." I take Leonard's scarf and consider stuffing it in his big mouth. "Go join the other card junkies in the den."

Leonard frowns. "Card junkies?"

"Would you rather I call you what Gran did?" I ask sweetly, taking his hat and coat.

"Iris Carlton was a great woman with not-so-great nicknames."

"She was perfection, and you know it." I pat his jowly cheek. "And I suggest you be nice to me, because lately I've been in the habit of carrying on her traditions."

"You inherited her crazy," the older man harumphs and shuffles into the other room with all the Mavericks.

"Now I'm curious." Leo stuffs his beanie in his pocket and unzips his coat. "I'm guessing she didn't call them the Mavericks."

"No, the Aceholes."

I'm not prepared for Leo's hearty laugh, but it helps warm the drafty spaces in my soul that have been left vacant since Gran's passing.

His amusement fades into something more tender. "I wish I had met her."

"Me too." Those two words left my lips with a husky delivery that did nothing to hide my emotion. Needing to lighten the mood for my sanity, I ask, "How long has this bromance between you and Leonard been going on?" I take his jacket. Catching notes of his cologne and resisting the urge to bury my face in the collar, I move toward the hall closest.

"He's been texting me since Light-Up Night. He got my number from your phone."

I whirl toward him. "He did not." I plugged Leo's number into my cell the day we decorated the store. The Maverick had my phone during the parade because he was *supposed* to connect the Bluetooth to the karaoke machine. We all know what happened there, but what I did *not* know was that the old codger was browsing my contact list.

A smile curves Leo's perfect lips. "He says I'm listed as *Mr. February.*"

I fumble the hanger, dropping the jackets onto the rug. Why can't I ever have a Hot Girl moment? Instead, I'm in my Unhinged Cringe era. Sadly, I don't think I've peaked yet. Well, there's something to look forward to.

Leo sweeps the coats from the floor and gently hands them over.

I hang them in the closet and say over my shoulder. "So ... you *are* in the calendar? Like for real?" I realize my tone's half-scandalized, half-accusation and completely high-pitched.

His head tilts. "Why wouldn't I be? It's for a good cause."

I shut the closet door and lean against it. "I, uh, didn't think you'd go for that kind of thing."

"Interesting." He flattens his palm on the wall, right above my shoulder, and leans on that outstretched arm. His smile builds into a wicked grin. "What exactly do you think the calendar's about, Greta Carlton?"

Fire climbs my spine, and his proximity is making my head swim. "The chief made me think it's ... you know, one of those."

"Mmm." He shakes his head, and his face dips closer. "I'm still not seeing it." His voice pitches low. "Just how are you picturing me?"

That's enough of that. I playfully push his arm away. "Shut up."

He chuckles. "Only curious where your imagination was going."

With a roll of my eyes, I lead him down the hall and pause at the archway to the den. It's at this moment, reality hits. This place isn't Leo-proof. I'm at once shy and feeling awkward all over. Beside me stands Remington Orileo Mathis from a prestigious family. The man's probably used to butlers serving him food, chandeliers winking at him, and dishes trimmed in gold leaf. We have red Solo cups that have Sharpied names on them. The names are necessary because once Pap accidentally drank Bruce's Sprite spiked with Metamucil. The hall bathroom has never been the same. Point is, this scene no doubt looks ridiculous. In the den, four card tables are draped with Gran's kitsch tablecloths and decked with paper plates. Around these card tables are eleven old guys in various shades of flannel.

Leo leans over and whispers, "Seems I'm not in dress code."

I huff a laugh. "Neither am I."

"No, you're cuter." He tugs one of my apron strings, bringing me closer to him.

Pap catches this exchange, and his eyes narrow. I brace myself for a rude comment, but instead, he waves me over. "Greta, come settle a dispute."

I don't budge an inch. "If this is about whether *Gremlins* is considered a Christmas movie, we've been over this. I'm not about to take another anonymous vote."

Pap's shoulders lower. "Denny rigged it."

Denny, the quietest of the golden guys, smiles slyly and continues scratching answers onto a crossword puzzle.

I face Leo and lower my voice. "You sure you're prepared for this?" I feel like any second now I'm going to hear "The Greta Carlton Show is filmed before a live audience."

Because—between the outdated decor and the antics of the golden guys—Leo no doubt thinks he stepped into an '80s sitcom. All we're missing is the laugh track. Though I'm sure Leonard could locate one fairly quickly.

I gesture toward the Mavericks. "I hope noise and inappropriate jokes told by old men won't spoil your pumpkin pie." Then I think to ask, "You already ate dinner, right?"

He shrugs. "There was leftover Domino's at the station."

I gasp. "Today is not the day for leftovers." While I love carbs in every form, I can't allow this. With a raised finger, I signal Leo to wait and address the Mavericks. "Okay, gentlemen, the pies are on the buffet. Mom's almost done with the topping. Then you can help yourselves." I turn to Leo. "You. Follow me."

He chuckles. "I like when you're bossy."

I don't think it's me being bossy as much as it is an impulse. A reflex. A need pops up, and I feel it's my duty to step in. I've been this way for as long as I can remember. "We have an extra guest," I call to Mom as we enter the kitchen.

She's scooping out the whipped cream into serving dishes, not glancing up. "Did Professor bring a date? He mentioned last week that he had the hots for the deli lady at Thatcher's Market."

Love and lunchmeat. I don't even want to know. "You remember Leo Mathis from the parade?"

Leo respectfully says hello, even as Mom's grin widens.

"Delighted you came!" There is so much inflection in her voice that she's practically singing.

He smiles. "Thank you for having me."

"I'm grabbing Leo a plate." I motion at the barstools. "Leo, you can take a seat at the counter if you want. Oh, and that's Oggy." The schnauzer lifts his head from the rug as if hopeful one of us will toss him a crumb. "He's harmless and surprisingly the quietest out of all of us." Seriously, the dog is too silent for his own safety, considering I nearly tripped over him last week. "Though he does have a penchant for burying things in the yard." Oggy tilts his head as if offended but is soon caught up in Leo's attention.

As Leo's preoccupied with Oggy, Mom leans to whisper in my ear, "Did you invite him?"

I'm thankful the dishwasher's running, keeping Mom's low tones from reaching Leo. "No, Leonard did."

"Is he single?"

"Leonard? Yes, I believe he's been single for about two decades."

She nearly swats me with a spoon. "You know who I mean."

"I know." I angle away from Leo. "But all I care about right now is making it through Thanksgiving without any fake body parts dropping onto the food."

Her face pales. "Please tell me that didn't happen before."

Glass eyeballs, toupees, and false teeth, to name a few. I warned Leonard not to buy his dentures off eBay because he needed a custom fit, but he never listened, claiming it was a steal. I dared not ask if they were used. "Enough for me to keep back a whole pie." I point at the lone pumpkin pie on the counter.

"The things that go on in this house amaze me." With that, she grabs the bowls of whipped cream and leaves.

Mom's oblivious to my Secret Santa duty. She has no idea that her mother was wealthy. Though I couldn't help but wonder, what if Gran had left Mom all the money? Would Mom leave again? It's sad that I can't answer this.

"Anything I can do to help?" Leo's question yanks me from my dismal thoughts.

Ugh, the poor man's probably starving. "I got it." I grab a plate from the cabinet and the covered dishes from the counter. I prepare him a plate large enough to induce a food coma and warm it in the microwave. Leo joins my side as I'm rinsing off the serving spoons.

"I feel bad you're waiting on me. Can I do anything?"

I move toward the beeping microwave. "You can grab a drink from the fridge, if you want. Coke and bottled water are in the bottom drawer. There might be some Sprite left." That is, if Bruce didn't steal it all. Those men act like teenagers, raiding the kitchen and leaving their shoes everywhere.

"Greta?"

"Yeah?" I grab some silverware and glance at Leo, who's staring into the open fridge with a bewildered expression.

"There's a hand in here."

I try not to wince. "Ah, yes. The mannequin." I reach inside and grab it by its chilly fingers. "Pap was looking for this. I've no idea why it's in the fridge."

"Do you usually have plastic appendages lying around?"

As if I needed another reminder that Leo's upbringing was a stark contrast from mine. We are from different worlds, but—I raise my chin—we share the same stars. I have nothing to be ashamed of. Mostly. "This is the Mavericks' esteemed trophy." I explain its concept and history, though I don't think I succeed at making the Mavericks seem less eccentric. But Leo's a good sport, and if he thinks we're all weirdos, he doesn't show it. We rejoin the others, and while Leo inhales turkey and mashed potatoes, Pap tries to teach him the rules of Hearts.

"You never want to be stuck with the queen of spades." Pap talks like he's instructing a five-year-old, making me snicker. "She's worth thirteen points."

Leo takes a large swig of his Coke. "And points are bad?"

"The fewer, the better. Your goal is to stay at zero." Pap makes an "O" with his hand as if Leo needs the visual, but what Leo really needs is an escape. These men are intense about their cards. "If you get the queen of spades, pass it along to your neighbor at the beginning of the round."

After some painful moments that involve a pop quiz and more monologues, I rescue Leo from Pap's clutches. I turn on the television so Leo can watch football—a game that actually makes sense to him—and go help Mom with the coffee. I approach Professor with a pot of decaf, and he holds out his mug.

"Ah." Professor leans back in his chair, a satisfied sigh escaping. "It's been a great week, Greta. First, I get what you kids call a *side hustle*, and then tonight, I have your Gran's pumpkin pie. You copied the recipe to a T."

"Side hustle?" I pop my free hand on my hip. "Leonard's not recruiting you for another pyramid scheme, is he?"

"The day I join Leonard Faulk in business is the day I say the Oxford comma's outdated."

"Wow, that's serious." I pour his coffee and hand the pot to Mom as she passes. I claim the vacant chair beside Professor. "Tell me, is this new job at the local delicatessen?" I wag my eyebrows, but the second I mention the deli, Professor's gaze turns distant.

"I wish." The poor man's got it bad. "The way Phyllis works the slicer is like watching poetry."

"Um."

"Sadly, no position at Thatcher's." He adds cream to his coffee, samples it, then adds more. "I get to channel my inner thespian and pretend to be an ailing parent."

"Ailing parent?"

"You know, Henry, who owns the hardware store across town?"

I scoot my chair closer. "I know of the hardware store."

"Well, Henry really wants a sunroom. You know, those fancy ones you see on those home design shows. He wrote the Silver Creek Secret Santa with a made-up story about his dying dad, and he asked me to pretend to be his father."

This has to be the letter I read. The one I picked! And it's a scam. "Professor, that's unethical."

"What's unethical is all those college kids using ChatGPS for cheating."

"GPT."

"What?"

"Never mind." I press a finger to my temple. Just when I thought I had it all figured out. "You shouldn't lie about that, Professor. Besides, what's in it for you?"

He leans forward and pushes his glasses up the bridge of his nose. "Henry asked for forty thousand dollars in his letter, but he already got an estimate for the sunroom for around thirty-five. So, he told me I can keep the rest. Can you imagine all the Cambridge texts I can buy with five thousand dollars?" He proceeds to fake-cough. "Does that sound believable? Maybe I should add a wheeze or two."

I pull his pie away, and he protests.

I keep it hostage with one hand, and with the other, I grab a carrot stick from the snack tray. "Here." I drop the veggie in front of him. "You don't deserve Gran's pie if you're going to go through with such a fraud." Which he won't because I'm definitely not picking Henry the Hustler. It takes several minutes, but Professor promises to relinquish his future life as a scammer, and I return his pie.

With Leo absorbed in the football game, and Mom roped into a round of Hearts, I duck into the kitchen under the guise of cleaning up, but, really, I need a moment. My mood drops even lower as I dip my hands into the sudsy sink. I feel duped. This morning, I was convinced I'd chosen the right candidate. Now, I am doubting my judgment.

Maybe I should donate the money to the chamber of commerce and let them take on the role. I blow out a slow breath, struggling against the tightening in my chest. I'm morally conflicted. Gran asked in her letter that I take on the task.

Footsteps sound behind me, booted and heavy.

Leo.

I glance over my shoulder at his handsome face, and he nods at the stack of plates. "Want some help?"

Despite my earlier disappointment, the sight of him has me feeling better. "Is football over?"

"No, I felt the need for company."

"Oh? I think Leonard and Bruce were swapping enema stories. I'm sure they'd love your input."

His smile slips. "You're too sweet to do that to me."

"Am I?" I arch a brow.

"I'll wash those dishes in exchange for *you* being my company." He approaches and smoothly tugs the dishcloth from my hand.

As if I'd ever deny myself the view of a hot guy doing dishes. "You're on. You wash, and I'll dry. Here." I grab an apron from the drawer and hand it to him. "I'd hate for you to get messy." As a connoisseur of clothes, I can tell his sweater is high quality.

He holds it up and reads the front, "Chop it like it's hot."

I sweep a hand over my own apron. "Clearly, we're all sophisticated at the Carlton residence."

He chuckles. "I prefer your version of refinement." He pushes up his sleeves, and yep, with those hot wrists, I know I made the right choice accepting his offer. He slips on the apron and plunges his hands into the soapy water. "Thanks again for tonight, despite not planning on me. Next time I'll interrogate Leonard a little better."

I laugh. "I expect someone like you to have more invitations than you can handle." I remember how those women flocked to him at the firefighters' benefit. Not to mention, those who practically elbowed me out of the way at the parade to get his attention. "I would've asked if I thought there was a chance of you coming."

"Would you?" A smile flicks across his face. "That gives a man hope."

Hope? My pulse thuds like the marching beat of a thousand nutcrackers.

"Greta, can I ask you something?"

"Of course."

A sudden buzzing noise makes Leo quickly dry his hands and tug his phone from his pocket. He glances at the screen, his face filling with regret. "It's the station. I'm getting called out." He removes the apron and sets it on the counter.

"I'll get your things." I start to pivot toward the hall, but then remember. "Didn't you arrive with Leonard?" If so, I might need to run Leo to get his truck.

He shakes his head. "No, I drove. We met here."

I nod and fetch his stuff from the closet.

He shrugs into his coat, stuffs his beanie on his head, then takes my hand. "Sorry I can't stay and help."

"It's totally fine," I say, my hand captive in his large one. "Better go out the back. The Mavericks can be a tough crowd to get away from."

He offers a small smile and withdraws his touch. "Will you explain for me?"

"Absolutely."

"Thank you." He pauses as if to say something more, but his phone goes off again. His eyes meet mine. "Goodnight, Greta."

"Be safe." I watch him leave, the glow from the porchlight carving out his form until he enters the night shadow.

A collective groan rises from the living room, followed by Pap's gruff rebuke, "Leonard, get your teeth out of the pie."

Stupid eBay.

CHAPTER 13

"IT'S A FALSE ALARM," I say when Leo steps out of his truck, meeting me the next evening in front of The Memory Bank. "The package wasn't your ceramic tree like I thought. It's babydoll clothes."

His gaze dips to the box beneath my right arm. "For Mitzy?"

"You know it." I found vintage doll outfits for an amazing price. It was too good to pass over. Plus I haven't seen Mitzy these last few days with her stroller. Not that unusual, since the temperatures have been below freezing. As if on cue, winter's icy breath pulses against my skin, making me glad I wore my heavier coat today.

He shakes his head, but his eyes shine with amusement. "So you're cool with being her enabler?"

I laugh. "Her babydoll addiction exists with or without me. Those dolls might as well be fabulously dressed." I soak in his warm smile but notice the faint lines fanning from the corners of his eyes. Guilt stabs me. He'd gotten called out last night, and I've no idea how late he'd been working. Did the man get any rest? "I texted you the second I opened the box and saw it wasn't your tree. But you must've already been driving."

"It's all good." He shoves his hands in his pockets and pops a shoulder against the lamppost. While Dean Martin is crooning through the speakers and the Christmas lights—swooping from the poles overhead—glitter against the darkness, Leo adds allure to the already charming scene. "It's okay to confess to wanting to see me. I would've stopped by without the ruse of the package." His teasing smile saves him from a retaliatory swat to the arm. Not that he'd even feel it with his thick coat.

"It totally was *not* a ruse." I shift the box to hold it under my left arm, but Leo swiftly relieves me of it. "I should've opened the package when Mark left it by the back door, but I was kind of busy. Today being Black Friday and all."

Leo drums his fingers on the sides of the box. "Who's Mark?"

"My FedEx guy."

His brows wing upward, disappearing beneath his hat. "*Your* FedEx guy?"

I roll my eyes. "Not *mine* mine. Mark's the delivery dude for all of Main Street." Mark also happens to be thirty years older than me and, more importantly, married with five children. "The point is, I'm sorry you came here, and I don't have your package. But I got an email that another delivery's scheduled for tomorrow." I raise my phone as if he could see the FedEx notification, then stash it in my tote bag slung over my shoulder. "I'll be sure to open it before texting you and not just assume." I'd thought for certain Leo's tree would arrive first, considering Jared had shipped it days before I even ordered Mitzy's stuff. But alas, nothing is ever predictable in both love and shipping ETAs.

His mouth curves into an easy grin. "It's seriously okay. This means I get another chance to see you tomorrow." He steps closer. "Have you eaten yet?"

I haven't had time to eat today. I don't get the foot traffic like department stores on Black Friday, but it was steady. Not that I'm complaining. Hours fly by on days like these. Though, come six o'clock, I was ready to lock the door. I'd only been closed for a few minutes before Leo pulled up. "No, but I've got a date with a giant bowl of Lucky Charms." And an entire evening's worth of reading Secret Santa letters.

He tilts his head, masking half of his face in shadows, his low voice the very essence of temptation. "Can I convince you to cancel that date?"

My vocal cords ice over at the heat in his voice. I flick my gaze to my shop's front window. It's not the twinkle lights framing my most recent Christmas display that I'm seeing. No, I'm glimpsing the ghostly memory of Greta from two weeks ago who determined to climb out of her mental and emotional rut. A swell of boldness overtakes me. "Maybe. It depends on what you're offering." This is a dangerous game. One where I don't know the rules but mindlessly participate anyway. "It's got to be something that can trump carbs and sugar. Those are my two favorite food groups." Granted, cereal isn't the best option for dinner, but my laziness will not be denied.

He laughs. "I know an Italian place with the best garlic breadsticks and lasagna. It's a town over, but worth the drive. Since you fed me last night, it's only fair I take my turn. You up for it?"

Oh.

Talk about taking an icepick to my fragile hope. He's not asking me on a date. He feels obligated to even the score, since he thinks he crashed my Thanksgiving dinner. Am I disappointed? Yes. Am I going to pass on a chance for a free Italian meal? I'm not that delusional. "You had me at breadsticks." My growling stomach confirms I made the right choice.

"Good."

"Care if I drop that off at Mitzy's first?" I nod at the package in his arms. "She lives above Zilo's Florist, but her entrance is around back."

"Lead the way," he says as if the flower shop isn't four store-fronts down, but it's sweet of him to join me.

Our breaths puff before us as we cut through a narrow alley and walk the short jaunt to Mitzy's. We climb the stairs, and I knock on her door, which has seen better days. We wait several seconds before I try again. I exchange a glance with Leo. "Maybe she's out."

Then I hear it.

A low guttural moan.

My gaze snaps to his, but he's already pounding on the door. "Mitzy," he calls. "Are you okay?"

Another groan, only this one's twice as loud.

"Something's wrong." I rattle the doorknob. It's locked. I can't even get help from the flower shop below because it's closed. "What do we do?" Panic pitches my voice higher. "What if she's seriously hurt?"

"Call 911 and get help sent over." His voice is calm and steady. "I've got something in my truck that can open this. I'll be right back."

My blood's pounding in my ears. "Okay."

He sets the box down, squeezes my shoulder, then flies down the steps, jumping the last several.

I make a quick call to EMS and give them the information. By the time I hang up, Leo returns with this metal knife-looking thing. He slides it between the jamb and the door in line with the latch. His profession undoubtedly makes him skilled at opening doors because within a minute, he pries it open without breaking the lock. We rush into the apartment and find Mitzy collapsed on the floor.

We both kneel beside her, but I let Leo take the lead.

"Mitzy." He's assessing her for injuries. "We called for help."

She moans, and her lashes flutter. She slowly opens one eye, then the other. Her dull brown gaze latches onto Leo. "Hello, handsome." Her voice is raspy. "What's happened?" She tries to sit up, but Leo gently holds her still.

"We found you on the floor," he says soothingly. "Are you hurting anywhere? This is important, Mitzy, because I can't have you moving until I'm certain you haven't sustained any injuries.

It'll make things worse." He gently strokes her hair from her forehead. "And we can't have that."

Mitzy expels a dreamy sigh, and I'm about to join her.

She takes her time to answer, no doubt soaking up all of Leo's ministrations. Smart woman. "I think I'm okay, young man." She squeezes her eyes shut, then reopens. "Just felt a bit woozy."

Leo runs his hands over her head and seemingly goes through a mental checklist before finally assisting her to a seated position. "Would you like me to carry you to the sofa?"

Mitzy's eyes sparkle. "Yes, please."

I'm not certain if she's truly unable to stand or just milking the attentions of a good-looking guy, but I think she made the right choice. Leo carefully gathers her into his arms and gently deposits her on a blush-colored couch. I grab the pillows from the adjacent chair and prop them beneath her.

After several seconds, Mitzy confesses, "I ran out of water."

"What?!" Leo and I say in unison.

Her gaze turns sheepish. "It's been too cold to go out, and I can't drink from my tap because of the rust in the pipes. So I haven't been drinking much." She glances to her left, where a babydoll is lying in a bassinet. "Plus, little Jacqueline had a case of the sniffles."

I'm already digging out my unopened Dasani from my tote. "Here."

She gratefully takes it, but her hands are shaky. I reach to help, but her gaze seeks out Leo. He dutifully holds the bottle for her while she takes measured sips.

Noise sounds on the stairs.

"That would be emergency services," I say.

"Up here," Leo calls, even as Mitzy's eyes widen.

Within seconds, two men stride through the door, and Leo takes control, explaining the situation. I guess he knows them, considering their familiar manner. Mitzy refuses to be transported to the hospital, but certainly doesn't mind the EMTs fussing over her, checking her vitals, taking her temperature, and asking her questions. Once she signs a release form, the medical team is on their way.

"Well, that was an ordeal." Mitzy leans back against the cushions. "I'm sorry to be so much trouble." Her chipper tone is the exact opposite of apologetic, making me wonder if maybe she's been lonely.

I finally glance around her apartment. I've been inside Mitzy's place barely a handful of times, but the space is as I remember it—quaint and tidy. I know that most of her dolls are kept in the spare bedroom, except for the select few she keeps out, such as the swaddled figure in the cradle by the armchair, the curly-haired doll in the wooden highchair, and the one she claimed has a cold in the bassinet beside her.

Which reminds me.

I grab the box of baby outfits that was abandoned by the door and place it next to her on the sofa.

She squeals in delight and rummages through like a kid on Christmas.

"Greta?" Leo waves me into the kitchen but remains close, as if we're sharing secrets. "She's stable now, but we didn't fix the problem."

I nod. "The water."

"Yeah."

I watch as he tests the faucet, then opens the cabinet beneath the sink. I never once thought to consider critical-thinking skills an attractive trait. But the way his hands flex at his sides and the way his brows furrow over a pensive gaze as he's mentally searching for a solution has my mouth going dry. He folds his arms over his chest and leans against the counter. "I can run to Home Depot and grab an under-the-sink filter system. That will make her water safe to drink."

"Good idea." Tilly's parents have one of those in their house. "I'll stay with Mitzy and see if I can get her to eat something."

His face softens. "Sorry about the Italian restaurant."

I'd completely forgotten. "Don't be." I smile. "I'm just glad we were here to help."

He watches me for several soul-stirring seconds before saying, "Me too."

"Oh, maybe I can get Mitzy to leak the name of her landlord. They really should be responsible for clean pipes." I briefly have the idea that Mitzy can be my Silver Creek Secret Santa recipient, but she needs clean water right away, not three weeks from now so Fletcher can get his coveted sob story.

"That shouldn't be a problem. I'm pretty sure Chief Todd owns this building."

"Really?" Garrison Todd is a pillar in this community. If his name's on that deed, then I'm pretty sure he has no idea about Mitzy's rusty water. He'll make everything right.

With our plan in motion, Leo heads to the store to get the water purifier, and I tend to Mitzy. She's dutifully drinking her water, and I do housekeeping tasks so she won't have to exert herself this week, like running the vacuum, dusting her furniture, and throwing in a load of laundry. By the time Leo returns, I'm heating up soup (from the cans I found in the cupboard) and making grilled cheese sandwiches.

Of course, Leo bought a top-of-the-line water filtration system that he spends the next couple of hours installing. I manage to get him to eat a little, but the man is on a mission.

It's nearing ten o'clock by the time we leave Mitzy's apartment. No soul is in sight on the back alley behind Main Street, but Leo insists on walking me to my door.

I gently bump his elbow with mine. "I think Mitzy loves her new tumbler." Along with her new water purifier, Leo bought her one of those expensive, temperature retention cups so she could always keep water nearby. It was ridiculously thoughtful. "She cradled it close like one of her dolls. I think you're her new favorite person."

He chuckles. "Yet she still scolded me for not saying goodbye to Jacqueline."

She totally did. We reach the bottom of the staircase leading to my door, and I'm surprised Leo climbs the steps alongside me. "Despite that, you're a good guy, Remington Orileo Mathis."

I expect him to smile at my words, but instead, his gaze is ... smoldering. I've never been *smoldered* before, and it's quite the heady feeling. My fingers are all twitchy as they wrap around the doorknob.

"I'm glad you think so." His voice pairs well with moonlight. "Sweet dreams, Greta."

CHAPTER 14

IT'S SMALL BUSINESS SATURDAY, and The Memory Bank is the busiest it's been all month. My heart's all aglow seeing my little space full of shoppers and antiquers. Out of all the various faces that have stepped into the store, I've yet to see the one I've been watching for. The Atlantic Mold ceramic tree did indeed arrive today. As a dutiful proprietor, I texted Leo letting him know, and he promised to swing by.

As I hand a receipt to a customer purchasing vintage baskets, the bell above the door jingles. My eager gaze zips to the front. Adelaide Springfield breezes in, her hands clutching a black velvet box. All my excitement deflates in a millisecond.

"Hello, dear!" Her giddy voice clashes with Perry Como's smooth baritone over the shop's speakers. "Do you have a moment to make a deal of a lifetime?"

No, I reached my scam limit for the week. "It's pretty busy today, so—"

"Exactly what I think too. Let's get down to business." Her boisterous tone draws glances from surrounding customers.

The slight fraying on the cuff of her peacoat and the bleeding of her crimson lipstick into the tiny cracks framing her mouth can trick the humblest heart into thinking Adelaide is a harmless middle-aged housewife with a misguided hobby. She's not. Adelaide's like a flamethrower in a room of ice sculptures. She makes a commanding entrance, incinerates everything in her path, and leaves your brain in a mushy puddle of confusion. I'm not saying her sole purpose in life is to ruin my day, but I'm also *not* saying I don't have the urge to staple the "CLOSED for Business" sign to my forehead rather than listen to yet another con.

She clears her throat. Twice. "Today, I have something you've never thought you'd *ever* see in your lifetime."

"I don't doubt it."

She reaches into the bag draped over her left shoulder and pulls out a pair of white gloves. With slow movements, she puts them on, finger by finger. "Prepare yourself."

"Believe me, I am."

She smooths a hand over the velvet box and then cracks it open. "Behold." Her awed whisper makes my eye twitch.

"Costume jewelry?"

"Not just any costume jewelry. This pearl necklace was worn by Donna Reed in the classic last scene of *It's a Wonderful Life*."

She might be trying to swindle me for thousands of dollars, but at least she made it seasonal. Without a word, I hold open my hand.

She retreats a step with a tsk. "You need gloves, dear. It just so happens I've an extra pair."

I wave her off. "Please set the box on the counter."

"Of course." She does as I ask but hovers close. "Don't you need a loupe?"

Adelaide is the cheese grater to my shredded patience.

"You know, those magnifying glass thingys that jewelers use?"

"Thank you, Adelaide. I know what a loupe is. I'm just ..." *Scraping for my sanity.* "Trying to gently inform you that this is not a piece from the '40s." Unfortunately for Adelaide, cinema wardrobe is one of my specialties. "The lobster-claw clasp, like this one, wasn't patented until the mid-nineties."

Her gaze narrows. "Are you certain?"

"Very."

"Hmm." She cautiously closes the box, which is probably worth more than the trinket. "I'll have to verify this from my source."

"Thank you for coming in." And because I can't help myself and my stupid soft soul, I offer her my voucher for a free entrée and dessert at the café. It's a small token, but maybe she'll grasp the hint that Christmas is the season of giving and not scamming. "This expires soon, and I won't use it. I remember you once saying how much you enjoy their cheesecake."

She brightens. "Oh, it's divine."

"Then enjoy." I smile, and as she says goodbye, a customer approaches me asking about a piece in the locked display case. I grab my keys from the register and follow her to where her daughter, I assume, is leaning against the case, typing away on her phone.

The mom points at an early nineteenth-century mirror. "We love this, but I don't see a tag."

"Ah, that's a Sylvia Stave piece. She was a silversmith from Sweden during the first half of the twentieth century. The art deco handle is beautiful." I can go on about the mirror, but judging by the younger girl's loud cracking of her gum and the older woman's rapid tapping of her boot, they don't seem like antique enthusiasts. "It's on sale for three hundred." Which is about half the cost of what they'd find at other shops. I unlock the case, retrieve the pewter piece, and let the ladies get a good look at it.

"We'll take it." She gives a quick nod and hands it back to me. "It'll look nice in my daughter's dorm. She's attending college in the spring and wants everything in a Roaring '20s theme."

"Oh, the mirror's actually from the '30s."

The mom lifts a narrowed shoulder. "Close enough."

"Great, I can hold this for you if you're still shopping or—"

"We're ready to check out now," she says, digging through her purse.

Walking to the register, I smile at the daughter, a spitting image of her mom with crystal blue eyes and dark hair. "What school are you going to?"

"Harvard." She cracks her gum again as if it's no big deal, but then adds, "Well, not officially. I didn't get accepted yet."

"But she will," her mother puts in. "We've got it all worked out."

"Oh, yes." The teen shoves her phone into her coat pocket. "It's what I asked Santa for. I mean, not like the mall Santa, but the Silver Creek secret one. A full ride to Harvard would be the best Christmas gift."

I inwardly wince. "Even though you didn't get accepted yet?"

She shrugs, then sneaks a glance at her mom, who seems to be answering a text. "If I don't get in, then I'll put the money from the Secret Santa toward a new car. My Jeep's a year old." She wrinkles her nose as if her car expired like rancid meat. Meanwhile, my Highlander's pushing twelve.

I'm going through the motions of the transaction, but my mind's disengaged. I vaguely recall a Secret Santa letter asking for college tuition, but I didn't imagine *this* scenario. I would think there are members of this community who need real support and are not just trying to get free cash. But how am I going to find that one? So far, I've already ferreted out two candidates who were frauds. How many more are in that folder? How can I tell? Leo said he learned over the years how to spot the phony in people, but I don't have the luxury of time. I'm on a deadline.

I finish up with the mother and daughter, exchanging goodbyes, as my business phone rings. I numbly answer, "The Memory Bank. Greta speaking."

"This is Jeff Reilly from Timeless Treasures. I was told you're on the hunt for a Vallerton Nativity."

I blink as the words sink in. The Vallerton. Leo's antique! The unicorn! "Yes," I say calmly, though my head's spinning. "I have an interested customer."

"I've got what you're looking for."

Say what? Pen, I need a pen. I sprawl across the counter and scramble for one. He gives me the address. Usually I would arrange the sale and have the owner ship me the piece, but one, this man isn't from my regular, trusted contacts. Two, there's no way he'll let that set out of his sight. Not that I blame the guy. "Okay, I'll pass this on to my customer."

Said customer is walking into my store even now.

My pulse races, but this time it has nothing to do with the Vallerton. Leo's smile is enough to make me forget a person is speaking to me on the phone.

"I can only hold this until closing." That brings me back to reality. "We lock the doors at seven."

I glance at my watch, and my stomach drops. It's already after four. "That doesn't give my customer much time, especially since your shop's over an hour away." Possibly an hour and a half.

"Well." He draws out the simple word into two syllables. "I'm certain I don't have to tell *you* how in-demand a Vallerton Nativity is."

Not sure I like his tone, but the man has a point. "I'll let him know." I hang up with a huff.

Leo approaches with a swagger I'm not exactly prepared for. He holds out a purple tumbler. "I realized I should've bought one of these for you too."

My jaw sags at the unexpected gift. "Thank you."

"I take hydration levels seriously." His tone is teasing, but I detect an earnestness in his eyes. After the scare with Mitzy yesterday, I've been much more conscious of my own water intake. I checked on our doll-loving patient before work this morning. She seemed disappointed to find me at her door rather than Leo, but other than a little pouty, she was doing great.

I lift my new cup in a *cheers*. "I promise I won't faint in your arms."

He dimples. "No, I'd rather you step into them willingly."

"You're such a flirt." I feebly swat him. "Okay. I've got good news and I-feel-like-throat-punching-someone news. Which first?"

He eyes me as if unsure if he should laugh or throw chocolate at me from a distance. "Let's start with good."

"I just got a call about the Vallerton."

His eyes widen, and a smile lights his face. "That's great. I was thinking it's a lost cause."

"Bad news is you have to leave, like, now. Because he won't hold it for you." Which is fair, but still. Leo doesn't know what to look for. There are many knockoffs, and I doubt Leo could spot a forgery. If only we could trade talents just for December. I could borrow his gift of spotting fake people, and he can have my skill in antiquing.

Or maybe we can strike a deal.

"Thanks for coming with me." Leo adjusts his hand on the wheel and sends me a smile full of wonder as if I'd told him I spend my evening hours watching *SportsCenter* and eating hot wings.

"Of course." I keep my tone breezy like it's no big deal to rearrange my entire schedule and recruit Tilly to tend the store. I caught her just as she was finishing up her shift at the café. Tilly has run the store for me on several occasions throughout the years. She knows nothing about antiques, but she can run a register and ensure nothing burns down. I for sure owe her one.

"I haven't been to Haviland in years. Gran used to go when I was younger. They had some great auctions there, and an amazing pizza place, if I remember right."

He checks the GPS on his dash and takes the next exit. "This will be my first time going."

"It's smaller than Silver Creek." Which he'll see in a matter of minutes because we've been on the road for at least an hour, and I still haven't worked up the courage to share with him about the deal I'd like to make. I grimace as snowflakes dot the windshield. "Though I think the town has its own charm." I've been keeping the conversation surface-level because I'm inwardly freaking out. In the shop, I had a brilliant plan of asking Leo to help me with the Secret Santa stuff in exchange for my help searching for the antique. But I realize my stupid mistake, we're literally on our way to get said antique. I have nothing else to offer the man, unless he wants to take sewing lessons. The last time I tried to teach someone, it was a Maverick's great-granddaughter, who had a habit of pressing the sewing machine foot pedal every time my fingers were near the needle. I shiver at the memory.

"You okay over there? Cold?" He turns up the heat.

"I'm good. Just thinking."

"About?" he asks with a wicked curl to his lips. "Unless you don't want to tell me. I know you've got that habit of thinking about what I wear to sleep."

"Yeah, it keeps me awake at night," I say dryly. "And you were supposed to forget about that." I swat his shoulder at his deep chuckle. This light teasing makes me see that I don't actually know much about Leo. Yeah, I don't need the details about his nighttime routine, but other questions remain unanswered. Like, who are these antiques for? He mentioned before that they weren't for him. As a rule, I don't get involved too much with my customers' personal lives, but this is different, isn't it? His grandparents passed, but what about his other relatives and family friends? I have no idea if he's an only child or how he lived before coming to Silver Creek.

"You realize I'm at a disadvantage here," I finally say. "You know more about me than I do about you. You told me you went to prep school, but after that, it's a question mark. Did you go to college? Do you have a string of ex-wives? Any felonies?"

"Yes, no, and no."

"Nope. You have to expound more than that, my friend. You've seen my eleven-year-old school picture." Which I would've totally taken down had I known Leo would be at our house on Thanksgiving night. It's hard to stay alluring when the man has an image of you with buck teeth, crooked bangs, and in a Big Time Rush shirt. "So yeah, I need more details and make it good."

"I went to Florida State, despite my parents wanting me to attend an Ivy League school."

"Major?"

"Finance."

"Did you like it?"

"Not really, but it's useful." He flicks the windshield wipers, clearing away the specks of snow. "I lived in Florida for a bit, then moved around a lot. My parents said I was restless." He shrugs. "Maybe I was."

He drifted from place to place while I dropped anchor in Silver Creek. "How'd you become a firefighter?"

"I was a volunteer in Florida. When I came back to Silver Creek, I ran into Chief Todd. He told me the department was in need of more volunteers, so I signed on."

Oh. He's not in a permanent position. That's good to know. "My Pap was a volunteer when he was younger."

Leo nods. "He told me at Thanksgiving. He also said he knows fifty ways to make my death look like an accident if I messed with you."

"He did not." I bury my face in my palms. "Never mind, I can totally see him saying that. Sorry."

"Don't be." His voice turns unexpectedly soft. "It's nice to have people who have your back."

I warm at his words because, despite Pap's gruffness, he has a loyal heart.

"Any other questions?"

"Well, there's always the dealbreaker ones, like your go-to karaoke song, your most embarrassing moment, and your stance on eating raw cookie dough. But those answers can kill a friendship, so I'll give you time to think."

He laughs. "I appreciate it."

Okay, it's time to dive into what I've been avoiding. I'm unsure if Leo will make a deal with me, but I need his help with this Secret Santa thing. "Since we're better friends, there's something I've been wanting to say."

"Shoot."

"So Fletcher wanted to see me …"

"Ah, I get it."

"Get what?" I've barely gotten started.

"You and Fletcher Thomas. I thought something was up with you two. It makes sense now."

"What? No. There's nothing between us." Why does everyone think that? "Also, what makes sense?"

He seems to be taking in what I said. The furrow in his brow has eased after my admission, but tension lingers in the stiff way he's gripping the wheel. Instead of answering me, he grows quiet. It appears I'm not the only one hiding something.

"I wasn't going to resort to this, but you leave me no choice." I lean on the console between us, brushing his arm. "I'm reminding you of our contract. You promised to answer all my questions."

"I did?" His gaze briefly jerks to mine, then returns to the road.

"Yeah, at the gala."

"That was only for the dance."

"Hmm, was it though?" I tap my jaw in exaggerated thought.

"I don't think I put an end date on that verbal contract. All I said was if I dance with you, then you answer *all* my questions."

He shakes his head with a good-natured scoff. "So now I have to answer your questions forever?"

"See, that's not hard to understand. Now spill. No, wait." My brain latches onto something I should've caught weeks ago. "Fletcher told me he'd known you since you were kids."

"That's right."

"Then why didn't you ask *him* about me? You know, when you missed our meetup. You said you asked around to see if anyone knew me. You should've talked to Fletcher."

"I did."

My mouth drops. "You asked him? You asked Fletcher Thomas if he knew me?"

He nods. "I talked to him a few weeks after you and I were supposed to meet. Told him everything. I mentioned your name, but he acted clueless."

"Fletcher would absolutely know who I am." But then again, could he have been protecting me? Like Mitchell had? This all happened around the time Gran passed, and Fletcher would know that I was grieving. Though he could've told me afterward. Something's off. "What about the gala? He introduced us like we were strangers."

Leo's jaw hardens. "He did."

"Why? Do you think your conversation with him slipped his mind?"

"Only Fletcher can answer that." He slows to a stop at a light. "But you can imagine my surprise when I arrive at the gala, and the beautiful woman on Fletcher's arm is the one he claimed he didn't know."

Beautiful? He can't casually drop that kind of remark and not expect my gaze to swing to his. I expect to see his playful smirk, but his expression is serious. Fletcher's actions must've really bothered him. "It's strange."

"Yeah."

"And frustrating." For an entire year, I thought Leo ditched me. Fletcher could've cleared everything up. Why didn't he? And the gala! I distinctly remember Fletcher's strained smile when Leo approached me in the ballroom. Tension simmered between the men, but I'll have to think on that later because we arrive at Timeless Treasures Antiques. And I still haven't told Leo what I wanted.

CHAPTER 15

LEO HOLDS the door to Timeless Treasures open, and I step inside, thankful for the pocket of warmth. We wipe our feet on the mat, and Leo fixes an amused gaze on me. "Are you humming 'Eye of the Tiger'?"

I freeze. "Am I?" The regrets roll on like the Polar Express. I press my lips together for a firm second as punishment for their rebel ways. "I blame Pap. It's what happens when one is raised by their grandparents." *Rocky*'s not from my generation, but Pap watched it religiously, so much that he could quote the whole film. "That song's ingrained in my psyche. He'd blare it before every important event. And for most every tense-filled moment I faced growing up. The day I took my license exam, he wrote in liquid chalk on my passenger window *I'm a girl with a will to drive.*"

"Nice." Chuckling, Leo adjusts his ball cap. "You expecting something I don't know, champ? Does it get wild in antique shops?"

"What happens in antique shops stays in antique shops." I loosen my scarf and square my shoulders. "Let's do this." I focus on my mission, refusing to allow myself to get distracted by the urge to browse the aisles. I love to visit other shops to get ideas for my own, but now's not the time. I approach the counter, Leo hovering near.

A middle-aged man with a bald head and bleached goatee is sitting on a stool and polishing cufflinks. He glances up with the standard, "May I help you?"

"We're looking for Jeff Reilly."

He stands and sets the tray of cufflinks on the counter. "That's me."

"I'm Greta from The Memory Bank." I offer a friendly smile. "You called me earlier about having a Vallerton."

"Ah, I didn't realize you'd be coming. I thought the piece is for your customer."

I don't bother to explain. "May I see it?"

"Give me a second." He disappears into a back room, and I allow my gaze to roam. Vintage sports things, like wooden golf clubs, leather football helmets, and a row of ice skates, line the far wall. My focus snags on a table next to Leo. "Do you want a souvenir with your name on it?" I point to the display of Remington typewriters.

His mouth tips into a flirty smile. "That's more your style. Would *you* like something with my name on it? You know, to remember our little adventure." He moves closer and drops his voice. "Though why buy that old dusty Remington when you can have the real thing cheaper? It'll move better and run longer."

I still. "Did you ... just quote Hitchcock's *To Catch a Thief?*" Okay, not an exact quote, considering the character from the film wasn't discussing typewriters, but Leo's remark was similar enough that I caught the reference.

His grin gentles around the edges. "It's what happens when one's raised by their grandparents."

He was too? I know he said that he spent summers with them while not at school. It seems they had an influence on him as well. I return his smile, then force myself to focus on the goal at hand. "These typewriters are all in decent shape. He's got quality merchandise."

"That's promising." Leo pulls out his wallet. "I should've stopped by the ATM. Think he'll take credit?"

Before I can answer, the owner returns, holding a single piece. "Here's what I got."

I glance at Leo and back at the owner. "It's the baby Jesus."

He places it on the counter. "The most important figure, if you ask me."

It is, but that's not the point. "I thought you had the complete set." When I started running The Memory Bank by myself, most people openly questioned if I had the expertise to oversee it. I've had longtime customers doubt and challenge my antique knowledge, but no one has ever looked at me with so much annoyance mixed with showy superiority as Jeff Reilly.

He leans on the counter, looking down at me. "Do you realize how difficult it is to get a Vallerton?"

Leo widens his stance in true alpha male fashion, but I press a hand to his arm.

"I do, actually." I lift my chin. "That's why I was surprised when you said on the phone 'I got what you're looking for.'" In this case, air quotes are necessary.

"I'm sorry for the misunderstanding, but this is all I have."

I gently pick up the figure and study it. The paint colors and glazing seem on point. No dents or scratches, which is amazing for an early twentieth-century piece. I turn it upside-down. "Oh."

"Oh, what?" The man leans over, getting into my space.

"We have to pass." I set the figure down rather than handing it to him. I don't want him intentionally bobbling the piece to make us pay for anything broken. "Thank you for reaching out."

His face reddens, which, coupled with his slightly oblong, bald head, makes him look like an oversized Christmas bulb. "Are you passing because I don't have the full set? I'll offer this to you for eight hundred dollars. The infant figure alone is worth a thousand. Any true antique dealer would know this is a steal."

I abandoned my store to come here. I'm hangry. And in my left shoe, my sock is slipping down my foot. So no, Jeff the Jerk, I'm not in the mood to coddle your ego. "Any *true* antique dealer would know your baby Jesus is a fake." I pivot on my heel, grab Leo's wrist, and stride toward the door.

"It's authentic," Jeff blusters.

"Check the hallmark," I say without looking back and make my exit with Leo glued to my side.

The second we're outside, Leo lets out a low whistle. "Nicely done, champ." He nudges my shoulder. "It's now confirmed that you do have a payback side." He threw back my words from the gala. "But I want to know if it's really a fake or were you pranking him for being an idiot?"

"It's a phony."

"Amazing." The corners of his mouth lift into an incredulous smile. "How could you tell? It looked like the picture I've got on my phone."

"The hallmark was all wrong. The stamped letters on a real Vallerton piece are farther apart." I shake my head. "It's a sad, sad world when people make impostor baby Jesuses."

"You, Greta Carlton, just saved me a thousand bucks. How about I start repaying my debt with dinner? Besides, I still owe you from last night." He put in his offer smoothly, but my mind's hung up on the fact that Leo would've bought that fake had I not been here. This brings me back to my initial deal. Will he go for it?

Leo unlocks his truck, but I'm rooted to the sidewalk. A knot puckers between his brows. "You okay?"

"Can we, maybe, walk for a bit?" I gesture toward Haviland's Main Street. Jeff's antique store is at the very end of the line of shops.

"Sure." He pockets his keys and rejoins my side. He takes the outside spot, closest to the street. While there's hardly any traffic, my romantic soul applauds this little protective gesture.

I brush off the remaining specks of annoyance from my exchange with the jerky shop owner and breathe in the moment, emptying my thoughts of everything but the scene spreading before me. "This"—I motion to the brightly lit surroundings— "has my heart. There's something about Christmas and small towns." While I'm partial to Silver Creek, this main street is charming. Speakers, attached to the iron streetlamps, are softly playing instrumental Christmas songs. The storefronts are aglow with seasonal splendor. The busyness, so attached to the holidays, doesn't exist here. A peace and stillness that whispers of bygone seasons hangs in the air. "Sometimes I feel like I was born in the wrong era."

His hand brushes mine. "I like you in this one."

I glance at him as the interplay of light and shadow flits across his face. "My tastes don't match my generation's. Probably because I was raised by my grandparents. I'd rather watch an Audrey Hepburn movie than scroll through social media."

"That's not a bad thing."

I shrug, uncertain what to say.

He pauses beside a bench nestled between a barber shop and toy store. "I never got to ask you the other night." The same intensity that made my chest squeeze in Pap's kitchen darkens his eyes.

My breath turns shallow. "Yes?"

"At the parade, I overheard your friend apologizing about leaving you alone on the fifteenth."

Oh. That. "Yeah. She's going to New York. She felt bad about canceling our plans." I offer the less-emotional version, but Leo's not having it.

"She mentioned the fifteenth. Does she know about last Christmas?" His gaze holds mine, then inches slowly over my face. He's fully focused on me, and I can't even enjoy his attention because he's digging into a moment I wish to forget. "The fifteenth was the night of our missed date."

"It was." I glance away. "But that's not what she meant."

A car goes past. The song over the speakers switches to "Jingle Bells." And Leo is waiting patiently for me to continue, but I don't know if I can.

He steps closer. "You can tell me." A breeze pulls a lock of hair across my cheek, and he knuckles it back.

I nearly slide my eyes closed at his touch. "The fifteenth is the night that Gran died. Tilly was apologizing for missing the first anniversary of her passing."

Leo pales. "You mean, your Gran passed the same night I didn't show?"

"Yeah." My bottom lip trembles, and I sink my teeth into it. This was painful, but maybe I need to voice it. Maybe talking will drain its strength. Or feed it. I don't know. "She woke from her nap and called for me. But she slipped back into sleep and then was … gone."

"You didn't get to say goodbye."

"No."

Before I can draw another shaky breath, Leo pulls me to him, wrapping strong arms around me. He buries his face in my hair and murmurs, "I'm sorry, Greta. You missed it all, and then I never showed. I can't begin to say how awful I feel."

This embrace isn't sensual or even romantic, but it provides the warmth my bleak heart needs. "Thank you." I angle back, peering up at him and savoring the comfort of his touch. "It's not your fault though. It's just one of those things." The notes of misery in his gaze make me press into him more. "This past year wasn't easy, but I'm learning more about her. Things I never understood before."

"Like?"

Here I go. "Did you believe in Santa when you were little?"

He's quiet for a handful of pulse-pounding seconds. No doubt from my abrupt switch in conversation. "I honestly can't remember. I think I did when I was really young." He releases me but remains close.

"I got made fun of in second grade because I told some girls at recess what I wanted from Santa. I came home crying and begged Gran to tell me the truth—if he existed or not. Do you know what she said?"

"Tell me." Leo leads me to the bench, and we sit.

"She told me about the real-life Saint Nicolas. How he gave to those in need. How he used his inheritance to help the poor." I can see everything so clearly now. "She told me to never stop believing in Santa. Not exactly the made-up one, but to believe in the message behind it, like the power of giving, the strength of love. She reminded me of that every Christmas since." Always believe. She even wrote those words in her last letter.

He strokes his thumb over my knuckle. "She was a wise woman."

"She was also the Silver Creek Secret Santa."

His brows rise. "Seriously?"

I nod. "I found out a week ago. I was shocked she never let on, but looking back, she told me in her own little ways."

He reaches over and adjusts my scarf, his thumb grazing my neck. "Your gran did a lot of good."

"She wants me to continue the tradition. But I don't know where to start." I exhale the air from my chest, feeling the pressure of the task. "I thought it would be simple. Like, just pick the person whose story hit me in the feels. I've already been duped twice." I tell him about my experiences so far. "Then I remembered what you told me at that gala. You said you could pick out the fake from the real. I thought … we can strike a bargain."

Interest lights his eyes. "What kind of bargain?"

I shift under the weight of his stare. "Maybe I can help you with your search for the nativity set, and you can help me find the right candidate. I feel so lost right now."

"Deal."

I blink. "Don't you want to, uh, think about it more?" At least longer than half a second.

His grin unleashes. "No. In this bargain, I'm the winner."

Time to wave the caution flag. "You might not be the winner because I can't guarantee we'll find an authentic Vallerton. It helps that Rene Vallerton was a local artist. It boosts our chances, though I can't promise anything. Only to help you search."

"Got it." He glances pointedly about, and I can't help but follow his searching gaze.

"What are you looking for?"

"Mistletoe. There's got to be some around here." His teasing smile steals my very breath. "So we can seal our agreement."

"A handshake works."

His head lolls toward me. "It lacks a festive touch, but okay." He sticks out his hand, and I slip my fingers in his. His hand's warm, calloused, and perfectly engulfs mine. "Does this make me your elf?" He gives a gentle squeeze. "Because I remember how you feel about elves."

I sputter a laugh. No doubt he was referencing my destruction of Josie's light display. "That was a one-time thing. I'm generally pro-elf."

"Good to know." He releases my hand. "When do we start?"

Oh man. Am I prepared to spend more free time with Leo? It's so tempting. *He* is so tempting. "I have some obligations at the beginning of the week, but, usually, I have Sundays and Mondays off. And most evenings free." Because I have no life. "I can also do early mornings before the shop opens."

"I can do Sunday and Monday night and any mornings."

"Perfect. How about we start Tuesday morning? Say seven? We can meet at the shop."

"Sounds great." He points to the restaurant across the street. "Should we celebrate our bargain over pizza?"

Monday morning finds me at Brewtiful Grounds, sitting across from Fletcher Thomas, who's sipping his peppermint macchiato made by the pageant princess herself. Tilly's behind the counter, giving me a thumbs-up every five minutes.

"I wanted to check in and see how you're doing." He sets his coffee down and graces me with a compassionate look. "A lot has changed since we last met."

"It's harder than I thought it would be." My mind's eye can picture the stack of letters still on my counter, taunting me. "But I have a plan in motion." Leo. He's the plan.

He smiles. "That's good. I'm glad you're adapting. It was a lot to pile on you."

I take a sip of my vanilla gingerbread latte. "Yeah, it was. Plus, you weren't entirely truthful with me." All this time. He knew something—a *huge* something—about Gran that I was clueless about. Though that wasn't the only secret he withheld from me. "Fletcher?"

"Hmm?"

"I kinda loathe you right now."

"You're very polite in your hatred. May I ask why?" After a second, his brows sink as if in realization. "Because I didn't tell you sooner about your grandmother? I wasn't allowed to with client confidentiality."

"Okay, fine. You can toss out legal jargon for that. But I was thinking more about Remington Mathis."

"What about him?" He leans back against the booth and stretches his arm along the benchtop, the picture of ease and relaxation.

"He asked you about me last year, and you told him you had no idea who I was. Really, Fletcher? Way to make a girl feel memorable."

"What?" His eyes widen. "You? You're Remington's mystery lady? The one he couldn't track down?"

"Do you know any other Gretas?" Maybe he does. I mean, I

don't own exclusive rights to the name. "Or am I that forgettable?"

He blows out a breath. "When Remington asked, he mentioned this charming, witty, beautiful woman."

I don't know if I should be flattered that Leo thought such of me or angered that Fletcher decidedly did not. "Fletcher, remember when I gave you that pep talk about how to talk to ladies? You're regressing."

He realizes his mistake. "No, no. That's not what I meant. You're all those things."

"Very convincing," I deadpan. "But continue. I'll give you a chance to redeem yourself."

He chuckles. "You *are* all those things, but only when people get to know you." He gives me a pointed look. "The first time we met—"

"I've known you pretty much all my life."

He leans forward, eyes on me. "No, I mean the *first* time we really spoke to each other. Do you remember?"

"Vaguely." I only revisited that encounter every night at 3 a.m. for months on end. "Something about me falling into a trash can. The details are kinda fuzzy."

He laughs. "You saw me and bolted. Like you wanted to avoid all conversation."

Sounds about right. "If only I could've avoided the trash can with the same finesse." In my hurry to get away, I didn't notice the giant plastic bin and landed headfirst into it. Not my finest moment.

"When I helped you out, you were covered in hives. Which you said was …"

"Allergies."

"More specific," he coaxes.

"High pollen count," I confess with a frown.

"And high pollen couldn't be the reason because …"

"It was December." I drop my head onto my balled hands.

"You're not helping me loathe you any less. You're actually fueling my disdain."

His smile widens. "I only mention this because I know how you are around people. New people in particular. You're more introverted."

Another valid point. If extroverted-ness was like cell reception, I'm the equivalent of one bar. And it's blinking off and on. "So you assumed that Remington's Greta couldn't be *this* Greta." I point to myself. "Because I have the social flair of a blind raccoon." Which is why I was amazed at myself when I could freely talk and flirt with Leo that night. It must've been the ambiance of the moonlit moment.

"Now I have a question. Are you Remington's Greta?"

"Huh?" I blink. "Yeah, I was the one who was at the park that night. Obviously, I didn't realize he never showed because he was fighting fires. We didn't exchange numbers or full names."

"No, I meant are you and him … a couple?" He takes a long sip of his drink, watching me over the brim of his cup.

"A couple?" I repeat like I'm some sort of robotic parrot. "No, we're not together."

He nods. "Probably for the best. I've known Remington my entire life. He never stays in one spot very long. As your friend, I thought you'd want to know."

CHAPTER 16

BEADS OF SWEAT roll down the line of my spine.

Five more to go.

I up the volume of my playlist and determine to finish this workout better than I started—which was me half-asleep and nearly dropping a twenty-pound dumbbell on my foot. After this, I have an hour to grab a shower, dress, and snag some breakfast before meeting Leo at the shop.

I nearly crest my chin-up when a brisk knock makes me jolt. I release the bar and land steadily on my feet. Swiping my forehead with my wrist, I glance at my door. Must be a delivery person. I'm expecting a few items for the store, and all the local drivers know to check upstairs if I'm not below.

It's a bit early to get a package, though shipping companies extend their hours during the holidays. I once got a toaster at 1 a.m. After a swig of water, I open the door and am hit with a blast of cold and the awareness that Leo's standing a few feet away.

"Uh, hi." I try to act casual even as a drop of sweat falls off my nose. Lovely.

His eyes scan over me in all my post-workout glory—which is me looking flushed, disheveled, and sporting perspiration stains in key areas. He clears his throat. "I knocked downstairs, but no one answered."

I usher him inside because the moisture's freezing on my face. Once I close the door, a surge of panic slices through me. Did I leave my bra on the couch? Is something disgusting in my sink? I sneak a sweeping glance. I'm positive my ceiling fan blades are fuzzy and the counter's cluttered, but nothing alarming strikes me. I did put up my Christmas tree the other day, so I don't look like a grinchy Santa. "I thought we were meeting at eight."

"Didn't you say seven?" He pulls out his phone, no doubt to check his calendar.

"I probably did." Crap. I really need to start writing things down. "Sorry, I got my times mixed up."

He takes my orderless ways in stride and offers a smile. "We can do this another time."

"No," I say a little too quickly. "It's my stupid fault. I don't have much time to delay with this Santa stuff." I grab the bulky folder off the counter. "Here are the letters." I watch his eyes widen. "Yeah, it's a lot. Hence, why I'm freaking out."

"We got this." Our hands brush as he takes the folder, which, under any other circumstances, would've sent a spike of awareness through me. But all I'm noticing is how slick and hot my skin is.

I resist the urge to use the bottom of my tank top to wipe my face. "Maybe you can browse the letters while I grab a quick shower. Is that okay?"

"Sure." He settles on my couch, and the nearby glow from the tree is working its whimsical sway because now I'm imagining Leo and me sharing buttered popcorn, watching Christmas movies with our feet tangled.

I hate to shake the daydream, but my reality needs addressing and more deodorant. "There's fruit and cinnamon rolls on the table if you want."

His mouth moves into a smile far too appealing for seven in the morning. "That's like two ends of the food spectrum."

I shrug, drawing his attention to my bare shoulders. "With me, it's either super healthy or junk food. There's no in-between. Anyway, I'll be right back." And I head off to take the world's fastest shower.

Less than ten minutes later, I return to the living room in sweats, my wet hair in a messy topknot.

Upon my entering, Leo glances over. Those dark eyes make a slow trek over my face, stirring me to wonder if any of those secrets swirling in his gaze are ever about me. I realize this is the first time he's seen me without makeup. Not like it's a big deal, but he told me authenticity in his world was scarce. Maybe a bare-faced Greta is a novelty to him. We're caught in this uncertain moment until my stomach growls.

Leo smiles.

Wonderful. I snag a cinnamon roll from the table along with a couple paper towels—because I know myself and my messy ways—and join him on the sofa.

He settles back against the cushion. "Can I make another suggestion?"

"Skip the hassle and run off to the Caribbean?" I have enough in my bank account now for a lifetime supply of SPF 75 sunscreen. "I'm joking. Mostly. Now tell me your idea."

"I think you need to be more organized."

"I'm fresh out of that skill, but can I interest you in some self-deprecating humor or witty deflections? I can roll those out all day long."

Leo's not falling for my redirection tactic. "I promise it'll make your life easier."

I groan and bite off a hunk of my cinnamon roll. This conversation needs a serving, or twenty, of sugary carbs. "I can try to do better. Though I think it'll be a failed effort." Like the time I tried to wax my own eyebrows. It was painful, and I ripped off half the arch of my right brow. I had to pencil the rest in for a couple of months. Sadly, my senior pictures were during that season. In the end, I learned to stay away from DIY wax kits, and Gran learned she could pay extra for Photoshop editing.

Leo glances at the folder between us. "A few of the letters were beat up. I couldn't read them."

"Ugh, yeah." I snatch my water bottle from the table and wash down my breakfast. "Some Scrooge swiped the letters from the café community mailbox and trashed them. Tilly salvaged what she could." But I agree. Some of those letters are hardly legible. What if one of those ruined entries was written by the perfect candidate?

"Might be wise to invest in locked, slotted boxes for next year."

I don't want to think about next Christmas. I'm struggling with this one.

"I started weeding out the letters that have no contact information." He lifts a small pile of papers. "Unfortunately, since there's no way to reach these people, you can count them out."

I nod. "Those are probably from people who submitted their letters at the in-store mailboxes. There's no envelope or email address on them to trace back." I grab my phone, open my notes app, and, like the recovering messaholic I am, jot down reminders for the future, such as discovering ways to ensure candidates include their contact info and Leo's suggestion about buying locked mailboxes. "Okay. We're making progress." I glance at the pile, then at him. "Do any of them scream at you?"

He exhales. "There are a lot of needs. I didn't get a chance to read through them all, but the ones I did are heart-wrenching."

"Right? And my main issue is how to know which are legit."

"Let's work through them, one at a time." He picks up the stack of letters. "We'll see how much headway we can make in an hour and go from there."

I appreciate him taking the time to help, but I feel bad. Yeah, we made a bargain, but I'm not sure I can hold up my end of the deal in finding him the Vallerton. Though just to let him know

I'm trying, I say, "I've reached out to several of Gran's old contacts in the antique world. I didn't before because many of them are retired. I'm hoping they might know someone who can give us a lead."

"Thank you." He gives an appreciative smile, but the skin around his eyes tightens. I noticed this shift in mood the day he'd first asked about the antiques. Something tells me there's a story behind this search, and, judging by his previous reluctance, it might not be one with a happy ending.

"I remember you saying the antiques aren't for you. Can I ask who they're for?"

He sets the folder between us on the sofa, a frown settling between his dark brows.

"If it's too personal, you don't have to tell."

"Last Christmas." He sits forward and clasps his hands between his open knees, his gaze fixing on the rug. "The house-fire that happened the night of our date. It was brutal." He exhales a ragged breath. "An elderly couple was inside."

I gasp, but he continues. "The husband came out first, thinking the wife was already rescued. When he didn't see her, he went back into the flames." Leo's large frame is rigid and tense, but it's the haunted notes in his glower that has my heart tearing at the edges. "What sucks is, the wife *was* rescued. The firefighter brought her out the back door. The husband didn't know, and he went on searching for her. By the time I got to him, he'd collapsed from smoke inhalation." He shook his head. "He didn't make it."

I cover my open mouth. How awful. "And his wife?"

"She survived, but she's heartbroken. They'd been married over sixty years."

My eyes sting. This couple shared a long love like Gran and Pap. Pap grieves his bride in his own way, and I know he misses her, especially during her favorite season. But this? It's tragic on so many levels.

"If the husband only waited another couple of minutes, he'd

still be alive." Leo's voice is heavy with regret. "He didn't think. Just ran back into the fire."

"Of course he did. Because love doesn't think. It acts." I glance away to swipe at the tears collecting on my lower lashes. "He did all he could to make her world right again. Even if it cost him. Because that's what sacrificial love does. It gives without a second thought." Leo's gaze is on me, and I'm unsure if it's because I got emotional or because I talked too much.

"I visited her a couple months after everything happened."

"Do you usually do that? Visit the families, I mean?"

He swallows. "Sometimes. This one was different. It was tough on me." He's staring at the rug again. "I hadn't lost anyone before. I replayed that night a thousand times, thinking about what I could've done to get to him sooner."

Then it clicks. This must be the *incident* Fletcher had referred to at the firefighters' charity event. "I'm sure you did all you could. My heart aches for the widow, but I hope you aren't taking any guilt."

He keeps quiet, which is an answer in itself.

"What happened when you visited her?" Surely, she didn't blame him.

"She honored his memory by telling me story after story."

"And you listened." One thing about Leo, he gives you his undivided attention.

"Yeah. She brought up the antiques, like the ceramic tree." He shifts, facing more fully toward me. "You know, the one you already found? She said that they would set it up every year together."

"And the Vallerton?"

"Her husband bought the nativity set as a wedding present." His gaze meets mine and holds. "That's why I want to replace it."

Now I want to scour the world for it too. If anyone understood this woman's attachment to a nativity set, it's me. I'm obsessed with my Garrick piece. Not because of the price tag. Its value lies in the memories tied to it. I purpose to amp up my search. Wait. Maybe I can make this widow the Secret Santa candidate. But as quickly as the idea fills me with sudden joy, reality sucker punches my hope. I can't guarantee I'll be able to locate a Vallerton. At least, not in this narrow timeframe. Leo doesn't seem to have a deadline, which is helpful, but I only have until the twentieth of December. While I can't consider her as the Secret Santa candidate, I can promise that ... "We'll do everything we can to find one."

"And we'll do everything to find the perfect recipient."

As if remembering our purpose, we reach for the letters at the same time, our hands meeting atop.

But instead of withdrawing his touch, he turns over his hand and threads his fingers through mine. "Thanks for listening."

"T-Thanks for telling me." I can't pull my stare from our laced hands. It's kind of silly. I'm not in junior high. I shouldn't be giddy over the interlocking of fingers or trying to memorize where the callouses are on his palms. But my reasoning doesn't keep my body from swaying toward him, and ... he matches my movement, leaning closer. His gaze is a slow meander over the contours of my face. When his hooded eyes settle on my lips, I measure my breaths, waiting for him to close the gap.

My eyelids feel heavy, begging for me to lower my lashes in anticipation, but I fight off the urge, needing to gauge his expression instead.

After what seems like forever, he squeezes my hand before releasing it and leans back against the sofa cushion. "You've got icing right there." He taps the side of his mouth.

Never fail. My awkwardness always ruins the moment. Or perhaps it wasn't anything, and I read far too much into the moment. I am *not* in a Hallmark movie. I'm in my apartment. Not in a chic outfit but wearing an oversized holiday sweatshirt with a puppy in a Santa hat above the words "Fleas Navidog." So yeah, no whimsical scene here. Just a girl with an overactive imagination on a sugar rush. Plus, I can't discount what Fletcher told me. Leo might not stay long in Silver Creek. Annoyed and embarrassed in equal measure, I trace the side of my lip with my tongue, tasting the sweet offender.

Leo doesn't miss the movement, his gaze hot on mine. There goes my daydream again. I refuse to fall for any illusions this time. "Did I get it?"

His eyes darken, and what I wouldn't give to know what he's thinking. "Uh, yeah. It's gone."

I devote myself to the letters as if it's my sole mission in life. Which, right now, it kind of is. Some entries are quick nos. Jokes, mostly. One student asked the Secret Santa to kidnap the school principal so he wouldn't have to serve detention. The author wisely left it unsigned. Other letters express problems I can't fix for all the money in the world, like the little girl who wished for her parents to get back together. After discarding two more, my attention snags on the most recent sob story. "What do you think of this?" I hand Leo the paper. "Does this say 'I'm trying to swindle you'?"

I wait while he reads it.

His brows pull lower. "She sounds genuine. Behind on her rent. Trying to make a better life for herself and her toddler." He hands it back. "You can scout it out." He lifts a lock of my hair and toys with the edges. "The letter says she's a hairdresser at Manes on Main."

The salon is only a few buildings down from mine. How have I never run into—I check the name—Brandy before? If anything, this Santa thing has caused me to look deeper into the heart of the community that has surrounded me my entire life. "Tilly cuts my hair. She'll feel betrayed if I let anyone else touch it." I rack my brain until I come up with a solution. "Ah, I can get an updo for the party."

"There you go." He smiles at me. "What party is it? Need a plus one?"

I should spray my heart with Leo repellent. Because the more I'm around him, the more I'm drawn. Which makes me nervous.

Especially if what Fletcher says is true. If Leo never stays in one place, we wouldn't work out. My roots, livelihood, and family are all in Silver Creek.

Leo and I aren't in that familiar place where I can just ask, "Hey, do you plan on sticking around for the next, say, seventy years or so? Because if you aren't, I don't want to fall in love with you." No, I'll have to figure out a way to discover this information. Let's hope I don't lose my heart first. I realize Leo's waiting for my response. "It's a holiday function at the senior center that the Mavericks host every year. Which means they try to best their fellow elderly friends in party games." I shake my head at Leo's chuckle. "My role is to help wrap presents for the seniors who have an Amazon Prime addiction and distribute snacks." Expectation fills his eyes, and—darn it—I want him near me. "You're more than welcome to come keep the Mavericks in line. Which probably won't happen but will be a noble effort."

"What day is it? And will there be karaoke?"

"Thursday at seven. And not if I can help it."

His expression falls. "I have to work."

"No worries. What you're doing is more meaningful than keeping Leonard from spiking the eggnog." My heart sinks, but this is good for me.

I can't get attached.

CHAPTER 17

"ARE YOU GRETA?" A twentysomething woman with piercing blue eyes and pink-streaked hair approaches as I'm waiting in the reception area of Manes on Main, flipping through a magazine featuring trendy haircuts. Because that's what one does at a salon. I don't make the rules.

"Yes." I smile. "You must be Brandy."

"Uh huh." She tucks her phone in a pocket on her smock and waves a hand, her glittery fingernail polish catching the fluorescent lights. "Come on back."

I've passed this place nearly every day for as long as I can remember, but I've never been inside until today. This building is old like mine, but whoever designed the interior cleverly blended the vintage with the modern. The original brick makes up a side wall, but the surrounding ones are sleek black. The silver tones from the exposed ductwork pair well with the dark hardwood floors. Of course, this space is all decorated for Christmas from the white twinkle lights framing the storefront windows to the tree nestled in the corner.

Brandy points to a chair at her station, which is overwhelmed with the tools of her trade, her cosmetology license, and pictures of herself and her daughter. "Have a seat, and let's talk about an updo."

"I have a Christmas party tonight and thought it'd be nice to get my hair done." I sit in the red chair and fight the urge to squirm. I can't blame the plush cushion. No, I'm not comfortable in my own skin. I hyped myself up on the way by imagining this task as undercover work, channeling my inner spy. Problem is, I don't have an inner spy. I'm a horrible liar and an even worse actress. My debut as the Star of Bethlehem in second grade didn't prepare me for casual espionage in the name of Christmas.

Brandy talks to my reflection in the oversized mirror. "Is this a formal event?"

"No, much more relaxed."

Her head tilts. "Ooh, something fun."

About as fun as menstrual cramps, but I nod anyway.

She bites her lip and stares at my hair as if envisioning her future work. "We can definitely do fun."

I give an enthusiastic thumbs up like I'm five. Apparently, I don't need much of a strategy because for the next twenty minutes, Brandy is braiding, curling, and pinning my hair while divulging her life story. How she considered a career on Broadway. How she lived in Las Vegas before ending up in Silver Creek. How she's raising a young daughter as a single mom. I keep encouraging her with well-placed questions. "And you say your daughter's two?"

"Yeah, a total terror. But a lovable one, ya know?" She turns my chair away from the mirror. "What do you think we spruce this up a little? I have the cutest Christmas accessories."

I shrug. "Do what you think's best." At this point, I don't care if my hair looks as if I'm going to junior high homecoming or a Comic-Con. I'm this close to getting the information I need. "It sounds like she's at a fun age."

Brandy pulls a small basket from a nearby closet. "Oh, I can't complain. I don't have half the problems I had a few weeks ago. My luck has turned."

"Brandy." A new, yet vaguely familiar, feminine voice enters our conversation, but my chair's turned so that I can't catch sight of anyone. "You shouldn't speak like that."

Brandy laughs and steps in front of me to slide a pin in my hair. "Well, my luck *did* turn. I got a house that's fully paid off." She busts into a dance move that makes me think she made the right choice in not pursuing Broadway.

"Yeah." The mystery voice continues, "But your uncle had to die for you to get it."

I suck in a quick breath, and my lungs protest with a coughing fit.

Unfazed, Brandy smacks my back. "Eh, he was old."

Her blasé outlook on her uncle's demise doesn't exactly give the "peace on Earth, goodwill toward men" vibe, but at least I got my answer. Brandy doesn't need help with her rent because she inherited a house, and I'm back to the proverbial drawing board. As I'm trying to consider my next move as the World's Worst Secret Santa, Brandy continues to work on my hair, piling it atop my head and dipping her hand into the basket of Christmasy hair stuff.

"I'm going to raise your chair and turn it the other way." She pumps the pedal beneath my seat. "I don't want you to see your hair until the *final reveal*." The sing-song emphasis on her final two words is somewhat frightening. She angles my chair to the left, and I finally glimpse the mystery voice.

It's Josie Dubois. My former nemesis.

She's getting her hair trimmed at the station beside mine.

No wonder I recognized her voice. Josie's chair's facing forward, meaning she's had a full view of the mirror, including my profile's reflection. So yeah, my presence isn't a surprise to her. However, currently, Brandy stands between me and the mirror, keeping me from sneaking a peek.

"Hello, Josie." I break the weird silence between us. "I haven't seen you in a while."

She averts her gaze and studies the floor. "Been a busy year." At first glance, I notice her skin tone is … normal. She doesn't look like a human Cheeto.

Her hairdresser grabs the thinning shears and addresses Josie. "Next time, you need to let me color your hair. Bring out those warm tones."

"I think I'll keep it like this for a while," Josie says in a soft voice. Her natural complexion isn't the only thing that's changed. Yeah, it's the same Josie, but with a different font—one that's far less flashy and softer around the edges. Sometime between last December and this one, the haughty glint in her amber eyes has dulled.

"Pssh. Your roots are an abomination. I can give you the glow-up you deserve. I've got an opening right before New Year's. Let me pencil you in." She reaches for her phone.

Josie sits straighter in her seat. "I can't right now."

Brandy scoffs. "A little splurge isn't going to make a difference." She looks at me. "Josie wants to get a service dog for her youngest brother. The sweet boy's on the autism spectrum," she says by way of explanation.

The pinch in Josie's brows tells me she's not thrilled with Brandy broadcasting her personal life, but the dejection lowering her gaze has me doing the unthinkable, offering my high school rival comfort. "I've heard service dogs are amazing companions for those on the spectrum."

Instead of stiffening up like a toy soldier at my words, Josie smiles sadly. "We're on a waiting list, but even if we're next, I can't afford it. Noah could really use one."

I've never seen Josie this … human. She's always worn the mean girl mask, carefully hiding the person beneath. This makes me wonder how often I tuck the truest version of myself behind a carefully curated front. Wait, wait, wait. Did she say Noah? Something feathers my mind.

I remember reading a Secret Santa letter from someone requesting support in getting a service dog for her little brother with cognitive disabilities. I had no idea it was from Josie because the bottom of the paper was illegible. It was one of the damaged letters from the café.

I'm trying to process this information while also responding to Josie. "Service dogs are expensive because of the extensive training involved. I know someone who just started—" An idea hits. Of course! My lips ease into a smile because I don't need to be the Silver Creek Secret Santa for this one. Though I *could* have Josie's brother as the candidate, except for the media coverage aspect. It bothers me that Fletcher insists on plastering the Secret Santa stuff all over the news. This little boy just needs a dog, not a camera in his sweet face. I know what I have to do. "Excuse me a minute." I stand just as Brandy is about to put … garland? … yes, garland in my hair. "I'll be right back." I grab my phone and find Patricia in my contacts.

"Hey, Greta," Patricia answers. "You finally taking me up on my offer to spend the holidays at our farm?"

"Not this time," I say graciously. "But I plan to stop by sometime and see where you hung the painting, if that's okay?"

"You know it is, girl! I can't thank you enough."

A family heirloom was accidentally sold at her aunt's estate sale. Everyone was flipping out because it was a framed landscape their great-great-grandfather painted. It took some time, but I was able to track it down and recover the piece. She promised me a *freaking huge favor*. Her words. So here we are. "I'm calling to see how the nonprofit is going. Hope Unleashed, right?"

"You know we got the funding. One litter just went through initial training, and we have another ready to go soon."

"Have you got the families selected yet?"

A pause. "Yeah, we did that pretty early on."

Oh.

"But funny you should ask, because we just had a family

back out. They discovered their kiddo was allergic to Labrador dander. They're looking into finding a hypoallergenic breed."

Hope billows. "Can I suggest a replacement family? I know someone who's looking for a service dog for her little brother on the autism spectrum. Her name's Josie Dubois."

"Does she know we're just starting out?" Patricia asks. "We can't officially assign dogs for training until after the new year."

I sneak a glance at Josie. Looks like she's nearly finished with her cut. As the hairstylist's removing her cape, I angle away and lower my voice. "I haven't told her anything. I wanted to talk with you first."

"Also, the family needs to be able to commit to at least a month of handler training."

"Okay, I'll let her know."

The following pause seemed long enough for me to recite "'Twas the Night Before Christmas" … backward. Not that I could do that. She finally says, "If they agree to fill out the paperwork and complete the training, then I think we can make it happen."

I jump up and down like a lunatic. Brandy yells something about my hair not being sprayed yet. "Thank you, Patricia. You're amazing."

"Be sure to give her my number. Then we'll start the process."

We hang up, and I approach a wary Josie, who's now signing a credit card slip at the counter.

I wait for her to finish with the cashier, then blurt out, "My friend Patricia owns a nonprofit service dog organization. She's got an opening for your little brother, if you want it?"

Josie claps a hand over her shocked mouth. Then, as quickly as the surprise hits, so does the skepticism. Her arm falls to her side, and she assesses me. "You're not pranking me, are you? This isn't the school cafeteria."

Okay. That's fair. I may have once replaced her mashed potatoes with art paste. "This is legit. Her name's Patricia Caffrey, and the organization is Hope Unleashed." I snatch a pen from the counter, write Patricia's number on the back of Brandy's lip-shaped business card, and hand it to Josie. "Call this number. She'll explain everything."

Josie's eyes well with tears, and I have a nanosecond to brace myself before she squeeze-hugs me. "Thank you, thank you, thank you," she squeals as she cuts off my air supply. "I can't believe you did this."

I can't reply. Mostly because I can't breathe, but also because I'm starting to see what Gran meant. It's a different sort of feeling to relieve a burden. To offer some sort of hope. This is more heartwarming than any Christmas movie. Instead of watching these kinds of moments unfold as a detached audience, I get to live it.

Josie practically floats out of the salon, and I'm smiling as I return to my seat. Contentment spreads through me as Brandy finishes my updo.

"Okay." She beams. "Just need the star."

The what?

CHAPTER 18

A CHRISTMAS TREE is exploding from my head. If that's the effect Brandy was going for, she nailed it. All my hair is piled atop my scalp. Brandy must've placed something beneath all those locks to give the updo height. Little plastic bulbs, snippets of mini-garland, and strands of tinsel are all pinned here and there. The crowning feature is the LED star bright enough to guide Santa's sleigh at night.

I look festive.

I look ridiculous.

And I don't have time to fix it. I'm needed at the Mavericks' Christmas party in fifteen minutes, and I'm going to be late as it is. I pay and tip Brandy for her creative efforts.

While I emptied my wallet for an updo that'll snag on doorways, I count this trip a success. I discovered Brandy no longer requires the Silver Creek Santa's help, and I was able to support a family in need.

That's why I'm smiling as I enter the senior center. I spot Mom across the cafeteria. She takes one look at me, and her eyes go wide. I guess Brandy also gave me the ability to make an entrance.

Noticing the stack of packages before Mom that need to be wrapped, I hustle over to her.

She sticks an adhesive bow on the corner of the gift she's working on and presses her lips together as if holding back a laugh. "Do I even want to know?"

"What, that I paid sixty dollars to look like the tipsy adult version of Cindy Lou Who? Probably not." I grab the next box, a roll of wrapping paper, and get to work.

"Leonard told me he tried to invite Leo tonight," she puts in with a side glance at me. "But said he had to work."

"Then Leo's story lines up. Because that's what he told me when I asked."

"Leo's popular." She smiles. "I know it's none of my business, but is there anything going on between you two?"

"Only friends." I can't tell Mom about our agreement because she has no idea I'm the Silver Creek Secret Santa. Or that her mother, my grandmother, had a hefty bank account. Or I should say bank accounts. I guess certain banks will only insure your money to a quarter of a million. As far as problems go, that's a nice one to have.

The seniors are playing "Guess that Christmas Carol" with Pap and Leonard showing flashcards of emojis. Although someone, other than a Maverick, should've checked the emojis to ensure everything is appropriate. Too late now.

Mom and I wrap gifts for an hour straight, then I join the festivities, making a Christmas craft and participating in the final game. *Participating* translates into being the humble prop. Brandy's exuberance is a hit with those over seventy. The seniors wanted to play a game where everyone stared at my hair for a full minute, and then I left the room. Whoever recited the most Christmas items on my noggin won the light-up star on my head. Being a good sport and really wanting this blinding thing far, far away from me, I agreed. So even more good has come from my salon trip. It's the gift that keeps on giving.

Needless to say, no one looks forward to snack time more

than me, especially since Brewtiful Grounds supplied the treats. Tilly's famous peppermint bark cookies are giving me life right now.

"Did you notice"—Mom reaches for a hot chocolate in a Styrofoam cup—"that we wrap gifts the same?"

"I didn't catch it." Mostly because I was busy thinking about my next steps as Secret Santa.

She takes a dainty sip and smiles at me. "Your gran taught me. I'm guessing she taught you too."

"Yeah." *Gran taught me everything*, I want to say, but the words sit like acid on my tongue. When Mom was absent, Gran had the job of schooling me on everything from makeup to boys to periods. Things that moms do. Gran never got to enjoy retirement because she was raising her grandchild. Did she miss out on something she wanted to do? Did she leave this life unsatisfied, feeling ripped off?

The cookies turn to cement in my stomach.

It's weird Mom never explained why she left. Why she *always* left. Gran stayed for me. Then I stayed for Gran. I regret nothing, but I do have some hesitancies about my relationship with Mom. Will it be anything like the relationship between Gran and me? Do I want it to be? Will we ever talk about the abominable snowman in the room? The giant beast of a topic we've been avoiding? I hate confrontation, but maybe I need answers more. I chew the inside of my cheek, taking in the festivities before me. This isn't the time or place. So I'll bottle the frustration and give myself a headache.

"You doing okay?" Mom places a gentle hand on my shoulder.

She's trying. I know this. It's the pressure of the Santa thing, the fact that this was Gran's favorite holiday, and the reality that she's not here—it's all getting to me. I can blame the gazillion pins in my hair, but it feels like everything stings. "I think I need some air."

Her brow lowers. "It's twenty degrees out."

"I've got my coat." Though with my stupid hair, I can't pull up the hood. I'll have to ignore the possibility that my ears might freeze off. I escape into the hallway and exit through a side door, my boots sinking into the blanketed-white ground. The skies had poured another layer upon the snow we'd gotten yesterday. I inhale deeply, trying to savor the quiet, but my mind's too loud. I have two weeks to find the perfect candidate. I have to help Leo find the Vallerton nativity set, and I feel like I've exhausted all my contacts. Plus, I have to navigate these chaotic emotions about my mom.

I step past a snow-laden dogwood tree—its branches stretching out like pale, gnarled fingers—and glance to my right, finding a familiar face. Santa's. Only he's a giant wooden cutout situated by the senior center sign. Floodlights are aimed at his jolly grin, but to me, his wide smile doesn't look like festive merriment. He's laughing at me.

"You think it's so easy," I say to the stupid decoration as I scoop up a handful of snow and pack it into something I can launch. "It's not." I hurl the snowball, and it smacks Santa's haughty mug.

Oh, that felt good. So I do it again. The tension seeps from me with every throw. I grab more snow and—

"You've got good aim."

I squeal and hurl my snowball at the voice.

It's Leo.

Snow covers his jaw and neck.

I suck in a deep breath, waiting for my erratic heart to slow. "You really have to stop doing this sneaking-up-on-me ninja thing." Did he not learn his lesson with the impaling elf?

After a smooth swipe of his hand across his face, he settles his gaze on me. "That, Greta Carlton, is the worst apology I've ever heard."

"Well, actually." I step toward him with a sweet smile. "I didn't apologize at all." I lift on my toes, watching his eyes brighten with surprise, and shake the branch above his head.

Snow falls right on his hat and shoulders.

A laugh spills from my lips, but then I catch sight of Leo's face, rather the way his mouth twists into a mischievous smile.

He stoops down for a scoop of snow, and I bolt.

I duck behind the giant cutout I'd just used for target practice. I pat Saint Nick's shoulder as if all is forgotten between us. "Mercy," I call while grabbing more artillery. A girl's got to be prepared.

"No mercy, Greta." His voice isn't as distant. Crap, he's getting closer. "I have snow dripping down the back of my neck."

I press my mouth against another laugh. "Do you really want to have a snowball fight right now?" I try to sound threatening, but I don't think it's working. "Because, fair warning, I'm in feral mode. Things can get ugly."

He chuckles. "I can handle you."

Oof. From his tone it sounds like he *wants* to handle me. But I can't think on that. I peek around Santa and launch a snowball. Leo shirks out of the way. Darn. Realizing I'm unarmed, he sprints toward me. I squeal and dash off, hoping to use the senior center sign for cover, but a snowball strikes my leg. I know he aimed lower on purpose. Because no matter how competitive he is, Leo can't help but be a nice guy.

He's fresh out of ammo, and I'm fast in gathering more snow.

I launch and miss again. "Ugh. Come on."

He has his arm poised to throw. "Are you going to tell me why I found you out here hating on a defenseless Santa?" He squints at me, and then his grin sparks. "I take it you, uh, went to the salon."

I forgot about my updo disaster! "Not a word, Mathis."

"You look very Christmasy."

I roll my eyes. "Are we calling a truce yet?"

"Says the girl with no snowballs." He takes a step closer and drops his voice to that husky timbre I've come to adore. "Or perhaps I can cash in on a seasonal technicality."

"What technicality?"

"Your hair."

"Yeah, it's ridiculous, but it's the price to pay to rule out Brandy."

"Ah, well done." Another step. "But the technicality is what's actually *in* your hair." He's so close I can reach out and touch him. Maybe snatch that snowball from his gloved hand. Though I can't move. His arrested gaze is on me, and it's like my smooth-soled shoes grew spikes and tethered me to the earth. "There's mistletoe. You know what that means, Carlton?"

"Huh?" My hands instinctively go to the ridiculous updo. "There's no ..." I keep searching. I pull out a bow, garland, a couple of plastic bulbs. My gloved fingers fish around for any sign of a parasitic plant. "No mistletoe."

His head dips lower. "You sure?"

I'm sure Leo's the king of mixed signals. He wears a crown forged from romantic energy but held together with friend-zone effort. And yet, I find myself wanting to pledge my loyalty to his kingdom. "Yeah." I'm breathless, and it has nothing to do with our previous snowball fight. "I'm mistletoe-less."

"That's too bad." He lingers for an excruciating second and steps back with a flirty smile. "But it was worth a shot."

I swat his arm. "Rude!" Mostly because I want him to kiss me. No, no I don't. He could be leaving. That's another item on my unending list of things I need to address. I'll get to it. Soon. Ish.

He drops the snowball and dusts off his hands. "Why are you out here and not at the party?"

"I thought you had to work."

"I got to leave early. Why are you out here?" he repeats, but this time, a softness threads his voice.

"I needed air."

"And to let off a little steam?" He nods at St. Nick.

"Something like that." The wind picks up, and I tug my coat collar closer to my neck. "I'm sorry I hit you with the snowball."

"No, you're not. But I'll accept your lie, anyway." Holy fruit-cake, that smile of his. "I shouldn't have sneaked up on you."

"It's a habit of yours."

"Yeah." He tugs me toward the senior center doors. "You're definitely becoming a habit."

"Can you video call me?" I type into the chat box to OldSoulSam and tap Send.

I woke this morning with the awareness that I forgot to check PastPort. PastPort is like an eBay for amateur antique dealers. I normally don't search the site because all I can picture are thousands of Adelaides wanting to make a killing on a faux piece.

But I'm desperate.

So during my morning coffee, I cracked open my laptop and searched PastPort for a Vallerton. After several rounds of using different keywords, I found a hit.

Someone with the handle "OldSoulSam" and a profile picture of a vintage film projector listed a Vallerton. Though it wasn't the entire set, only Joseph, Mary, and the baby Jesus. While the wisemen and shepherds are noticeably missing, it's the most progress I've had, and I'm not about to dismiss the chance to secure the key figures.

The price seems fair, but the pictures are fuzzy. Since I never buy sight unseen and flying to Nebraska to inspect them isn't going to happen, I request a video call to see the pieces. I go to work, checking the site throughout the day, but receive no response.

What I *do* get is a text message from Leo inviting me to Ivy Hall tomorrow for dinner. Since the firefighters' gala, I haven't indulged my imagination about what could possibly be inside the legendary estate. I didn't want Leo to think I was using him to gain access. It sounds silly, but after Leo expressed that people are more interested in his possessions than him as a person, my heart did an about-face.

I'm to bring the Silver Creek Secret Santa letters, so I can't actually call tomorrow night a date. After last night's party at the senior center, I can admit to myself that I have a crush. I don't know whether to feed it or smother it with a pillow. Fletcher's words haunt me like the Ghosts of Christmas. I can't entertain the idea of a future with Leo if he's prone to roaming. Long-distance relationships can work, but the end game has to be both of us in Silver Creek, and I can't be certain this is where he wants to settle.

When I return to my apartment to reheat my exciting dinner of leftover casserole from the party, my PastPort mailbox chimes.

"I have pics posted of the items," is all OldSoulSam reponds.

Really? I waited all day for *that*? Anybody can pull internet pictures of the set. I need something more substantial. A virtual call will help determine authenticity, and so I type that.

I wait a few minutes and get another response, including a video-call invite set for five minutes from now.

A knock sounds at my door.

"It's me!" Tilly calls. "I'm armed with eighty-sixes!"

"Say no more!" Eighty-sixes are the foods the café makes that are not suitable to sell to the customers. Mostly, it's a cake that fell flat, a soup that isn't thick enough, or a salad on its last leg. It doesn't matter because Tilly's leftovers are far better than mine. I run to open the door. Tilly of course has a key, but she's burdened with boxes. "What happened?" I was expecting maybe a couple bags, but Tilly has enough food to last all week.

"One of the businesses booked us for catering, then canceled. So we have fifty finger sandwiches and pastries for dessert." She smiles. "Which is great because I'm starving." She places the load onto the counter.

I notice the pastries have a company's logo on them, no doubt the reason they can't be sold at the café. "I have to make a video-call first."

She grabs plates from the cupboard. "To whom?"

"Some guy I just met on the internet."

"Ha. Ha." Tilly reaches into a box and grabs some sandwiches. "Who is it, really?"

"Seriously. Some guy who claims he's got an antique I'm looking for. It's on PastPort."

Tilly gasps as if I've told her something scandalous. "PastPort?" She hands me a plate full of food. "That hopeless, huh?"

See, she knows my brain. "Yes. I'll take any lead at present." I log into the video-call platform and click Enter Meeting.

A man's face fills the screen, but his phone camera's tilted up on a table or something. So basically, I have a personal view of OldSoulSam's nostrils. Grimacing, I put my sandwich down. I might never have an appetite again.

"Hello?" I say. "Can you hear me?"

"Yep. What can I do for you?"

"You claim you have the Vallerton nativity set pieces. I'd like to get a closer look."

"Hold on." He picks up the phone and walks with it to another room. Meanwhile, I'm struggling against motion sickness. He angles the camera at the pieces, and I can spot the bottom edges of the Mary figure. Unlike the rip-off piece at Timeless Treasures, this hallmark is legit. Okay. Promising so far. He shows me the hallmarks of the other two pieces.

"Thank you. Can I see the rest of the figurines?"

"Yeah." He shows me the bodies, placing them close to the camera. They *look* how they're supposed to. It bothers me that I can't test the weight. However, this is the furthest I've gotten in this search. OldSoulSam is holding the tops of the pieces, so I don't yet have a clear glimpse of their heads. "Can I see their faces?"

"Faces?"

"Yes. What's underneath your hands."

He's quiet for a second, then repositions the camera back to the nostril angle. "You're about to see something spectacular," he gushes and adopts a transatlantic accent. "These pieces have transformed from stuffy antiques to interpretational art." He aims the camera on the full figures.

My mouth drops.

Tilly gasps over my shoulder.

"They have *no* heads." I stare at the once beautiful figures.

"Ah, this is where the magic happens. You can imagine the Madonna in your own mind's eye. See the Christ child with your heart instead of your vision."

"What I see is a collector's set that lost all value." Someone decapitated the figures! The culprit could be a monster with a vendetta against valuable antiques or a kid who found their dad's hacksaw. Either way, the set is worthless.

"I'm willing to negotiate," OldSoulSam continues.

"I appreciate your cooperation, but I'm not in the market for headless figurines. Thank you for your time." I disconnect.

Tilly, who listened to the entire exchange, hands me a scone. "You might need to have dessert first."

I bite off a chunk. But even a triple-chocolate pastry can't lift my spirits. I know finding this set is pretty much an impossibility, but I have to try. I just hope Leo didn't mention this hunt to the dear widow. Because it's looking like we might need a Christmas miracle.

CHAPTER 19

I PRESS the buzzer at the gate to Ivy Hall. I've never spoken into an entrance intercom before. What's the protocol? Is it like a Wendy's drive-thru where you wait to be greeted before ordering a combo? Right now, I can go for a large order of confidence with a side of wit. I just really want to get through this evening without making a fool of myself.

"Look at you being on time."

I mock huff at Leo's teasing through the speaker. "I only confessed to being disorganized. I will not have you insulting my punctuality." Although my chaotic mind has made me late for things. But I stated my point and am bound to defend it.

He laughs. "Come on in. You can park right under the porte cochere."

"Port what? Is that another language or rich-person talk?"

"I hear that sarcasm. Just park by the front door."

A beeping sound precedes the gates swinging back. As I pull up the sloping drive, pathway lights frame the paved road, giving a soft glow. It's only six o'clock, but it might as well be midnight for how dark the sky is. I take in the snow-capped trees surrounding a palatial-looking home. My lungs squeeze at such opulence. The sprawling brick structure can easily be featured in magazines. However, the best sight is Leo leaning on the open front door as if he's been waiting for me all day. A large overhang, supported by pillars, shelters the entrance. Must be the port thingy. However, I can see why Leo wants me to park here. My car won't get dusted with snow or iced over. The weather seems tame, but snowfall in Ohio is unpredictable from October to March.

I step out of the car, making sure I grab the Secret Santa folder, and meet Leo by the entrance. He's all casual in gray sweatpants, a hoodie that says, "Silver Creek Fire Dept.," and—my kryptonite—a backwards hat. An unexpected shyness courses through me. Probably because it's only been twenty-four hours since I acknowledged my feelings for him. "Hello." I hate the little quiver in my voice.

"Hey." He smiles and eases back so I can step inside.

At first glance, the Mathis mansion lives up to the town gossip, at least in terms of extravagance. The high-vaulted entryway tempts me to say something loud to check if my voice echoes. But mostly, I'm thinking the recessed lights must be a pain to change. Not everyone needs extension ladders to switch out a lightbulb.

My boots click against the marble flooring as I follow Leo farther into the foyer. I unbutton my coat, hoping I picked the right outfit. I didn't want to look like I was trying too hard to impress, especially since this wasn't a date. On the other hand, I didn't want to appear as if I didn't put in any effort. My mood called for a red sweater dress and black leggings. I swept up the left side of my hair with a vintage comb from the 1940s, a past birthday gift from Gran and Pap.

Leo takes my coat and scarf and hangs them in a closet. A grand staircase is before us, its wrought-iron balustrade making a bolder statement than the one in *Gone with the Wind*.

He glances at his phone, then pockets it. "The food should be here in about twenty minutes. I thought DoorDash would be good. That way we can get to work." He nods at the folder I'm holding.

"Sure." I'm standing too stiff, too wooden, like some over-grown nutcracker. Okay, deep breaths. Get the focus off me. "Can you give a quick tour? I need to verify if the rumors are true."

His mouth takes on an amused twist. "Ah, the Mathis lore. Enlighten me, 'cause I only know of the suspected dungeon with a tunnel leading to an underground crypt."

"Wait, you're saying that's a myth?"

He laughs. "Sorry. No skeletons or torture devices here."

I snap my fingers in an "oh, darn" gesture. "Bowling alley made with the wooden slats from JFK's bedroom?"

"No bowling alley."

And the best for last. "A gallery full of sconces salvaged from the Titanic?"

Another shake of the head.

"Well, I better be going then." I playfully turn toward the door, and that's when I spot it. "Leo?" I say in a hushed tone.

"What's wrong?" His hand's at my elbow, and he's glancing about as if I'd encountered a giant spider.

"Your hall side table." I walk tentatively toward it.

He's stuck to my side. "What about it?"

I inhale and brush a hand reverently over the rosewood top. "Do you know this is a Meeks?" I tamp down the urge to hug the pedestal table from the 1840s. It's stunningly preserved.

The corners of his mouth tip up. "I did not. Is that good?"

I gape at him. "The J. and J.W. Meeks company is like the Tiffany's of the furniture world."

"Got it." He gives a brisk nod. "So you're saying I shouldn't toss my keys on it anymore."

"No!" I swirl around and move between him and the table, as if protecting the gem. "Reform your ways, Leo Mathis."

He chuckles. "I think you might like to roam around the rest of the house. It's filled with this kind of crap"—he retreats a step at my glare—"I mean, treasure. Have at it, Greta." And he turns me loose.

It's like an antique scavenger hunt plus a vintage wonderland as I explore the rooms. A Herman Miller chest of drawers. A Drexel Heritage buffet. A Baccarat vase? Are you kidding me? "This is like a museum," I say to him on our way up the steps. Seriously, Leo has a better inventory than I do, and he had absolutely no idea. I try not to be jealous.

"I spend more time up here." He opens a door to a personal gym that puts my weightlifting equipment to shame.

"Wow. Impressive." Not as impressive as the Baccarat vase, but I emphasize my words to placate him. He seems proud of this space.

"I thought you'd like this setup. Seeing that you love to strength train."

Ha! Good one. I don't contradict him, but apparently my face alerts him to the falseness of his words.

He raises a brow. "You do like to train, right? You have all the equipment."

He would think that, since he interrupted my morning workout the other day. I lower onto a weight bench. "Yeah, but it's not for me."

"That's not your gear?"

"It is. But I don't strength train for myself. I did it all for Gran." I pick at a fuzz on my sleeve. I never told anyone this, not even Tilly. "A few years back, Gran started to lose her mobility. There'd be times when she couldn't get out of the bathtub or stand up from her chair. Pap couldn't lift her, so it had to be me. Which meant I needed to get stronger." In more ways than one. I had to build up my muscles, but also my emotions. It was a time for Greta Carlton to toughen up.

He sits beside me. It's not a large bench. One of his thighs is against mine. I don't hate it. But I do feel uncomfortable under the weight of his stare.

"What?" I finally ask.

"You." He gives a tender smile. "I don't know anyone more selfless than you."

"I did what I had to do."

"What about now?"

I scowl. "What do you mean?"

His gaze slides to my exposed neck, then back up. "You still work out."

I get what he's saying. Since Gran's passed, there's no need to keep up with the vigorous routine.

"Why keep lifting if you hate it?"

The answer springs to my mind so quickly that I clamp my lips together to keep from spewing it. Word vomiting is a thing. While I can't tell him the entire reason, I can offer a partial truth. "I work alone at the store. I lift and move heavy stuff all the time."

"I'm here, you know. If you need help."

Though for how long? I wisely keep that to myself and mutter a "thank you."

He looks like he's about to say more, but a buzzer sounds. "That will be the gate. Our food's here."

Leo takes care of everything, and I follow him into the large kitchen where he sets two huge bags of food on the counter.

"I hope you're hungry. I picked pretty much everything off the steakhouse menu." He gives a sheepish smile. "I didn't know what you liked."

"You could've asked."

He shrugs. "Whatever you don't eat, you and I can use for meals this week."

Yes, because I always have filet mignon on my lunch break. But it's a sweet gesture. He unloads the bags, then hands me a plate. His selection is far better than the food from the firefighters' gala. My taste buds applaud him. Once our dishes are full and we get our drinks, Leo suggests we eat in the living room by the fire.

"The dining hall's always cold," is all he says before leading me to the family room. This space is more relaxed, making me suspect this is where Leo spends a lot of his time. The giant TV between two bookcases is a pretty good hint.

Leo sets his food down on the coffee table and carefully pulls it farther from the couch. He plops down on the rug beside the table—as if he's done this a hundred times—and pats the space next to him. "It's easier to sit on the floor than balance a plate on your lap on the sofa."

I appreciate his logic and join him. Although I do inspect the coffee table first to ensure it's not a Chippendale or any other brand worth an entire year's salary.

While we eat, I update him on the Vallerton search and explain the PastPort fiasco, which he finds hilarious.

"It hurts to think someone destroyed those beautiful pieces." I press a hand over my heart, as if rubbing a physical ache. "I'll check in again with my contacts, but I keep hitting dead ends."

He downs the rest of his Coke. "It's all good. I'm sure something will come up."

I hate to dash his optimism, so I only nod.

"Now what about the letters?"

I grimace at the folder on the table. "Let's hope we can find 'the one' tonight." I read through more sob stories, and my heart's both torn and wary. It's a conflicting task. You want to believe these people, but it's tough to tell if they're being honest. I blow out a breath. "How's it going with you?"

"I like this one." Leo hands me a letter.

I quickly scan it. A woman is asking for help on behalf of her neighbor, whose husband was injured at work. The couple is trying to adjust to their new circumstances. It doesn't exactly specify the need, but I assume it's financial. "Why this one?"

He shrugs. "Because the writer isn't trying to pitch a 'woe is me' story. She simply states the facts. If anything, she's underselling, like she's embarrassed to ask. I think there's more to the story."

Hmm. It's an interesting take. I put a blue "maybe" sticky note at the top of the letter.

"What about you?" he asks. "How's it coming?"

"I've been able to reject at least ten. People ask for extravagant things without a solid reason. Some dude wants a boat just because he loves summers on the lake. Well"—I glance down at the paper—"Justin Dodd, that does sound fun, but you don't see me buying a fifty grand Sea Ray."

Leo sits forward, a sudden interest brightening his dark eyes. "What *do* you want?"

"Huh?"

"You're always looking after other people and their needs. Caregiving for your gran. Weightlifting to help others, even though you hate it. Volunteering at the senior center. Talking up your best friend instead of taking any attention for yourself."

I send him a questioning look.

He gives a guilty smile. "I overheard you at the gala tell some guys that your friend was the fifth runner-up for Miss Ohio or something like that."

Tilly would faint at the demotion to fifth place. But still, I understand what he's getting at. "Ah, yeah."

"Not a word about yourself."

"I don't mind. I'm her hype girl."

"You're everyone's hype girl." He gets up and leaves the room. I have no idea how or why the topic switched focus to me, but I sense the need to play some conversation dodgeball to duck away from it. He returns with a sheet of paper and a pen. "Here you go."

"What am I doing, exactly?"

"You're creating a list of what you want." He takes the pen and writes *Greta's Christmas Wish List* at the top.

I don't reach for the pen he's offering. "Why?"

"It just seems like a question you never ask for yourself."

"You're right. I don't." I glance at the stack of letters. "I'm grateful I don't have huge needs. But as for wants?" Gran gave me the store and the apartment above it. I'm taken care of. "I guess I really don't want anything."

He's not letting this drop. Instead, he seems more invested. "What about *want* in terms of hopes and dreams?"

"Is this some kind of psychological strategy to get me to pick the right candidate?"

He drops next to me on the floor, far closer than before. "No, this is only me being interested in a girl and wanting to know what makes her happy."

Oh my gosh. If I was blank before, my mind's definitely empty now. "May I get back to you on this?"

He eyes me for a second, then relents with a smile. "Yeah."

"Good." I fold up the paper and slip it into my purse. "Now it's my turn to pick you apart."

"Can't wait," he says good-naturedly.

"Your house is beautiful." I look around. "Seriously, it's stunning. And yet ... it lacks something." Listen to me criticizing a million-dollar home filled with expensive antiques. When I said it reminded me of a museum, I meant it. "It just doesn't seem lived in. There aren't any personal touches. Nothing that makes it stand out as a safe haven. Which is what a home's all about."

He presses his lips together. "You're right." He kicks his legs out and crosses his ankles. "It has the personality of my grandfather. Cold. Detached."

"That's how he was?"

"When I visited as a kid, I hardly saw him or my grandmother. I was with nannies. Then as a teen, just left to myself."

Add that to what he told me about his parents always being abroad. "Wow, you must've been lonely." As an only child in the house with older guardians, I certainly understood that isolated feeling. Though Gran and Pap always made sure to include me.

"I didn't know any other way." He glances around as if looking at the place with fresh eyes. "When I returned to Silver Creek, I debated moving back in here. It doesn't really hold good memories for me."

A surge of boldness overtakes me, holding for a breathless moment. "You can create some."

His gaze pierces mine. "I can see that."

It's warm. Too warm. And to avoid his intense focus, I avert my eyes to a bare spot by the fire. "You don't have a tree." I suddenly realize. "You don't have anything Christmas-y."

He expels a heavy sigh. "I bought a tree and stuff last year but never took anything out of the boxes. The fire kinda threw me."

The man fights fires regularly, but he's referring to *the* fire. The one that claimed an elderly man, leaving behind a broken-hearted widow. "Do you still have the tree?"

"In the garage." He catches on to my reasoning. "Want to help me put it up?"

I brighten. "You helped me decorate The Memory Bank. It's only fair."

He stands and helps me up. "Let's get to it then." He leads me to the garage, where he hoists the massive tree box on his shoulder like some lumberjack. I grab the designated containers of decorations.

We return to the living room, and he clears space for everything. Using a knife, he slices through the box and opens the flaps.

"Stop," I say as he begins to pull out the artificial limbs.

"What's wrong? Don't tell me I'm already messing up?"

"Traditions!" I exclaim like a madwoman.

His face resembles the Leo of Last December. The confused brow that makes my fingertip tingle in want of smoothing it out, and my heart yearns in want of him to experience all he's missed out on growing up.

I try to coax him along. "When putting up the tree, don't you have certain things you do?"

He glances at the tree box, then at me. "Like spreading out the limbs to make it look more natural?"

"No. Creating memories and traditions go hand in hand. Like

when I put the tree up at my house, I always watch *White Christmas* because that's what we did every year."

"Yeah, don't have any of those." His tone doesn't hold traces of regret or hurt. It's steady, like he's only stating the facts.

"Okay. Will you humor me?"

He meets my gaze. "I told you before, I'm yours to command."

I sputter a nervous laugh. "Let's start with this. What's your favorite Christmas music?"

"I like the traditional ones. But nothing in particular."

"Okay, Christmas movie?"

"Easy. *Home Alone.*"

I clasp my hands together. "Nice! We can watch it during or after we put up the tree."

He pauses.

I still, my skin flaming. "I'm doing that again, aren't I? Where I'm too much?" It's my impulsive nature that always wants to help. "You can tell me to chill. I won't get offended."

"No." He stands and steps close. "You, Greta, can never be too much. In fact …" His knuckle is a whisper along my jaw. "I don't think I can get enough."

I want to tattoo his words onto my soul, so the next time I find myself looking inward, I'll see the truth and remember this moment.

He cups my cheek for a pulse-pounding second, then drops his hand. "Let's watch the movie as we set up everything."

I smile, liking the idea that he wants to start a tradition—and I get to be part of it. "Okay."

Leo pulls up *Home Alone* on a streaming service, and we begin putting together the tree. He ends up getting a stepladder because the thing is twelve feet tall. There aren't nearly enough ornaments or decorations for trimming the monstrosity, but it's cute he tried. With Kevin McCallister's antics as our soundtrack, we work as one, arranging the tree. He leaves the lights unplugged, so we can have the full effect once the final ornament has been hung. Leo slips on the last bulb from the box and steps back, joining me in assessing our work. He slings an arm around my shoulder. It's a total *bro* move, but I savor his touch anyway.

"Ready to plug it in?" he asks. "I'm pretty sure that was the last of the ornaments."

Ornament. Oh snap. "Wait. I almost forgot." I step out from under his touch. "I brought you something." Nervous about his reaction, I don't look at him but grab my purse from the sofa. "Don't get your hopes up. It's nothing jaw-dropping or anything." I withdraw the tissue-papered gift and hand it to him.

He accepts with a surprised smile and unwraps it.

"It's a sled." I rush to fill the silence. "Obviously not a real one. It's an ornament." Remember my goal of not making a fool out of myself tonight? I doused it with kerosene and lit the match with my stupid tongue. "I made it at the senior party." The painted brown popsicle sticks and hot-glued pipe cleaners for the rails now look ridiculously cheesy. Why did I think this was a good idea?

He turns it over and reads my Sharpied script, "Leo's Maiden Voyage." His gaze darts to mine with a grin splitting his face. "It's our sled."

The way he says "our" makes my heart jump, like soaring over the ridges on Killer Hill.

"You even snapped the rail." He chuckles low at the mangled pipe cleaner.

"I'm nothing if not detail-oriented."

He grabs my hand, sliding the ornament ribbon over one of my fingers and around one of his. "Let's put it on there together. Another tradition." His free hand settles on the small of my back, guiding me forward.

"Where at?" I ask softly.

"Front and center." He raises our joined hands, and we hang the sled on the bough.

We're so close I can note the curl of his lashes and a small scar near his cheekbone.

"Now it's finally ready." He steps behind the tree and plugs it in. The bright white lights illuminate the space.

Leo rejoins my side, and I smile at him. "Beautiful."

"Very beautiful." His smoldering gaze makes my skin burn. "Thank you for my gift."

"It was either that or a pipe cleaner elf."

"In honor of how we met." If his voice rumbles any deeper, I will melt into a Greta-shaped puddle. He catches my hands in his and tugs me to him. "Why are you like this?" His lips brush my temple.

My breath shallows. His nearness. His touch. It's unraveling my knotted defenses. "Like what?"

He eases back, and his thumb glides along my lower lip, his gaze tracking the movement. "This perfect." His eyes darken with intent, and I react with a small nod, giving him the go-ahead.

His mouth is on mine, hungry, tender, and so very scorching. He anchors me against him, gripping my waist, even as my arms twine around his neck.

The fire crackles behind us, but it's no match for the flames of heat igniting my body. His lips skim my throat, and the scratch of his late-day stubble against my soft skin pulls my pleasured sigh. I'm instantly embarrassed, but my reaction only encourages him to up the intensity with every sip of breath.

In the glow of the Christmas tree lights, Leo Mathis kisses me thoroughly.

I've imagined him holding me over a hundred times, but nothing prepared me for this moment. The heat of his left palm through my clothes, the press of his strong arms around me, the tangling of his fingers in my hair, I memorize it all. But it's not until he murmurs my name against my lips that I realize he wants this. Wants me.

Could this really be happening? Could I have a future with

Leo? Something warm unfurls in my chest, and it feels a lot like hope.

We move in delicious waves of give and take until I can almost hear Fletcher Thomas at the edges of my mind.

Leo never stays.

Shut up, Fletcher. I don't care. I don't care if Leo leaves. I want this moment. I need it. I kiss the man harder. Fiercer, as if in spite. Leo instantly responds, matching my fervor. Yet the chanting echoes louder, and the truth is getting bolder, like wearing an ugly Christmas sweater at a black-tie event, itchy and an overall bad idea.

I know me. I can't just *not care.* Which has always been my downfall.

My knees weaken.

Leo grips me tighter and gently walks me toward the couch. My legs didn't buckle from the swooniness of the moment, well, not *mostly.* It's that gripping fear I've known all my life that I can't explain even to myself right now.

I pull back, my breathing ragged, and place my hands on his shoulders. I want to stay, and Leo will always want to go.

His eyes are hazy, no doubt resembling my own. Then his mouth curves into a slow, satisfied smile. "We didn't even need mistletoe."

I give a nervous laugh, but I'm inwardly freaking out. "I should go."

He blinks. His gaze—seconds ago so beautifully hooded with the languid pleasure of our kiss—is now alert and ... confused. "Everything okay?"

"Yep. Just jolly over here." *Jolly?* Who says that? Other than Santa Ned after his smoke break? Why am I so weird? Probably because my entire body is humming with the residue of Leo's touch. I feel fire and ice in tandem. Happiness and sadness. With shaky limbs, I grab my purse and beeline for the foyer, Leo trying to keep up with my crazy pace.

He gathers my coat and scarf and hands them to me.

I force a bright smile. "Thank you for tonight."

He steps close. "Greta, talk to me." His voice is a deep timbre like rich cocoa—smooth and hot. But I can't stomach any more of his sweetness. "Are we good?"

"Yeah, all good. I just didn't know the time." Which is true. I still don't know the time. "I should be heading back."

He nods, his gaze still hesitant, and opens the door for me. "Goodnight, Leo."

CHAPTER 20

MY MIND HASN'T BEEN this disharmonious since the Mavericks' impromptu Christmas caroling jaunt. It happened five years ago, and I'm still haunted by their tone-deaf version of "Blue Christmas." But this morning, I'm in no mood for Christmas songs. After church, I need to teach Mom how to access Pap's online medical portal to get prescription refills. I also intend to grab the tub of antique ornaments Gran gifted me in her will. I've been slow in getting them, but I want that reminder of her right now.

Oh, and I need to figure out what to text Leo without sounding dumb.

I left the Secret Santa folder at his place, and I'm not going back to his house. Him and his backward hat, and gray sweatpants, and perfect words. And even more perfect kissing.

It's like when I was eleven and got a sewing machine for Christmas. I'd been saving money working at The Memory Bank but didn't have enough to get the Brother SE400 model. Though that didn't stop me from dreaming of all the creations I'd make on it. The machine could sew and embroider. It came with an LCD touch screen display and an automatic needle threader. To me, every other machine didn't measure up.

When I woke that Christmas morning, a large box, covered in green paper and topped with an enormous bow, sat beside our tree. I wanted to tear the gift wrapping to shreds but also savor the moment. Because this—this!—was my every wish, my every expectation, and, somehow, I knew my life wouldn't be the same after I opened it.

Last night, I had that same sensation. Leo's kiss is my SE400. The weight of his hands on my back, the pressure of his lips, the tightening of his arms around me was everything I didn't know I was missing. Those minutes made me see that every kiss before fell way short, like some dollar-store version of the real thing. Okay, not that there were *many* prior kisses. I don't have Tilly's long list of exes. Am I being dramatic in saying that Leo not only ruined every past kiss, but every future one if he's not the other participant? Maybe. I don't know. But I *do* know that—just like opening that present years ago—things aren't going to be the same for me.

Especially now, since I destroyed the experience with my rashness, leaving Leo in a state of confusion.

When church lets out, I head straight to Pap's and pull in the driveway. Mom's already opened the garage door for me. After ditching my high heels at the entrance, I find Mom in the kitchen making lunch.

She smiles brightly. "You look nice."

"Thanks." I stoop down and pet Oggy behind the ears, but he seems more interested in what Mom's cooking. "It's jumpstart jumper day."

"It's what?"

Oh, that's right. She wouldn't get it. I scored this wool jumper from the '70s at a flea market across the state. I only wear it when I need a mental boost, so Gran coined this my Jumpstart Jumper. I'm not saying that the vintage outfit cures brain fog. But also, I'm not saying it doesn't. Though today, I've had no such luck. "Never mind," I mumble, not having the energy to explain.

"You hungry?"

"No, thanks." I haven't had an appetite since last night's steak dinner. With Leo. Who kissed me, and I ran from the room like the floor turned to lava. I don't understand why I got so triggered. I shouldn't have flipped out. Yeah, it was an amazing kiss, but it's not like Leo proposed marriage. We aren't even dating. Maybe after I teach Mom how to access Pap's prescriptions, I should just call him to get it over with. Or leave the country. Perhaps buy property in a remote land and raise bunnies. That's how it is with me, chasing one illogical thought after another. Although, is raising bunnies truly an outlandish idea? Because it's kind of growing on me.

"Oh, guess what?" Mom flips over her grilled cheese. "I figured out how to navigate that portal thingy. So I refilled Pap's prescriptions."

"Great." Yep. Wonderful. I'm no longer needed. I can go home, and my mind can replay my life choices on an unending loop before going to Tilly's for our scheduled girls' night. I'm already dreading telling my best friend. Though I don't think she'll be overly surprised at my making things awkward between Leo and me. While she's the beauty queen, I'm the vibe assassin. We're good at what we do.

I venture into the living room to say hi to Pap, but he must be resting upstairs. Mom enters with her plate and bottled water.

"I'm sorry I can't stay long," I say as she sits in the recliner. "But I want to grab Gran's ornaments. Pap told me the other day he set them by the door to the garage. I didn't see them."

"Oh, you mean the tub of Christmas bulbs and decorations?"

"Yeah, that."

"I moved them to the utility room. I was shining them up for you. Some were grimy."

No.

No, no, no. "What do you mean *shining*?" But I can't wait for her reply. I bolt into the small utility room, and my heart sinks at the sight of the blue bottle. "Mom, please tell me you didn't use Windex on the Hummels?" I drop to my knees beside the tub and pick up a Christmas bulb lying atop packing filler, finding my answer.

"They were dirty, honey."

"Then you use a very, *very* diluted dish soap and water solution. Not Windex. Never Windex." I gape at the peeling paint. It's ruined. I can't help the burning in my eyes. How many more are—

Oh, no.

I start unpacking wadded newspaper sheets and plastic bags used as cushioning material, horror filling me with each rapid heartbeat. "The Garrick. Mom, did you touch the Garrick?"

Her blue eyes widen. "I-I'm not sure what that is."

"The nativity set. It's in this tub." It's worth more than anything I own. But more than that, it's tethered to core memories, making it valuable beyond any dollar sign. "Did you clean that?"

"No." She shakes her head rapidly. "Just a few of the bulbs."

I exhale in relief and release the Walmart bag I was strangling. At least the Garrick's safe from Mom's cleaning binge.

"I'm sorry." She puts the Windex in the cupboard above the washer and gives an apologetic smile. "I didn't know."

A tight band stretches between my shoulder blades. "But you could have."

She looks at me. "What, honey?"

"You could have known. You could've known that you never use ammonia on antiques. And that I wear this jumper when my mind's foggy." I sweep a hand over my person in an exaggerated fashion. "That I freak out in front of crowds. That I hate raisins and feel strongly they've no right to be in cookies. Mom, you could've known all of this ... if you hadn't left."

Her fingers flit to her parted mouth, but I'm not done. "Was I not worth staying for? Me? Your only daughter. Your family. I got to see you for a few weekends and holidays. That's it." I press a hand to my heart, but it's too late. It's crumbling, and there's not enough fight in me to hold it together. "I stupidly thought I might have more pull when I became an adult. You'd answer my texts, give the occasional call. But you didn't want a relationship. It took Gran dying—dying!—for you to come home."

Her eyes fill with tears. "I know."

"I don't think you do. You can't begin to know the damage it's caused." I can't enjoy a kiss with a guy without getting triggered that he's going to leave. Something that should be no big deal is *huge* to me because of her. She always left. And I always stood there, helpless, watching her pull away from the drive, never knowing if or when I'd see her again. An uneasy gnawing in my stomach would hit me every time. A feeling I'd only had in those moments. I blink, my haunted thoughts of the past smacking me in the present. That exact sensation struck me last night. That's why I panicked like I did. It was because of mommy issues. "I know I'm emotional, and it's probably best to talk when I've a cooler head. I'm not angry. Well, I kind of am, but I think I need answers more than anything."

My cell rings. It's Jared, the one who sent over Leo's ceramic tree. "I have to take this," I tell Mom and duck into the hall, needing space. "What's up, Jared?"

"A lead on your set."

"Really?" I jolt my head back and knock a sconce off the wall, the bulky candle landing on my foot. Though I feel nothing. Either my adrenaline's pumping from my exchange with Mom, or my body's still numb from last night. I'm not used to this much drama. Which is probably why I'm not overly optimistic about this call. "The Vallerton?"

"Yeah, my aunt's got it." Then Jared says that.

Game changer. "You're going to say Midge, aren't you?" Jared comes from a huge family who all deal with antiques. Midge is the scariest of the bunch, but she's also good at what she does.

"The very one. So you know the urgency."

"I do." Midge Saunders is an old-school antique dealer. She

doesn't do any business online, no website, no social media pages. What she does have is a customer base that trusts her. Gran trusted her. If Midge has a Vallerton, I know it's authentic, but I also know how she operates. "Thanks, Jared."

Just to be sure, I verify Midge's store address, hours, and contact information before disconnecting. I punch in the number Jared gave me for Midge's store and prepare to barter, beg, or offer my own version of *Let's Make a Deal*. Anything to persuade Midge to break her own rule and hold the Vallerton until I can get there. A busy signal pulses against my ear. Because of course she has a landline. With a sigh, I return the sconce and candle to their proper place and find Mom in the living room, her grilled cheese untouched. "I have to go."

Her expression falls, and I feel bad. I needed to say what was on my heart, but my execution could've been a little less emotional. "It's unfair of me to dump all this on you, then bolt. But it's really urgent, or else I'd stay." I soften my voice. "I know you didn't mean to hurt me, but you did. We need a long talk."

"Yeah, it's overdue." She pulls in a breath. "I'm sorry about the bulbs. I'm sorry for a lot of things." She glances out the window, reluctance marking her brow. "Do you really have to leave? It might snow."

It's Northern Ohio in December. The sky always looks like that. "Yeah. It's important." I give her a hug because, while I have questions, I'm an adult. I grab the tub, trying hard not to think about the damaged ornaments, and rush out the door. "Time is of the essence" sounds cliché-ish but totally accurate. Midge's store is in Sugarvale, about two hours away.

I check the clock on the dash. It's half past one. Since Midge's store closes at five, I should get there with moments to spare. Problem is, with Midge, it's first come, first served. If someone else knows about the nativity set, it's a race. And I don't intend to lose.

I punch the gas.

The sweet widow will get her Vallerton set.

After forty minutes on the road, I realize Mom missed her calling as a meteorologist. The skies unleash fluffy white stuff. I flick on my wipers to the level just above lazy and right below dramatic. As I drive, the weather gets worse. The whole "dashing through the snow" thing is great in theory, but it sucks on Rt. 11.

I've driven in snowy conditions since I was a teen. I can handle it. What I can't handle? Ice. So I slow my speed because even four-wheel drive isn't awesome on slippery roads. The freeway is eerily empty. Needing to fill the silence, I call Tilly over Bluetooth.

"I have all the things set for tonight" is how she answers.

I lean over the steering wheel as if it will help with visibility. "I might be late."

"Where are you?"

"Heading toward Sugarvale."

"Uh, why?"

"To get Leo's nativity set. An antique shop has one, but it'll go fast." Might be gone now. There's no way of knowing because I can't get ahold of Midge. "It's snowing hard, so I'm basically crawling."

"Take your time."

A deer darts onto the road.

"Oh crap! Move!" I squeal and swerve, so I don't hit the stunned beast. I lose control and skid. A pump of the brakes. A jerk of the tires. No success. The car skids off the road into a snowbank. "No!" I slam my hands on the steering wheel.

"What happened?" Tilly screams into the phone. "Are you okay?"

"I'm stuck in a snowdrift on the side of the road." I shift the gear into reverse. The engine growls with the spinning of tires. It's obvious the car is on a slight incline—no doubt due to packed snow—but even gravity doesn't want to help a girl out because I'm still stationary.

"Are you hurt?"

"No. Not at all. But I can't get the car to move." I put the car in park, roll down my window, and stick my head out to help assess the situation. Snow is pushing against my door, but I can easily open it. Question is, do I want to step into two feet of ice crystals to vainly tug on the bumper? No.

"What can I do?"

"I have roadside assistance."

A pause. "That might take a while, since the roads are horrible."

I check my fuel gauge. "I'm good on gas." Pap once told me a car can idle for over sixteen hours on a full tank. Not that I want to test that theory. "And my phone's at ninety percent. I should be fine." But can I still get to Midge's before five? "I better hang up and call."

"Okay, keep me updated. Oh, and lock your doors! I heard a story on a true crime podcast about a woman—"

"Maybe another time, Tilly." I already have enough chaos cramming my brain, so irrational paranoia gets put on a waiting list. I say goodbye and disconnect.

After getting the number from my insurance app, I call roadside assistance and am promptly placed on hold for half an hour. It's after two now. Time is wasting. I finally speak to a dispatcher, and the earliest a tow truck can reach me is around four. I'm currently about forty-five minutes from Midge's door. That's cutting things close, but what choice do I have?

I call Midge's again. Busy. I check the radar on my weather app, and it seems like things are calming down. The snow has shifted from rapid bursts to gentle flurries. Hopefully the worst is past. Wanting to save my battery, just in case, I put my phone in the cup holder and try to occupy the time by mentally composing a list of who I've left to buy gifts for. The answer's easy—everyone. I try not to think about my emotional exchange with Mom, but it's useless. When she first walked through Pap's door months ago, I knew this conversation was bound to happen. At the time, I was wallowing in my grief and didn't have the energy to confront her. Then I felt bad. She was making an effort. So I piled on excuses, avoiding the issue. Deep down, though, I understood the true reason I never confronted her. Because I feared she'd leave again.

A car door slams from behind, and I flick the rear window wiper to clear the view. Thank you, Tilly, for placing true crime scenarios in my brain. Instead of a potential murderer, I spy a familiar truck.

Leo? I blink to ensure I'm not seeing a snow mirage. I'm not sure if that's even a thing. But my confusion gives way to pure relief as he lifts a hand in greeting.

I suspect Tilly's behind this. Beautiful, wonderful Tilly.

I don't often relish the damsel in distress role, but I have to say, it does have its perks. Like my current view being the late afternoon sun carving out Leo's figure as he strides closer. Though I don't mistake the concern etching his face. I open the door, pushing against the pressing snow, and peek out.

His gaze fuses to mine, and his shoulders lower, as if his every joint has locked tight, only giving way when he sees I'm unharmed. "Everything okay?"

"Yeah." Which I'm thankful for. All things considered, it could've been a lot worse.

He stands on the edge of the snowbank, eyes raking over my car. "Any damage?"

"I don't think so." I shake my head. "I missed the deer. But I got new accommodations in this nicely furnished snowdrift."

He smiles at my sarcasm.

His wool coat's covering up his shirt, but I can tell from his khaki pants that he's more dressed up than usual. The backward hat is noticeably absent, and his wild waves are subdued. Was he … on a date? I don't like the clawing in my gut, but I currently have bigger issues—like getting my car off a mound of snow. "I called roadside assistance."

"Cancel it. We'll have you out."

"We?" I twist in my seat and see Mitchell jumping out of Leo's passenger door.

Mitchell grins with an exaggerated wave as he nears. "Hey, Greta. Did you lose sight of the road?"

I huff a laugh. "Sorry to pull you away from duty. Think of all those jaywalkers running amok." Dressed in sweats, Mitchell definitely isn't on patrol, but it's nice to get jabs in when I can.

He rolls his eyes. "I see your mishap hasn't affected your attitude. Tilly called and asked me to get ahold of a Remington Mathis from the fire department. Who turns out to be your Killer Hill friend."

I ignore Mitchell's eyebrow wag and glance at Leo, who's cutting through the snowbank, the powder coming to his knees. I shiver just watching him approach.

He reaches my open door, and for some reason, my heart swells with emotion. It could be the awful morning I've had, or the fact that he came for me even after I acted like a weirdo. I blink away the moisture and smile. "Thank you for being here."

His eyes scan my face. "Nowhere else I'd rather be." Then he glances at his snow-clad legs. "Well, maybe not in this exact spot." He flashes a grin, even though he's probably losing feeling in his lower extremities. "I'll carry you out. Wrap your arms around my neck."

I grab my purse, and Leo scoops me from the car like some kind of avalanche avenger. His arms tighten around me, and a surge of heat chases the chill from my fingertips.

While Leo's trudging through the snowdrift, Mitchell is grabbing the kinetic rope from the truck bed.

I glance up at Leo, noting the snowflakes catching on his stubble, in his hair. "Was Mitchell grumbling the whole way because this pulled him away from football?" Growing up, Tilly and I would deliberately plan Jane Austen movie marathons on Sunday afternoons just to commandeer the television. It probably was mean, but Mitchell always got us back, one way or another.

Leo scoffs. "I don't know who was more worried about you. Me or him." He looks down at me, his lips hitching into a smile. "What is it with you, Greta the Charmer of Silver Creek Men?"

I snort. "Hardly." Though I'm oddly touched he adopted my quirk of tacking on descriptors.

He manages to open the passenger side door to his truck while holding me and gently sets me inside. "Don't downplay your influence." His eyes are hot on mine. "Because you've got a chokehold on me."

It's freezing. I can't feel the tip of my nose. But Leo's words are a warm jolt, a shot of fire to my adrenals.

He saves me from coming up with a clever response by reaching across me and grabbing a travel blanket. He spreads it across my lap. "Sit tight. We'll get your car out." He opens the glove box and pulls out a Snickers. "You must be starving."

That's it. The man has my entire heart. That beating gushy thing landed into Leo's palm as he plunked chocolate into mine. "Thank you," I casually say as if I'm not going to devour it in three bites once his back's turned.

He opens the cab door and grabs … the folder I'd left at his house. "Here's this too."

I flush as he gently drops it onto my lap. "Thank you."

Leo and Mitchell get to work, connecting the rope to my Highlander, then to Leo's truck. The remainder of the human race seems to have decided to stay out of the elements because we have the entire stretch of road to ourselves.

I check my phone. It's almost three. Two hours until Midge locks her doors.

Mitchell hops into the driver's seat of my car, and Leo jumps behind the wheel beside me. He gives a reassuring smile. "Here goes nothing." He does some skilled maneuvering and success-fully frees my car from its snowy prison. I give a victory whoop, and he laughs. As a firefighter, he probably has to do things like this a lot, but I'm glad to have a front row seat to his heroics.

I watch as Mitchell backs onto the road and flicks on the hazards.

"What now?" I turn to Leo.

He shrugs. "Up to you. Mitchell and I can head back to Silver Creek, and you can choose wherever you'd like to go. Though I recommend following us back because it's getting bad out. Or Mitchell can take my truck to the station, and I can hitch a ride with you."

Simple answer. "Option B. But with an addendum."

"Shoot."

"I have to get to Midge's by five, and I want you to drive me there." I'm so ready to be a passenger princess.

"Midge's?"

"Yeah, she owns an antique shop in Sugarvale. She's got your nativity set and—"

"Greta," he says with a gravelly undertone. "You drove out here in all this." He jerks a thumb outside. "Because of me?"

"Of course. I told you how crazy difficult it is to find that set. Midge is a trusted dealer."

He rakes a hand over his face. "I don't know whether to scold you or kiss you."

I freeze in my seat, and I spot the second he catches what he said. If I expect him to get embarrassed about the topic of kissing, I'd be wrong.

His smile builds slowly. "Though now that I think about it, I know exactly which one I'd choose."

My skin heats, and my mind places me back in his arms in front of his tree. The ambiance of it all. The passion in his touch. "Uh …"

A tap at my window makes me jump.

Mitchell. "Forget about me?"

I totally did. I open the door and hop out. "You're unforgettable, Mitchell." I reach up and pat his cold cheek. "Thank you for helping."

He nods. "Stay home next time," he says in his cop voice.

"Doubtful." I grin, then give Leo the come-hither look—that's less romantic and more *let's go before we're too late*. Not sure if he catches all that, but I prop myself in the passenger seat of my car all the same.

After a minute, he tosses his bag in the back, then settles in the driver's seat. It's like we're playing musical cars. I wave at Mitchell as he drives off in Leo's truck.

Leo amps up the heat. "You sure you want to attempt this?"

"It's like a thousand-to-one chance that we find this set. More or less. My mathing is iffy, but I think we should try." The only reason why the odds are higher in Ohio is because Rene Vallerton was a local artist. So one may pop up occasionally, but again, they go fast.

"And if we get stuck in the snow again?"

"Technically, I didn't get stuck because of the snow. It was a rogue Rudolph," I say this as the plow truck barrels past, laying salt down and splashing my car with slush in the process. "Look, he's clearing our path. How convenient."

Leo puts the car in gear, and we're heading toward the prize. Everything's going smoothly. We're making excellent time, and the skies have cleared. I'm just getting comfortable when Leo turns down Michael Bublé and clears his throat. "So are we going to discuss last night?"

I look pointedly out the window and ask in my most inno-cent voice, "What about it?"

"You know what I'm talking about. The kiss."

"Oh, that." I give a wave as if I make out with gorgeous guys on the daily.

"Yes, that." He flicks the wipers and tosses me a look. "I didn't mean to upset you."

"You didn't." Which is the truth. "It wasn't the kiss that freaked me out. The kiss was ... perfect. It was something else. Something I didn't realize until just today, in a total epiphany moment." I lean forward, peering through the snowfall. "Oh! There's our exit."

He exhales as if he's not entirely happy I changed the subject. Not that I blame him. But we can't miss the exit. One thing about Ohio highways is that if you miss your turn you have to go approximately twenty to a million miles to the next exit to turn around.

I place a hand on his arm. "Let's get the Vallerton, then I'll explain everything."

He agrees with a simple nod, and I direct him through the small town, trying not to get caught up in the wintery scenery. We pull onto Midge's Antiques's lot with twenty minutes to spare.

CHAPTER 21

MIDGE'S SHOP is scented with dust, cinnamon, and nostalgia. The layout is exactly how I remember. I'd visited Sugarvale often as a child, but not much recently. The last time I was here was six years ago for a summer antique show.

Beyond the sun-drenched memories with Gran, something else strikes me. "It's busy." Crazy packed, as if Midge thinks the maximum occupancy number is a loose estimate of her inventory and not a fire code.

Leo and I glance outside as if we somehow missed twenty other cars crowding the lot. Nope. Only a few minivans and a sedan.

Leo brushes snowflakes from my scarf. "Did they walk here?"

"I think there's a hotel down the street." Though I don't recall it being a hotspot, only a small-town inn near the main thoroughfare. "I never tagged Sugarvale as a touristy place."

"Is that Iris Junior?" A raspy voice calls from a couple of yards away.

"It's me." I smile and snake around people to reach the white-haired, chain-smoking, antique guru. "How are you, Midge?"

She scowls. "Getting old stinks."

I offer a commiserating smile. "Gran used to say that."

"Sorry for your loss, pup." She gives a solemn nod as she moves behind the counter. "Iris was one of the best."

"She was."

Leo's hand goes to the small of my back, and my pulse pounds at his sweet show of support.

Midge's sharp gaze bounces between us. "Boyfriend?"

My neck prickles with heat. "Not exactly."

Leo slings an arm around me and tugs me close. "I'm trying to convince her that I'm a great catch. It's been a challenge."

"Because she's smart. You're too good looking." Midge sniffs and pins Leo with the glare she reserves for those who swap price tags. "The hot ones are cheaters."

Leo bristles, and I place a hand on his chest since I'm still curled into him. He's not used to Midge's rash opinions. When I was a kid, she told me my nose was too big for my face. In my teens, she said I looked like a Vegas showgirl, though I was wearing shorts and a Snoopy tee. Midge is one of those people who says things for shock value, trying to get a riled response. "Midge, leave him alone. It's not his fault." Then I pat his chest with a slow shake of my head. "The poor guy can't help his hotness. It's his burden to bear."

His hand skims under my coat and tickles my waist. I nearly squeal. "Anyway, we came here for—"

"Ah, ah. First things first." She props her elbow on the counter.

I groan. "Seriously? I'm not going to arm wrestle you."

Leo coughs.

"For old times' sake," she demands.

Someone knocks me from behind, and Leo steadies me. After smiling my thanks, I adjust my purse strap, which slipped off my shoulder with the jostle. "Midge." I address her over a couple talking loudly about teacups. "Maybe another time. You've got more bodies here than a zombie movie."

She ignores my remark and wiggles her fingers. "There's still life in these suckers."

Leo rubs a hand over his mouth as if it's all he can do not to burst out laughing.

Never mind Midge is pushing seventy and looks like her arm would snap like a gingerbread cookie. The woman is stubborn like Gran. She won't discuss the Vallerton until she gets her way. "Fine." I take off my coat and set it on the counter with my purse and scarf. "But I better get what I came here for."

She nods and waves Leo over. "All right, sonny, count us down."

He's still struggling to keep a straight face, but he quickly sobers at Midge's glower. He places his hand over Midge's and mine. "Ready. Set. Go."

I determine to keep things at half-muscle, but Midge has a surprisingly strong start. She tips my arm to the right, and I quickly counter her progress. It's almost too easy, but my conscience isn't sold on giving an old lady a wrist fracture. I purposefully slack and let her gain ground. She grunts with a final push, and I give her the win.

"Ha!" She raises both arms, then takes a victory lap around the counter, nearly plowing over a man with a walker. "Still the champ."

"Way to go, Midge. Though I did put up a good fight."

She dismisses me with a half-hearted shrug. "Eh, you were okay."

"Thanks," I say dryly.

Leo's gaze narrows, suspicion marking his every feature. I angle toward him with a finger to my lips.

I reface Midge. "Can we talk business now?" I retrieve my things and drape my coat over my arm. "Jared called me about the Vallerton."

"Ah, yes. The nativity set. You know, that's from my personal collection?" She launches into the backstory as if there isn't a growing line of customers behind us. "It's been sitting in storage for years. I bought it off some chump who had no idea what a fortune it's worth." She snickers. "But the Vallerton was never my style, so I thought I might as well put it up for sale."

I smile wide, a lightness flooding my chest. Within seconds, I will have completed my end of our bargain and fulfilled my promise. "I want to take it off your hands."

"Too late."

My world goes gray. "W-what?"

"Sold it an hour ago."

"No." My throat thickens, making my words rusty. "You don't have another?" That's like asking Shakespeare if he has extra *Hamlets* lying around.

"Sorry, hon." She waves me to the side, so the next customer can approach the counter. "You know how this business is."

Frustration soars, but mostly, I'm crushed. "Thanks, anyway," I manage with a forced smile and Leo helps me into my coat. "I hope you have a wonderful Christmas."

"You too. Come back for a rematch." She pats her bicep, unaware of my misery.

Leo grips my hand and leads me to the car, even as a numbness spreads through me. That was, in all probability, our only and last chance.

He starts the ignition and twists toward me. "You okay?"

"If it wasn't for that stupid deer ..." I would've been here long before the competition. I would've gotten the set. I'd almost be to Silver Creek by now with my treasure secured in the back. "I'm sorry." I can't look at him. "I messed it up."

He gently cups my chin and softly nudges until I meet his gaze. "No, you didn't." He slides his hand to frame my face, stroking my cheekbone with his thumb. "What you did today"— he shakes his head with a disbelieving smile—"goes above and beyond. Thank you, Greta." He leans closer, withdrawing his touch but not breaking eye contact. "And for the record, I'm not a cheater."

I keep my voice soft. "I never thought you were."

"But you are." He flashes his palm at my sudden jolt. "In a totally different way. You let that lady beat you. You could've whipped her soundly."

"Midge is a sore loser. If I'd won, she might not have been willing to negotiate. Not that it mattered."

"I think it's more than that." He absently toys with the edge of my scarf, but there's nothing flippant about his gaze, searching mine as if he wants to gather all my secrets and hold them close. "I think you were saving her pride. Because that's the kind of person you are."

He leans closer, but his phone buzzes, interrupting the moment. He grimaces at the screen. "More bad news."

I slump in the seat. "Do I want to know?" Seriously, if I had a punch card for all the terrible things that occur in a week, I could've had a free appetizer by now.

"We're in blizzard conditions. Whiteouts are expected throughout the night. I won't risk driving back. Not with you." His tone tells me this is non-negotiable. "You said there's a hotel down the street?" He glances both directions as if he could spot the Sugarvale Inn from here.

His protectiveness is sweet, but I want to go home. I'm hungry, tired, and devastated about losing the Vallerton. As if this trip hasn't already cost me emotionally, now it's going to hit me financially. I don't want to pay for a hotel room. But white-outs are no joke. I'd only experienced it once when walking down Main Street. The sudden rush of snowfall can reduce visibility to the point that it's hazardous, especially when driving.

I direct Leo where to go and notice the snow's coming down harder and faster. Now that the sun's down, the drop in temperature will make the roads slick.

What should be a quick jaunt down the street takes us longer because of the weather. We finally reach the hotel, and I blink at the full parking lot. "What's going on?" I can't imagine all these cars are here because their drivers wished to escape the snow. Sugarvale doesn't get *that* kind of traffic in the winter.

Leo finally finds a parking spot. He grabs his bag, and we race toward the automatic doors.

A "Welcome to SugarFest!" sign greets us as we enter the lobby.

"SugarFest?" I say aloud as I take in the space. Large gumballs—basically multi-colored inflatable balls on fishing line—suspend from the ceiling. Floormats shaped like chocolate squares lead to the front desk. A rainbow balloon arch resembling Skittles stands at the far left. This place is like Candy Land on steroids. People are wandering about, talking and laughing. Well, this explains the foot traffic at Midge's. A man dressed as an old-fashioned soda jerk, wearing a red-striped hat and holding a megaphone, announces some sort of event that is about to start.

"Event?" I look at Leo, who only shrugs.

"Let's just see about some rooms."

Leo and I approach the front desk.

A lanky man around my age puts his phone down with a sigh. "Can I help you?"

I open my mouth to speak, but Leo beats me to it. "We need two rooms for tonight."

"Sorry, we don't have any standard rooms left. It's SugarFest, if you haven't noticed." The man—Dorian, as his name tag reads—clearly snoozed during his training video on customer service. What's worse, no vacancy. No room at the inn. Cute. Our situation is far different than Mary and Joseph's, but I'm convinced our dislike for our respective innkeepers is mutual.

Leo takes the man's sarcasm with a good-natured nod. "Yeah, I see that. Are you saying you don't have anything?"

"Well …" Dorian's mouth twists, and he flicks a glance at me. "We do have the Sugar Rush Suite."

Leo opens his wallet. "We'll take it." I tug his elbow, drawing his eyes to me. "What's wrong?"

"This sounds pricey." I keep my tone low, but out of my peripheral, I note Dorian leaning to catch my words. I retreat a step, pulling Leo with me. "And it seems like he's being difficult just because he can. Like a kid who got bullied in high school for bad acne but has since developed amazing skin. So now he criticizes everyone's complexion."

Leo tilts his head as if he's unsure whether to laugh at my unhinged assumption or snag me another Snickers bar. To be fair, I'm uncertain too. It's been a day.

He smooths a lock of hair from my face. "Is there another hotel close?"

"Ugh, no." Though I'm sorely tempted to return to Midge's and demand a rematch. Winner gets to camp at her store. I totally spotted a Chesterfield sofa that looked comfortable.

"This is probably our best bet." He squeezes my hand.

With a grimace, I return to the counter. "What exactly is the Sugar Rush Suite? And how much is it?" I'm hoping the accommodations include more than one option for sleeping. Perhaps a pull-out sofa, a couple of beds. Maybe an extra room entirely. Gran and I once stayed at an Embassy Suites, and the front desk manager upgraded our room because the air conditioner had broken in the one we booked. I ended up having my own space with my own bathroom. It was almost like a tiny apartment.

Dorian's beady gaze settles on me. "It's fifteen hundred dollars. Plus tax."

"What?! For a single night?" Do they have diamond-studded toothbrushes? Bed sheets woven with gold-silk thread? For the love. "Why so much?"

"It's the honeymoon package."

Oh gosh.

He lifts a flyer and reads in a monotone voice, "The Sugar Rush Suite is designed to enhance romance. The amenities include a heart-shaped jacuzzi and private balcony." He pauses to yawn. "It comes with a three-hundred-dollar credit to the hotel shop, which has everything from nail files to formalwear. And two tickets to tonight's Dough Ball."

I'm not about to ask what the Dough Ball is. "Can't you depackage it? We don't need all that extra stuff." And I'm trying very hard not to think about staying in one room with Leo.

"Sorry, miss." Dorian does *not* look sorry. "I'm just the front desk agent."

"Can I speak with a manager?"

"She's judging the Sugar Cookie Icing Competition. It may be a while." A petite brunette walks past, and Dorian totally checks her out, following her with his gaze until she disappears down the hall. He seems to remember we're standing here and shrugs. "Since I'm unauthorized to hold the room without a deposit, I can't guarantee no one else will claim it, considering it's the last one we have and the weather's getting worse. So …"

"I hope all your zits return."

"What?"

"We'll take it." Leo presses his palm to my back, and with his free hand, gives Dorian his card.

My shoulders slump, all fight is lost. "Are you sure?"

"It'll be okay," he says soothingly. I know fifteen hundred dollars is nothing to someone like Leo, but I can't even fathom paying this much for a hotel room. Maybe for one in Paris overlooking the Eiffel Tower, but not in Northern Ohio with a view of a rusty water tower.

While Leo's paying for the room, I text Tilly, letting her know I won't make it for girls' night. She suggests we reschedule for tomorrow. I don't tell her about my new lodging situation with Leo. I'm still trying to process it myself. We have no extra clothes. No things whatsoever. Well, that's not exactly true. I slap a hand to my forehead. The antiques! "I'll be right back," I blurt before darting back into the cold. Of all the days to wear heels instead of boots. If anyone looks out their windows, they'll see me high-stepping as if I'm reenacting my marching band era. All because my wimpy ankles protest being submerged in snow.

I grab the Christmas decorations from the back of the car. It's less about someone stealing a boring-looking tub and more about the extreme cold. Mom may have ruined the paint on a few bulbs, but temperature fluctuations can make glass susceptible to cracks and brittleness. So I lug the bulky container into the hotel and meet a confused Leo by the elevator.

He pushes the up button, then lifts the tub from my hands. "I would've gotten this for you." He seems mildly offended I didn't ask. "I take it that whatever's inside is worth rushing outside in a ten-degree blizzard."

The doors ding open. "Those are Gran's antiques. Long story, but it was a rescue mission," I say as we step into the elevator. "I got them from Pap's this morning before dashing off in a competitive fury." Which was all for nothing. "Antiques don't hold up well in extreme temps. I didn't want to risk it."

He nods and hits the floor button with his elbow. "Good idea."

I fix my tired stare on my shoes, trying not to think of how I got here. The elevator starts, and my stomach flips. Though I'm unsure if my roiling gut is caused by a turbulent lift ride or the fact that I'm spending the night with Leo. "I'll, uh, split the room cost."

"It's all good." Something sparks in his dark eyes. "Fifteen hundred dollars is a small price to make your dreams come true."

My shocked squeak bounces off the walls. "Leo Mathis, what are you talking about?"

His grin turns mischievous. "You're the one who's been dying to know what I wear to sleep. You finally get your answer."

Then I realize what he's doing. He's trying to nudge me out of my hazy funk. All day I've been … off. Like the second I get close to finding my equilibrium, something knocks me off balance. Oddly enough, Leo's teasing helps ground me.

I playfully knock his shoulder with mine. "Well, I'm looking at what you're sleeping in. We don't have any extra clothes."

"Says who?" His smile is smug, and I have the unholy urge to kiss it. "I have clean hoodies and sweats in my gym bag."

My skin nearly screams to get out of this jumper. A girl can only wear wool for so long. "Are you planning on sharing the goods?"

"I am."

I look at Leo like he's a Fabergé egg. "Thank you."

The elevator opens, reminding me of our destination. The honeymoon suite.

I follow Leo down the hall and sputter a laugh. "I'm guessing the door with the vinyl conversation hearts all over it is the Sugar Rush Room." My gaze skims over the bold colored words shaped like the popular candy—Luv Machine, Bae-Watch, U R My Boo Thang.

Keeping it classy, Sugarvale Inn.

"You'd be correct." He carefully places the tub on the floor and inserts the key card in the door slot. The corners of his mouth lift. "Want me to carry you over the threshold?"

I snort. "Don't you dare. I'm freaking out as it is." I meant it as a joke, but the smile drops from his face.

"You're safe with me." His tone's both soft and adamant. "You know that, right?" I've read novels where the hero declares to set the world ablaze for the heroine, as if it's some romantic gesture to incinerate humankind on a woman's behalf. With Leo? He'd be the one to carry me out of the flames, to do everything in his power to protect me from the fire.

I place a hand on his arm, reassuring him. "I know." And with that, I step into the honeymoon suite. "Uhh … Wow."

Leo trails behind, bringing in my tub and closing the door. I turn to watch his initial reaction to the space and am not disappointed. His eyes widen in a what-is-happening kind of way.

Iridescent inflatable chairs shaped like gummy bears are positioned on a waffle-cone-print rug. The king-sized mattress is framed by four bedposts wrapped in red and white crepe paper to resemble peppermint sticks. Mr. and Mrs. Claus sugar cookies are on fluffy marshmallow pillows. A strip of multi-colored LED lights runs around the entirety of the space, where the walls meet the ceiling.

It's gloriously tacky.

Leo palms his neck and sighs. "Looks like someone had fun on Temu."

I laugh. "It's so ridiculous, it almost doesn't feel real." But it is. Today has officially clenched the title of the weirdest day of my life. And I've had some strong contenders.

The infamous heart-shaped jacuzzi tub is in the far corner, but thankfully, there's a shower in the bathroom to the right.

Leo slides his gym bag off his shoulder and sets it by an oversized gummy bear. He removes his jacket, revealing a button-down shirt. My sneaking glance must be more obvious than I think because he catches me. "What?"

"You're dressed up more than usual. Did you miss something important today?" A date, maybe? Not that it's any of my business.

He shakes his head. "Something for work, but it's not a big deal. Are you hungry?"

"Famished."

"Me too." He moves to the desk that is surprisingly normal, as if the design funding got cut off once they reached the far side of the suite. "Let's get room service."

"You've spent enough already. Can we subsist on vending machine junk? It's a challenge I'm willing to accept."

"It's fine, really." He plucks a menu from the desktop. Along with the menu, there's an agenda for the SugarFest events and a brochure with "Things to Do" around the area.

I pick up the brochure. It's outdated, the pages are wrinkly, and I wince at all the germs no doubt layering every inch of this thing. As I leaf through it, a familiar storefront catches my eye. "The Antique Emporium." I show Leo the picture. "I completely forgot about Alice's place."

"Who's Alice?"

"She's another antique dealer. I haven't been in contact with her for years, but it might be worth checking with her for the Vallerton. She's old school, like Midge. No online presence." I point to where there's only an address and phone listed. "I'll call her in the morning when she reopens."

He nods. "Maybe we can hit the place tomorrow before we head back."

In my search for the Vallerton, I've neglected my Secret Santa duty. I left the folder in the car and am not motivated to retrieve it. Maybe I can take a break from everything tonight. Yet I'm running out of time as it is. Today's the seventh, which means I have less than two weeks to find my recipient.

"Looks like we need a Plan B." Leo's voice cuts through my overthinking.

"What do you mean?"

"There's no room service tonight because the kitchen's preparing for the Dough Ball." He picks up the SugarFest flyer.

I join him in reading the paper. The Dough Ball is a fundraiser event for next year's SugarFest. "It's a weirdly clever play on words."

His eyes meet mine. "The room package comes with two tickets."

I scoff. "You seriously want to attend?"

He flicks the corner of the page. "They're serving sirloin and shrimp."

"Enough said." But then. "Wait. Is there a dress code?" I glance at Leo's dirt-stained pants, which I doubt qualifies for ballroom attire.

"Ah, but don't forget." He grabs my hand. "We also have store credit."

I catch on to his reasoning. "Which, according to Dorian the Dubious, has everything from nail files to formalwear."

Time for shopping.

CHAPTER 22

"I THINK Dorian should've specified the formalwear is not from this century." I grimace at an evening gown with shoulder pads so large I can easily pose as a linebacker. You know, if linebackers wore rhinestones. Because this number is glitzed up.

In all the times I've visited this town, I've never had a reason to go to the hotel. I know from reading the flyer that SugarFest is an annual event that's been steadily growing, but I have so many questions. What's the draw? And why does an inn in rural Ohio sell evening attire? Hotel shops should have nail clippers shaped like flip-flops, license plate keychains with names on them, and T-shirts with sayings that were trendy five years ago. While I do spot a sweatshirt that reads, "Powered by Cane Sugar and Bad Decisions," it's literally hanging next to a tiered chiffon gown that reminds me of a macaron.

I can't make it make sense. Such has been the theme of my day.

"Nice." Leo grins. "I can complement you in this." He raises a neon pink button-down shirt.

"Gah! My eyes!" I hold up my arms, fingers splayed, as if Leo's aiming a high-intensity searchlight at me. "That is *not* formalwear. It's hideous."

He appraises it again. "It might not be pretty, but it has an amazing personality."

I laugh. "They take this SugarFest theme a bit too far." I hold up a gown labeled "Cotton Candy Chic," but nothing about this dress is posh. It's blue, pink, and lavender tulle thrown together with a sequined bodice. If I wear this, I'll rival a giant puff ball and get caught on everything.

"Yeah, but you can't find this just anywhere." He holds up a deep red, crushed velvet—imitation, mind you—dinner jacket with jeweled buttons resembling gumdrops.

I lean back with a hand to my chin and study the jacket as if I have my own fashion reality TV show. "All you need to complete the look is a top hat, and you'll be the next Willy Wonka."

He points to a shelf beside me that has, indeed, a top hat.

I gasp at the insanity of it all, but that doesn't stop me from snatching the hat and holding it out to him. "I dare you."

"Want to make it a true dare?" He asks this in a tone that makes me think of a heated kiss by a Christmas tree.

"It depends on the terms."

"We pick each other's outfits."

A laugh bursts from my lips. Okay, not expecting that. "You're willing to take that risk? It could be dangerous with my creativity levels." I return the hat to the shelf but give a pointed nod at a bright orange suit coat that can moonlight as a creamsicle.

"I told you I like your kind of danger."

He said that the day we met. My chest squeezes, but I'm never one to turn down a challenge. "Okay, Mathis. You're on." I tell him my size, and we go to work outfitting each other. I've never dressed a full-grown man before. Well, not entirely true. I've sometimes set out Pap's clothes for doctor appointment days to ensure he matches, but I'm much more invested in this dare than I ever was in grabbing an argyle sweater from Pap's closet. After a while, I stumble upon the perfect jacket and trousers for

Leo. They're not the highest quality, but they're the best I can find. I discreetly make the purchase, and the cashier covers everything with a dark blue garment bag.

"Meet you back in the room," I call saucily to Leo but don't realize how I sound until the cashier lady snickers. I was referring to the dare and how I finished shopping first, but, of course, she knows we have the honeymoon suite. And now I'm running into a mannequin wearing a peppermint swirl bikini. Nothing crashes, except my dignity. I scuttle out of the shop, Leo's deep chuckle following me.

I zip up the side of the dress and study my reflection in the bathroom mirror. Leo picked out the "Sugar Plum Princess," and I actually love it. The gown's a deep purple, bodycon maxi with crystal beadwork mimicking sugar-frosted glass. Since the fabric is a polyester and spandex blend, the dress hugs my curves but has some stretch. I sported a braid all day, so my hair has a wave to it. I swipe lip gloss over my mouth and now … this feels very date-y. Before, we had our little bargain as a buffer. Even when Leo invited me to his house, it wasn't an official date, but to review the Silver Creek Secret Santa letters. Tonight, that folder is in the car, and the Vallerton is gone. Our agreement's on hold.

I promised earlier to discuss the kiss, but my brain can't focus on anything except the clump of mascara on the edge of my right lashes or how I wish I had better deodorant than the reserve one from my purse. I adjust my bra straps, so they'll stay in place, then wet a wad of toilet paper and wipe the mud from my black heels, smearing white nubs all over them instead. I spend the next five minutes controlling my breathing while picking soggy paper from my shoes.

Leo and I are just grabbing dinner downstairs because room service is a no-go. That's all.

After one more calming inhale, I open the door and step into the room.

Leo's gaze sweeps over me. "I'm calling it. I won." He seems to consider his words as he lounges on a marshmallow-shaped bean bag. "Or maybe you won. I don't even care. All I know is that you look amazing and that slit will torment me all night."

While I was getting ready, it was like open mic night in my brain, with all my insecurities elbowing for center stage. My physical defects on full display, like how my right front tooth is slightly more forward than my left front or the small scar near my hairline from when I smacked my head off the monkey bars in elementary recess. How, when I get chilled, my skin turns freakishly translucent, and the blue vein lines and goosebumps make my arms look like raw chicken meat. Because of this, I nearly struggle to believe Leo's sweet words if not for the arrested expression on his face.

Too bad I can't switch off my screaming insecurities. "Really?" I hate the wobble in my voice.

He misses nothing and approaches me like a man on a mission. "Yeah, really." He catches both of my hands in his. "You know why I picked this dress?"

"Because it came with a pack of Nerds?"

His smile is the stuff of poems. "No, it reminded me of your dress at the firefighters' gala. I nearly choked when I saw you from across the room."

"That's because you weren't expecting me."

"It was more than that." Hunger flashes in his eyes, but it's gone so quickly that now I'm wondering if I imagined it. "You're beautiful, Greta. And if you're doubting yourself, I'm not doing a good job as your hype guy."

Oh great. Now he feels forced to give me compliments. "You don't have to be."

"Ah, but I want to." His thumb slides over my knuckles, slow and rhythmic. "You're the only one on Earth that I will wear purple pants for."

My laugh is small because my heart's doing some big things right now. Like writing Leo's name all over it in permanent marker. "I wouldn't call them purple. More like lavender."

His nose wrinkles as if that's worse.

Smiling, I smooth a hand over his lapel. "You fill out this jacket nicely." Almost too nicely. He's wearing an ivory coat with trim that's the same shade as his trousers. "Look at us." I gesture at our reflection in the mirror above the dresser. I find it amazing we both chose colors that blended well. "We unintentionally match." And I realize that sums up our relationship. Nothing about our meeting last Christmas had been planned. Two random strangers from two different worlds collide beside one old street clock. Yet, somehow, we're good together.

"We do." He looks at me as if he understands the subtext. His hand slips around my waist, the warmth of his palm seeping into my skin. We're smiling at each other with this unreserved energy like we're in fifth grade, and he just asked me to sit by him in the cafeteria, during the last week of school. Growing up, we always had assigned lunch seats except for those final days. That was when everyone asked their crushes to meet them at their table. The gossip would fuel the summers. But here Leo and I stand, aware we'll probably spark rumors in Silver Creek— because that's just the way it is in small towns—but we only seem to care about sharing our chicken nuggets. Figuratively. Although if he ever literally offered me nuggets, I would do my part.

We make our way downstairs and, after we surrender our Dough Ball tickets, we're granted entrance into the convention hall. I expected the room to be gauche, like our suite, but it's surprisingly pretty.

The recessed lighting is dim, allowing rows of bistro bulbs to offer a soft glow. The pillars framing the room are wrapped in pastel pink and ivory fabric. A wide center row leads to the dance floor in the back area, with a DJ station sitting to the side. Tables, draped in ivory with crystal candied centerpieces, are strategically situated throughout. While this aesthetic is top tier, I've come expecting to see pastries and baked goods in abundance, considering it's called a Dough Ball. To my disappointment, I only spot one dessert table. What's up with fancy events not delivering the good stuff?

I blow out a sigh and resort to people-watching as we wait in line for food, which is a buffet-style ordeal. Attendees are either dressed absurdly, like the woman wearing a gingerbread crown, or elegant, like … "Candy Cane Kelly," I blurt.

"What?" Leo dips his head close to hear me over the music.

"Nothing." Except there's a woman, speaking to a group of guests near the dance floor, who looks exactly like my Hallmark Barbie Collection ornament that Gran got me when I was little. She's wearing an A-line silhouette in crimson with white panel cutouts that swish about her long legs. Even her hairstyle is the same, her dark waves cascading down her back with a few locks framing her face. She's stunning, in a way that women stare, trying to find fault, and men stare because there isn't any. I'm also thinking she's someone important because, yeah, she's got that air about her.

Leo and I load our plates as if we hadn't eaten in weeks. I snag the last two-person table while Leo fetches our drinks. A man walks by wearing a cellophane jacket, making him look like a giant candy wrapper. I press my lips together to stifle a laugh, but his *clothes* make that all-too-familiar crinkling sound as he passes, and I'm too tired for self-control.

Leo returns, placing my Sprite in front of me.

I smile my thanks. "This feels otherworldly." As soon as Leo sits, I'm reaching for a roll. Ah, hot carbs. "It's like we're extras in a live action of Candy Crush."

Leo shakes his head with a laugh. "Yeah, I don't think anyone would believe us if we tried."

We are both absorbed in our food, which is actually good, but then, I sip my Sprite and nearly spit it out.

"What's wrong?" He sets down his fork.

I examine my glass. "This tastes like salt."

"The fountain must be out of syrup. What else can I get you?" He's already up on his feet before I can protest.

"Anything's fine." I just want to get this bitter flavor from my mouth.

He strides toward the drink station, and I allow my gaze to follow him as he moves effortlessly through the crowd, that is, until he gets stopped by Candy Cane Kelly.

She's smiling at him, not in a seductive or even a flirty way, but like she knows something he doesn't. I can't explain it. I take another bite of my roll and watch as they chat like old friends. Maybe they are. I'm expecting jealousy to twist my gut because she's gorgeous and probably never in her life compared her skin to raw poultry. But there's no twisting.

Because of Leo.

He's offering polite smiles and contributing to the conversation, but he's not looking at her the way he looks at me. As if he can sense my thinking of him, he glances my way and unleashes that signature grin. They finish their discussion, and Leo retrieves another drink. I don't care if it's bitter Sprite or flat Coke because I don't think I'd be able to taste the difference. I'm numb in the best kind of way.

"Here you go." He sets my drink down and reclaims his seat. "Guess who I was talking to." He jerks a thumb toward Candy Cane Kelly. "That's Mrs. Langston."

My mouth drops. "The pie lady? No way!" Mrs. Langston Pies are to Ohio what Marie Callander's desserts are to the rest of the country. Since this state is all about loyalty to their own, households have been buying Mrs. Langston Pies for decades. I squint at her. "How does she not look a hundred years old?"

He laughs. "Because she's not the original Mrs. Langston. She's the granddaughter."

"Ah, that explains it."

"It also explains this event. The Langston family owns this

inn." He cuts into his steak. "She told me her grandmother once worked in the kitchen here and—"

"It's where she made her first pie." Because of antiques, I'm always fascinated by origin stories. "And that's why they celebrate SugarFest."

He smiles at my enthusiasm. "Right on both accounts. Most of the attendees are Langston employees or vendors."

"Which is why it's so crowded. And probably why we look so out of place."

"As to that." He tugs his lapels. "The reason she pulled me aside is because of my coat."

"See? I told you that you fill it out nicely," I tease and take a bite of potatoes.

"Her mother designed it. She recognized the style. I guess the second-generation Langston wanted to be a fashion designer but couldn't make a go of it."

"So all of her creations ended up at the Sugarvale Inn's shop." And why the formalwear looks like it's straight from the eighties and nineties. Because it is. "Finally, it makes sense. All our mysteries from today are solved."

"Not all." His gaze fixes on me. "Not the most important."

Oh, the Vallerton. Of course that would be at the forefront of his mind.

He leans close and drops his voice. "You promised to explain about the kiss."

CHAPTER 23

GRAN ALWAYS SAID, *"Be careful when you issue promises because the delivery costs are high."*

So yeah, I'm paying for my past words. I really don't feel like stirring up those emotions. But I owe Leo an explanation. "I told you that it wasn't your fault, right?" I shift in my seat. "That the reason I left in a hurry had nothing to do with … the kiss."

He nods, though remains quiet, letting me talk.

"It's kind of a long story." Just then, my phone buzzes. It's a text from Mom. As if she knows I'm about ready to uncork this pressurized bottle of memories, spilling my feelings all over the place.

> **MOM**
>
> Sorry about the Windex. Sorry about everything.

I slide my eyes shut with a weighted exhale. The chatter of the room, the blaring of some Spice Girls' song, the clinking of utensils off plates. The surrounding noises seem to intensify and bounce around in my head. I count to three, then slowly lift my lashes.

Leo's watching me.

"Sorry. It's my mom." I lift my phone with a little shake. "She's apologizing for this morning. And every morning for the past, oh, twenty-some years."

"That's a lot to be sorry for."

It really is. "This is why—*she* is why—I ran out on you last night." I press a fingertip to my temple, my thoughts piling in my head like today's snowfall, threatening a whiteout of complete blankness. "I know that doesn't make sense, but hear me out." I force myself to sit straighter, like I'm about to plead my case. "You know how I mentioned the rescue mission at Pap's this morning?"

"The antiques?"

"Yeah. My mom was using Windex on some Christmas bulbs. Ammonia on antique glass works like paint stripper."

He cringes.

"Exactly. But I reacted with big emotions. Because, yeah, the antiques were ruined, but it went beyond that."

He puts his fork down, giving me his full attention. I never realized what it's like to be someone's sole focal point, but I can easily get addicted to those dark eyes steadied on me.

"Remember when you asked why I keep strength training, even though I'd rather shave off my eyebrows than lift weights?"

He smiles at my exaggeration. Well, it's mostly an exaggeration. "Yeah, I remember."

"It's because I'm waiting for my mom to leave."

He's quiet for a second. "You want her to leave?"

"No, but that's just it. Growing up, I never wanted her to leave, but she always did. When I became an adult, I had this hope that maybe she'd come around more. But no. It messed with me, you know? Like what's wrong with me that my own mother doesn't want a relationship?"

Leo reaches across the table, taking my shaking hand in his calm, strong one.

"Then out of nowhere, she comes back after Gran passes and

expects me to be okay with everything. Problem is, I don't know how to be okay. I don't know how to ignore all those years of her not being here, of coming in and going out of my life. So now, I expect her to go. It's a reflex, I think. Then, eventually, I'll be left caring for Pap. Which is fine. I'd do anything for him." I give a small shrug like it's no big deal when it's anything but. "So I keep weightlifting in case I have to resume my role—"

"As a caregiver."

"Yeah. It's like, I know it's coming, but don't know when."

He gently squeezes my hand and lets go, as if he can tell when I need space. "Why don't you ask her?"

"Ask her when she's leaving?"

A server comes by to pick up our plates, and Leo waits until she walks away. "More like, ask your mom if she plans on staying for the long haul. Then maybe you can ask her why she left in the first place."

I want those answers but … "I think I'm afraid of her response. Which is probably why I hold her at arm's length. Why I hold everyone at arm's length." Even Leo.

He leans forward, resting his elbows on the table. "I understand that. You know that I grew up in boarding schools. I hardly saw my parents. I didn't even have a relationship with them until just a few years ago."

"What changed?"

"I did. I made more of an effort to understand them. I still don't agree with their choices. I would've rather had a steady upbringing with present parents, but I can't change the past. Our relationship still has hiccups, but it's getting smoother as we keep trying."

His words give me hope. "Where are they now?"

"They spend most of their time at their villa near Lake Como."

My mouth parts. "Italy?"

He nods. "They're supposed to come to the States in January."

If they plan on visiting after the new year, that means Leo might be alone for the holidays. "You're welcome to spend Christmas with me. I always go to Pap's. The Mavericks will be there, of course."

His head tips slightly back, as if the invitation surprised him. He smiles at me. "Thank you."

My conscience nudges me to finish what I started. Here goes. "Circling back to what we were talking about. Now that you know a little more about my background, I hope this makes more sense." I force myself to breathe, so my words don't all run into each other. "I rushed out last night because of something Fletcher said. He warned me that you never stay in the same place for long."

"Ah." His eyes light with understanding. "And given what you just told me about your mom always leaving—"

"It shook me. That same twist in my gut—the one that always hit me when she left—came back full force last night. So I ignored confrontation and ran. That's kind of my defense mechanism." That and self-deprecation. But I can only deal with one personality defect at a time. "It was less about you and more about me getting my head on straight about my mom. In a way, it was good for me."

His grin sparks. "Which is basically saying kissing me was good for you." He leans back in his chair with a satisfied smirk. "Say the word, and we can work on this self-awareness thing whenever you want."

I laugh, needing a break from the heaviness. But also, having the freedom to kiss Leo any time I'd like makes me heady. It's best not to think about that too much to avoid spontaneous combustion.

As if realizing the conversation hasn't yet reached full closure, he says, "Fletcher probably said that about me because of how I grew up. I was always moving around, shuffled here and there. Then as an adult, I drifted because I never had a permanent home." He shrugs. "Or maybe he said it because I'm only a volunteer at the fire department. Who knows. But just because I'm not tied to the job doesn't mean I'm going to leave." His eyes take on an intensity that makes my breath turn shallow. "I have the strongest reason to stay. I'm not going anywhere, Greta."

My heart leaps in response.

Some slow song—that I can't remember the name of—filters through the speakers, and Leo extends his hand. "Dance with me?"

I shoot off a quick text to Mom, explaining we'll talk soon, and I answer Leo's question by slipping my fingers into his waiting ones. He leads me to the dance floor and, keeping our hands intertwined, he wraps his right arm around my back. Our rhythm syncs, and I note how this dance is far different from our first, when I was furious with him for thinking he deceived me. But the one thing that hasn't changed is the spark between us, which seems to burn fiercer with every touch.

I rest my head on his shoulder, and he presses me close.

"Greta?"

I feel rather than hear the rumble of my name. "Hmm?"

"A week from Monday …"

I know exactly what that day is. "The fifteenth?"

He dips his head lower, his late-day stubble skimming my temple. "I know it's the anniversary of your Gran's passing. What can I do?"

I slide my hand from his shoulder to his neck, feeling the strength there. "Be with me." I intend to spend the day with Pap, but he always turns in early. I tell Leo this.

"What if—and this is only if you want—we meet again at the park? By the street clock, just like last December? Only this time I'll be there." His voice is so full of promise I can hardly breathe.

I smile up at him. "I'd like that."

"I'm not sure if you realize this." He grips me tighter. "But I'm struggling to get you out of my head."

"Do you *want* me out of your head?"

"No," he says, and I feel his smile on my skin. "I don't want you out of my arms either."

I press against him. "Well, what are you going to do about it?"

"I'm going to tell you how much I like you."

"That's a good start."

"Then ..." He eases back, and his hooded gaze is filled with the hunger that I feel. "I'm going to point your attention to what's hanging over our heads."

I glance up and laugh. A fake, candied-looking mistletoe is above us. "Did you pick this spot on purpose?"

"Would I do that?" He gives me a look that says he totally did. "You know how I've been hunting for mistletoe these past few weeks."

I lean in, my mouth hovering close to his. "We don't need it." And I kiss him.

After our mistletoe moment, we are in constant contact, either by dancing, holding hands, or trading heated kisses that start with the brush of lips across my bare shoulder and end with me being pressed against a side-hall wall for a dizzying stretch of time.

Just when I start thinking I've stumbled into some kind of Candy Land fever dream, my bladder reminds me—nope, still real life. So while Leo's picking at the dessert table, which I plan to attack later, I head to the nearest ladies' room that is blessedly without a line. I'm thankful Leo didn't pick the Jellybean Jumpsuit I spotted earlier at the hotel shop, or else I'd be in trouble. I'm washing my hands beside a frazzled woman dressed like a cream puff, currently assaulting the paper towel dispenser.

"It's jammed," she says as if I were some sort of bathroom monitor.

It's the same model as the one at Brewtiful Grounds. "There's a trick to it." I dig in my purse and slide out a business card.

"The roll backs up, but there's a spot … right here." I slide my card in the narrow opening and work free the paper. "Voila." I smile at her, but she still seems slightly hostile, so I step back and let her reach for a towel.

"Thank you, young lady." She gives me a cursory glance, then doubles back. "I saw you on the dance floor." She rips off a paper towel with a swift swoop. "You and your husband look very much in love."

I don't correct her. "Thank you." I'm about to ask her if she works for Mrs. Langston Pies and if she knows how I can score free samples, but she's not finished gushing about my fake marriage.

"Hold onto that." She wipes her hands as if she wants to sweep away not only the moisture but also several layers of skin. "Because all too soon, you're married twenty-four years, and your husband decides to spend several thousand dollars on something he has no right buying. At least without consulting you first."

This got weird fast. I gently tug my business card from the dispenser, but it slips through my fingers, kind of like this conversation.

The lady picks it up, and her hazel gaze catches. "Is this you? You own an antique shop?"

"Yeah, in Silver Creek?" I don't mean for it to sound like a question, but her tone's slightly intimidating. I blink and regroup. "My shop's about two hours from here."

She studies the card like I'm going to pop-quiz her on my contact info. "Can I keep this?"

"Of course. Are you interested in antiques?" I ask to create small talk and keep her from giving unsolicited marital advice.

"Not really. I don't know much about them. But I do know more than my husband."

And we're back to that again.

"Do you know what he did? We've been looking for a certain thing for our daughter. She's had some serious health issues, and she recently got the *all clear* from the doctors." She explains how her daughter had been born with a heart defect and details all the hurdles her daughter had to overcome. By the time she finishes her story, I've got unexpected tears in my eyes.

"I'm very happy for her." There's something inspiring about those who defy the odds and persevere. "And you."

She accepts my well-wishes with a small nod. "We wanted to get her a gift, something nostalgic. She wants one specific item, but we couldn't find it anywhere." She exhales a weary sigh. "Sal, that's my husband, and I'm Candace, by the way. Candace Whitman. Anyways, Sal thought he found it this afternoon, but he bought the *wrong* thing. Did he call me? No, because I would have told him that set wasn't a Garrick. Now we can't return it. I've been giving him the cold shoulder all night. Not that he noticed. He's been trying to schmooze Mrs. Langston, but she hasn't given him the time of day to hear his proposal. Did you know her real name's Chloe Ferndash?"

"A Garrick?" Oh. It was all clicking into place. "Did your husband happen to buy a Vallerton set at Midge's Antiques today?"

Her eyes widen. "Yes … well, I'm not sure if it's a Vallerton, as you call it. But he was at Midge's Antiques. He told the lady he needed a nativity set from the early 1900s that was pretty rare. But like I said, he bought the wrong one. How'd you know?"

In her husband's defense, the sets debuted around the same time and are both rare and valuable. I can see how he made the mistake, especially if he didn't know what he was looking for. "I've been searching for a Vallerton set. They're hard to come by." And just like that, every whimsical feeling that's been swirling through me over the past hour shrivels dead. The sole reason we're stuck here in Sugarvale is because I had one goal— get the Vallerton.

"Ah, I see. They must be just as rare as Garricks. But that's all she wants. We once had a set when she was younger and lost it in a move."

"That's disappointing," I hear myself say, as if my voice is outside my body.

"Yeah, I didn't know it was worth that much." She glances at my card again. "I'm not sure what we're going to do. The woman at the store won't take back the set, and so I guess we'll have to give it to our daughter. Though her heart was entirely fixed on the other."

"I have a Garrick."

CHAPTER 24

I TAKE a hot shower but can't get rid of the stinging chill. It's settled in my bones. I should be happy, ecstatic even. The other day, I thought we'd need a Christmas miracle to get the Vallerton, and it happened. The miracle being me in the right place with the right nativity set to trade with Candace Whitman. She gets my Garrick and Leo gets the Vallerton. I fulfilled my end of the bargain.

And I'm absolutely crushed.

Mostly, I'm disappointed in myself. When Candace mentioned needing my set, I offered it up without hesitation. The words spewed out of my mouth before I realized what I was doing. It scared me, to be honest. Why is my default to surrender without thought? Like if someone needs a new brain, I'd say, "Oh, here, take mine!" Though it doesn't matter now, since I feel I officially lost it anyway.

Just as I lost the Garrick.

I'll get over it. I faced a bigger devastation with Gran's passing … but then, why does it feel like losing her all over again? I know the answer, yet I don't have the headspace to acknowledge it.

I slip on Leo's hoodie and sweatpants. They're both too big, but I roll down the waistband and fold up the sleeves. I should probably dry my wet hair, but I only want this day to be over. Topknot it is. Drawing in a ragged breath, I exit the bathroom.

Leo's watching college basketball highlights and scrolling on his phone. My seating options are a marshmallow bean bag or an inflatable gummy bear. I choose the bean bag.

His smile broadens as he takes me in. "You look cute in my clothes."

I press the cuff to my face and inhale. "It smells like you." That will probably embarrass me come morning, but all my filters are scattered downstairs on the women's bathroom floor. I haven't been the same since I walked out of there.

"I'm not getting that back, am I?"

"I'm glad we understand each other." I try to match his teasing, but my tone falls flat.

If he notices my dampened mood, he kindly gives me a free pass. He holds out his phone, showing me the weather radar on the screen. "The bulk of the snow has stopped. I say we take the turnpike tomorrow. It should be clearer than backroads."

"Agreed." I glance at the tub of antiques, which has one less Garrick nativity set and one more Vallerton. It's a good thing. I did a good thing. Christmas is a season of giving. Look at me— I'm embodying the whole Santa Claus thing.

"You okay?"

I suddenly realize that Leo's turned off the TV and is staring at me. He doesn't know about the trade, and tonight I'm going to keep it that way.

"Oh, me? Yep. All good." Just a bit of emotional scar tissue that I'm hiding beneath forced smiles and rapid nods.

He reaches out and sweeps a rogue lock of hair from my cheek. "You sure?" His touch sends a shiver through me. "Cold?"

"Very."

He goes to the thermostat. "Kicked up the heat. That should help."

Maybe with the chill, but not the numbness. That will go away with time. Hopefully.

"You sure you're all right?"

I must look awful. "Yeah, I'm overtired." I move slowly toward the bed, but Leo intercepts my hand, tugging me to him.

"I'll take the chair." He brushes his lips across my forehead.

I slide my eyes closed, taking in his touch. Forehead kisses are underrated. After several deep breaths, I pull back. "No way you're sleeping on a plastic gummy bear." Never thought those words would ever come out of my mouth. "There's room on the bed for both of us."

"You sure? You're acting a bit weird."

Of course he would think my strange behavior is because of our sleeping arrangements. "Weirdness is ninety percent of my personality." Apparently the other ten percent is impulsivity, considering I offered up my Garrick before I could clamp my mouth shut. I could knock on Candace's door and say I've made a colossal mistake, ask for my antique back. But the expression of unbridled joy on her face when she saw the nativity set makes me pause. Her family has been through a lot.

Maybe I'll feel better about it in the morning. I glance up at Leo. "I'm sorry I'm out of it. This day has been long." In so many ways. "And yes, I'm sure. I trust you. I'm just not feeling my best right now."

"You need sleep." He guides me to the bed and turns down the comforter and sheet.

I scoot onto the mattress, and he tucks me in with such care that my heart squeezes. He kisses me softly, then grabs another blanket from the closet. It's about half his size, but he doesn't seem to care. I hear him move to his side of the bed, the mattress dipping with his weight. He stays above the covers, and I'm touched at his sweetness in respecting my space.

"Goodnight, Greta," he says and switches off the lamp.

"Night," I whisper, but it's a long time before sleep claims me.

In every rom-com I've watched where the story features the one-bed trope, the heroine always—always!—wakes up with her head on the hero's chest *or* they both rouse in a tangle of limbs.

I wake to an obnoxious knocking at the door.

Leo groans and flops onto his back, an elbow across his forehead. "Maybe they'll go away."

It seems Leo is not a morning person.

Another knock. "Breakfast," an overly bright, feminine voice calls.

I blink until the room comes into focus. "Dorian the Deceitful forgot to mention breakfast service is included in the Sugar Rush package."

Leo chuckles, his voice still rusty with sleep. He grabs his phone off the nightstand. "It's only seven. If we were really on our honeymoon, I'd be ticked."

I fight against a blush. "Think on the bright side. Maybe there's waffles." I get up and catch a glimpse of Gran's tub. Last night's events come rushing back—swapping the sets while Leo was in the shower, seeing the pure relief and happiness on Candace's face, handing over a chunk of my heart. I roll my shoulders and open the door.

The chipper hotel person left one of those rolling tables by the door. I wheel it into the room. Leo's sitting on the edge of the bed, looking handsomely disheveled. I have no idea what my appearance is, but I've never exactly had that "I woke up like this" caption-worthy face.

I lift the stainless-steel dome lids like some French waiter. Shriveled eggs, hashbrowns that could pass for rubber pellets, and two bagels that haven't been toasted are tossed onto the plates. I wrinkle my nose. "The Dough Ball food was so amazing, and this is …"

"Crap," Leo finishes.

I nod. "I hope they don't expect a five-star review with this breakfast."

"Your vending machine idea has some merit." He glances over, and I want to memorize the soft curl of his mouth. "Good morning, by the way."

"Good morning." I return his smile.

"You're too far away." He crushes me to him and breathes me in. "Your hair smells amazing."

"That would be the provided vanilla-sugar shampoo. Very on-brand of them, I think." I slip my arms around him. He has no clue how much I need this hug. After a long minute, he releases me, and I instantly miss his warmth. "Think the roads are all right?"

"Most likely. Trucks had all night to plow and throw down salt." His gaze is a slow crawl over my face. "You seem sad."

"I think I'm hungry." And regretting life choices. You know, the usual.

He grabs his wallet and leaves to raid the vending machines, giving me a second to find my emotional equilibrium. I wash my face and brush my teeth with the toiletries from the hotel courtesy basket.

Leo returns with protein bars, pretzels, and Pop-Tarts—the three Ps of every balanced breakfast. We drink the orange juice that came with the meal, which does not mix well in the aftermath of bubblegum toothpaste. Lesson learned. We scarf down our food and go to the lobby. Leo takes one glance at my current fashion statement, which I dub "hoodies and heels," and wisely keeps any remarks to himself, though I do see him sneak a smile. He's holding the tub of antiques, and I'm trying to imagine a way of telling him how I got the Vallerton that doesn't involve my tears. Or me looking like a lunatic.

I'm drawing a blank.

We check out and head toward my car. The sun's out, making the snow sparkle like diamonds. A minivan pulls up as we're about to cross the parking lot, and the passenger window rolls down.

It's Candace.

She smiles brightly. The man in the driver's seat, who I assume is Sal, nods at Leo.

Candace pokes her head out the window like a middle-aged turtle. "I wanted to say thank you again! You made our daughter's Christmas."

I wave her off, but I can't control the tremor in my hand. "Don't mention it." Like, please, do *not* mention it.

"I really hope you're happy with the Vallerton. It's a great set but not what we wanted. Thanks for trading."

Feeling the weight of Leo's stare, I scramble for a reply. "Uh, yeah. It'll work wonderfully. Well, safe travels."

Candace is not catching my hints. "Hope you have a Merry Christmas!"

Sal points at Leo. "Remember what I said."

Huh? Sal never said anything, especially to Leo. Unless I zoned out for a second, which is entirely possible. Leo only dips his chin, and they drive off. I feel a gusty chill, and it has nothing to do with the December breeze.

"What was that about?"

"Oh, I met her last night in the bathroom at the Dough Ball." I offer a quick smile and hustle toward the car. "Are you driving, or am I?"

He pulls out my keys and unlocks the doors. "I got it." He opens the hatch and sets the tub in the back. In seconds, he's behind the wheel and pulling off the Sugarvale Inn lot.

His frame's rigid. "Why didn't you tell me you got the Vallerton?"

"I was going to." I force a bright tone. "It was supposed to be a surprise, but now that's ruined."

He softens somewhat. "She said you traded."

I sink lower in my seat. "Yep."

"What did you give her?"

"Oh, just an antique from that tub. It worked out that I brought it along."

His brow lowers. "We were together the whole time. When did you do this?"

"When you were in the shower. I went to her room." Now I feel icky and busted, like I was caught smoking behind the bleachers in junior high.

He nails me with a look. "What antique, Greta? Be more specific, please."

Ugh. "The Garrick."

Leo pulls to the side of the road and brakes. "Your inheritance?"

I suck in a quick breath. "Who told you?"

"Your Pap at Thanksgiving. He told me the Garrick was the first antique you and your gran found together. Said it sparked your love for antiques."

"Yeah."

He puts the car in reverse. "I'm turning around. We're going back."

"What? No."

He keeps his foot on the brake and his heated gaze on my face. "Greta, I can't let you give up that set."

"It's too late. They have a daughter who had a health battle. All she wanted was that set."

"And *you* have a grandmother who passed, and that piece is meaningful to you."

My lips quiver. "They're no doubt long gone."

"I can catch them." His voice is steel.

I lean over and press my hand to his arm. "Listen, I traded the Garrick for the Vallerton. The Whitmans get the Garrick for their daughter. Your sweet widow gets the Vallerton. Everyone's happy."

"No. Not everyone."

"Yes. Right. I see that." My words are choppy like my breath. "You're obviously not happy. I overstepped. I didn't want to miss the chance. I should've talked to you because you might not have wanted to spend—"

He throws up his hands in the universal "what the heck?" gesture. "This isn't about money, Greta. Because whatever number you have in your head, I guarantee you, I was willing to spend at least four times that much. No, I'm not talking about my happiness here." He cups my face in both his hands, his gaze imploring. "But yours. You're the one I care about most."

I swallow. This is not how I wanted to hear this declaration. "I made my decision." My voice is reedy. "Nobody forced me."

His thumb swipes my cheekbone. "It's your nature. You see a need, and you'll surrender anything. Even if it costs you."

I blink. "You say that like it's a bad thing."

His hands drop from my face. "It's not. But it's also okay to say no."

"That would be selfish." I'm feeling defensive, even though I've shared the same reservations. My emotions are all over the place, not even a GPS can track them down. "Isn't Christmas about giving? Isn't that the point of the season?"

He looks at me like that's the biggest load of festive fluff he's ever heard. "I want to know why *you* always have to be the one who sacrifices?"

"I don't mind."

"Really?" He leans close. "Then tell me why you were upset last night and this morning?"

"I ... uh."

"I'll tell you why. Because you felt awful about giving away your gran's Garrick. One of the biggest things that connects you to her."

"This was for you," I say emphatically. "I promised you I would do everything I could to get the set, and I did. I never go back on my word."

He rakes a hand through his hair. "I wish you would've talked it over with me."

Is there a right answer to this? I don't even know. "And what would you have said?"

"That sometimes you need to speak up for what you want."

CHAPTER 25

LATER THAT NIGHT, Tilly walks through my apartment door for our rescheduled girls' night. "Oh my gosh, you need to see this." She's waving something in the air, and it takes me a full second for my brain to make the connection.

"Is that what I think it is?" I sit up from my reclined position on the couch. I've been home since eleven this morning, but most of the day has been a blur. I've been self-medicating by becoming a blanket burrito and vegging on CRMs (cheesy romance movies), while trying not to feel sorry for myself. The last part is a colossal failure. I lost my Garrick and most likely any chance with Leo.

"You know it! The firefighters' calendar. My manager gave them out today. I guess her sister's a dispatcher." She practically skips over and holds open the calendar to … February. "Is this not the hottest thing you've ever seen?"

My heart catapults into my throat. It's Leo, of course, but he's in his firefighter gear, sans helmet, holding a dog. The caption reads that Leo Mathis rescued a Yorkie named Boots from a burning house, and even after the fire was out, the dog wouldn't leave his arms. *I get it, Boots.* If I concentrate hard enough, I can feel the ghostly pressure of his muscles against my back. I want to crawl into that embrace so badly.

All this time, I thought the calendar consisted of a lot more skin with strategically placed extinguishers, and yet, it's highlighting how the firefighters serve the community. As if I need another example of how my mind always gets it wrong.

As I'm studying the warm tones in Leo's expression, Tilly inhales sharply.

She lowers beside me on the couch, her eyes bulging at the pile of wadded Kleenex and empty Queen Anne Cordial Cherries boxes. Yes, boxes. Not my proudest moment. "Okay, what's wrong?"

"Everything." I slump into my mound of blankets. Tilly worked all day, so I didn't get the chance to relay all that's happened. "I made a huge mistake."

"We need hot chocolate for this, I think." So while Tilly's pouring Ghirardelli powder into warmed milk, I'm cleaning up snotty tissues and telling her about trading the nativity sets and Leo's reaction.

"Have you talked to him since this morning?" she asks softly.

I toss a cordial cherry box into the garbage, wishing I could trash the consequences from my stupidly rash decisions just as easily. Too bad life doesn't work like that. "No." After our emotional discussion in the car, he was quiet the rest of the ride home. He wasn't rude or angry. Just silent. Which was probably the worst reaction I could imagine. It'd left the space between us filled with tension, my brain filling the time and stillness with too many fears about what he was thinking. After he retrieved his truck at the fire station, we went our separate ways. He didn't take the Vallerton, which speaks volumes. "It was all for him, but I think I ended up scaring him off."

"Honestly ..." Tilly hands me my mug, and we return to the sofa. "I think he hates that you gave up so much."

If Pap hadn't told him how special the Garrick was, Leo

would've never known. Worse, Leo's right. That nativity ignited my love for what is now my livelihood.

When I was ten, Gran taught me about antiques and how fun it was to hunt them down, like a historical scavenger hunt. As a challenge, she asked me to pick out an antique and we'd search for it during our spare time. Because it was around Christmas, I picked the Garrick nativity set. Little Greta didn't understand antique specifics, such as condition, rarity, and market demand, but only thought the artist made Mary really beautiful. It wasn't until Pap had taken us to Nashville, nearly a year later, that I spotted the set. We traveled there for some random estate sale, and the Garrick was sitting between yellowed doilies and salt and pepper shakers shaped like roosters. I'll never forget how Gran's eyes misted at my excitement. It was like I finally found my thing. The price of the set was a steal, making Gran even prouder. "Yeah, he knows the story behind it."

"It's more than that." She sets her mug on the coffee table and brackets my shoulders with both hands. "I love you—you know this—but sometimes you're absolutely oblivious."

I can't argue with her there. I thought I was doing the right thing when I traded the sets.

"Girl, the man's in love with you." She shakes her head, her gaze squinting as if my ignorance is physically painful to watch. "And not some grade-school crush either. Mitchell told me when he called Leo about your run-in with the snowdrift, the man was having lunch with Chief Todd and Mayor Perkins. He abandoned his superiors to go save you." She splays a hand over her heart with a dreamy sigh.

"He said it was a work thing and wasn't a big deal."

"To him, it probably wasn't. Not compared to you."

Did he miss an important meeting? It would have to be something huge if Vernon Perkins was involved. No doubt Silver Creek's mayor didn't appreciate Leo's disappearing act. And he did it for me. "I think I messed up."

"As I said, he probably hates that you sacrificed so much."

Her head tilts, her dark hair spilling over her shoulder. "Why exactly *did* you give up the set? Tell me, what was going on in your head? I'm struggling to see why you handed over a valuable family heirloom to a total stranger."

When phrased like that, I look like an idiot. "It was automatic." My brain's been replaying those moments all day but without supplying any answers. "I can't explain it. I felt like it was expected of me. Which is stupid because the woman didn't know I had a Garrick until I told her."

"Almost as if … you're conditioned to act that way."

I look at her and can practically hear all the disjointed pieces of my life finally clicking into place. "I'm the queen of spades."

"Um, repeat that." Tilly shifts closer, making a crumpled tissue—one I must've missed in my rushed clean-up job—topple onto the floor. It's gross, but I'm on the edge of an epiphany. "Because for a second I thought you said you're—"

"The queen of spades." I can see it so clearly. "I have the queen of spades complex."

Tilly grabs her hot chocolate mug, cupping it with both hands, as if gleaning from its warmth. "Are you just making up complexes or are you in full-blown crisis mode?"

"It's from the game of Hearts. Nobody wants to be stuck with the queen of spades because she costs you the most penalty points. If she's in your hand, you pass her off. She gets shuffled around until someone is eventually stuck with her."

"Okay. I'm with you so far, I think."

"Mom didn't like the hand she was dealt. She didn't want me. She passed me on to Gran and Pap. They were stuck with me, and I did everything I could to be good, so they wouldn't see me as penalty points."

"Oh, honey." She sets her mug down and wraps an arm around me. "Is that how you really feel?"

"Growing up, Gran constantly complained about how selfish my mom was. My little brain understood that selfishness disappointed Gran, and I guess I disciplined myself to act the opposite. I thought of myself last. Which isn't always a bad thing but …"

"There's a difference between giving from your heart and giving as a default response."

"Tilly!" I hug her. "How are you so good at this?"

"I told you that a barista is like a bartender. I hear problems, I assess. I give people advice and sometimes an extra shot of espresso. But since I know you, this one was easy. Now." She sets a hand on mine. "Can I offer a suggestion?"

"Of course."

"Talk to your mom." Tilly gives a compassionate smile. "She might not be as selfish as Gran thought. She could have a valid reason behind her choices."

"You're right." I've thought the same before, but the hurt would often blur my logic. "I'm planning on talking to her after work tomorrow. I need to make up for emotionally unloading on her, then running off to Sugarvale."

"Another suggestion? Since I'm on a roll here. You might want to book a chat with Kennedy."

I nod. "Good idea." Kennedy Graham is a family counselor who attends our church. She wears Louis Vuitton and has the uncanny ability to peer into your soul. Mom and I should consider making an appointment with her.

I look at my best friend, grateful she's here. "Thank you, Tilly."

She smiles. "We've had each other's back since first grade."

Yeah, we have. Which is why I need to explain one more thing. "I've been keeping another secret."

Her eyes widen. "Yes?"

"You know how we thought the Silver Creek Secret Santa is Fletcher Thomas?"

"It's Leo, isn't it?!" She swipes the calendar from the coffee table and raises it high, as if I need a visual. But really, it's distracting because … wow. Leo holding a puppy is the dopamine shot my weary system craves but can't get. Because, like the picture, the man himself seems out of reach. "Tell me it's Leo!"

"Uh, no." I force my gaze off Mr. February and onto Tilly. "It was Gran. And now it's me."

Her mouth drops. "What? How?"

"Let me explain."

When I finish detailing everything, she lets out a whistle. "Girl, you've had a wild month."

"I still don't have a candidate yet." I retrieve the folder from the desk drawer I shoved it in earlier and hand it to Tilly. "Here are the letters. The top one is Leo's pick. A woman submitted on behalf of her neighbor. She's brief and to the point. I'm leaning toward it, but I want to know your thoughts."

As she reads the letter, her head tilts, then she gasps. "I know this lady. It's Elana Keller." She shakes the paper. "She comes to the café every Thursday morning around nine."

"What's she like?" I reclaim my seat. "Is she one to spin stories?"

"No, not at all. Elana's the blunt, honest type." The CRM goes to commercial, and Tilly grabs the remote. "Ugh, I hate these." It's a pharmaceutical ad that offers a product with a gazillion side effects. "Your eyes might bleed, but at least your armpits won't itch. Mute!" And she does. "Now, back to Elana and the letter."

"She doesn't mention the neighbor's name." I scan the page again as if it will magically appear. "Do you know who she's talking about?"

"I don't." She crimps her mouth together with a shake of her head. "Maybe you should do some Secret Santa stalking. I'll text you when she comes to the café."

"Hmm. I can't leave the store unattended."

"Oh." Tilly clasps her hands together, her eyes brightening. "I'll tell my manager I need to take my break early, then I'll come cover for you. You only need a few minutes, right?"

"Probably. But wouldn't that be really early for a break?" Tilly would only have been at the café for two hours.

"Yes." She pats my hand. "But it's time you let other people help you."

I won the best friend lotto. "Are you mad at me for not telling you about the Secret Santa stuff?"

"What, you think I'd get upset over you telling Leo before the girl who's been like a sister to you for twenty years?" She folds her arms in an exaggerated huff, then cracks a smile. "No, I'm not mad. I just wish you had said so sooner because I could've helped you."

"Leo said the same thing."

"Ah, wise dude." Her gaze turns empathetic. "Maybe this is your hint to let others carry the load with you. Maybe even *for* you sometimes. Not because we have to, but because we want to."

The next evening, I turn on M*A*S*H in the living room for Pap, who's cradling Oggy on his lap in the recliner, then join Mom in the kitchen. It's been a long day. Still no word from Leo, and I'm trying not to freak out about it. He probably needs some space, but how much is too much? I sigh and take a seat at the table, eyeing the plate of cookies before me.

Mom claims the chair beside mine and gestures toward the desserts. "Not a raisin in sight."

"My stomach thanks you." I grab a chocolate chip cookie and take a full bite before launching into my apology. "Sorry about the other day. I shouldn't have lost it like I did."

She gives a sad smile. "Yes, you should've. I deserved everything you said and owe you an explanation."

"My main question is *why*? Why did you stay away for so long?"

"Because I was scared." Her blue eyes dim. "And ashamed."

"Of me?"

"No," she admits quickly. "Never of you. I was ashamed because I had you so young. I was only fifteen when I got pregnant. I couldn't even drive, and here I was having a kid. I don't even know who your father is. What kind of mom can't even tell her daughter who her dad is? There's been a lot of shame for a lot of years." Her voice shakes, but she holds my gaze. "When I would visit, I felt like an intruder, an outsider."

I'd be lying if I said I wasn't overly curious about my dad's identity. Gran and Pap never discussed it, and I never felt my relationship was solid enough to ask Mom. My dad has always been this fuzzy shadow in my mind's eye. "But you're my mother."

"A mother who had no idea how to parent. I was a kid myself. As I grew older, I felt in the way and didn't want to interfere with how your grandmother was raising you. A sense of failure hung over me every time I'd visit. When I'd leave, it would go away, but not the ache. The ache stayed with me." Her eyes fill with tears. "I missed my child, but I feared messing up again. I know Gran thought I only wanted my freedom. Truth is, I was scared."

I let her words marinate in my brain, processing. "So you were afraid of being a bad parent?"

She runs a finger over the handle of her teacup. "I didn't want to mess up your life like I did mine. I was scared I would make bad decisions that would hurt you. With Gran and Pap, you were safe. I know it doesn't make sense, but my mind wasn't always in a good state."

"And now?"

"I've been trying to get my life in line. I renewed my faith and have been going to counseling. I'm nowhere near perfect, but I've come a long way."

I set the rest of my cookie on the plate. "I understand your fears and hesitations when I was a kid, but I've been an adult for several years." I keep my tone free from accusation, but I'm sure

Mom can read the emotion in my face. "You didn't even try until Gran passed."

"Gran didn't want me around, and that was its own kind of pain. To know that I'm a disappointment to her. But I should've tried to repair our relationship. I could've at least been around you more. My fears held me back. I should've been brave, but I didn't know how."

I guess Mom and I aren't too different in that respect.

"When your gran passed, I knew time was slipping away. I had to try. I know I returned like a whirlwind, swooping in and wanting to help any way I could. I thought if I could help you, then I maybe could learn how to be a mother along the way."

I swipe a tear from my cheek. "I'm sorry I didn't know how to talk or act around you. I'm learning too." I tell her about the counseling idea, and she readily agrees.

She grabs my hand and squeezes. "I hope you know that I love you. I'm so proud of the woman you've become."

"Thank you, Mom. I love you too." In time, I'll learn to trust her. I'll tell her stories from my childhood she'd missed. Eventually, I'll inform her about Gran being the Silver Creek Secret Santa. An absence of twenty-five years can't be healed in five months, but if we both put the effort in, I can see us growing closer.

I'm unlocking The Memory Bank doors on Thursday morning when my phone buzzes in my pocket with an incoming text. I already know it's Tilly, but the uptick in my heart rate tells me I'd hoped it was Leo. After my talk with Mom Tuesday night, I returned to my apartment and repeatedly checked my phone for anything from him. Nothing. I kept my cell by me all Wednesday until finally I couldn't stand it. I called him and got his voicemail.

These last three days have been an awakening of sorts. Past

Greta would've projected her suppressed feelings on a new sewing project or binge-watching a Netflix series. Present Greta is healing. While dissecting my psyche has not been the happiest of pastimes, it's been good for me. Good for me like doing cardio or drinking a kale smoothie. It's not fun or even palatable, but future me will be grateful. I swipe to open my phone and read Tilly's text.

TILLY

Operation Elana!

Ah, Elana Keller, the lady who nominated her neighbor, is at the café. This means Tilly is about to take her break and come cover for me. I don't know what I'll tell Elana, but I need more information about her neighbor. My goal is to at least get the name. Thankfully, I don't have any customers, so I run back to the office and grab my coat and gloves.

Within a minute, the bell above the door jingles. "I'm here," Tilly calls.

I'm shoving arms through my coat while hustling to the front where she's waiting. "Thanks for doing this."

"How many times did you listen to 'Eye of the Tiger' this morning?" Tilly tugs off her gloves. "Don't lie."

"Whatever you think is overkill, it's one less than that."

"Okay, basically, you had it on repeat." She squeezes my shoulder. "You got this. Elana's at the counter in a bright pink sweater. Platinum blonde. Can't miss her!" She shoos me out the door.

The cold air stings my face. We haven't had any more snowfall since Sunday, but the temps have been hovering around twenty degrees with a wind chill of negative hundred. Slight exaggeration. I dip my chin into my coat collar and do that scuttle-walk thing people do when they want to get somewhere quicker, but don't want to break into a full-fledged jog. I'm so focused on getting to the café that I nearly bulldoze Fletcher Thomas.

He grabs my elbows, steadying me. "Good morning, Greta. It's a little early for women to be falling into my arms."

I roll my eyes. "You were blocking the entrance, and I was about to take you down, but whatever."

He chuckles. "How's everything?"

I know what he means. *Everything* meaning my festive mission. "Okay, I guess." It's going horribly, but Fletcher doesn't need to know that. "Hey, have you heard from Leo, uh, Remington, lately?"

Fletcher shakes his head. "Chief Todd said Remington's out of town." He adjusts his collar against the wind. "I told you the man can't sit still."

"Ah, I see." No, I do *not* see. Why didn't Leo tell me he was leaving? Especially after I shared about my background? I'm sure it's only temporary. Not like he up and moved away. I want to say this to Fletcher, but he's already retreating.

"I have to get to the office." The wind picks up, disturbing his perfectly styled hair. "If you need anything, let me know."

I give a parting smile, but my mind's on Leo. As if my whole system malfunctions, I stop just inside the entrance of the café, next to a potted plant covered in twinkling lights. My brain scrambles for possible scenarios. What if ... Leo's tracking down my Garrick? The thought launches into my brain, then flies right back out. I never told him Candace's name, first or last. The man couldn't even locate me last year with full knowledge of my first name *and* my hometown. No, he must've left for another reason, and I truly hope it's not because I scared him off.

All momentum for Operation Elana is lost. I can't think straight, let alone be clever enough to glean information from the woman. But time is ticking. Tilly only has a half hour before she has to return. I need to get something right this week. After a few deep breaths, I spot Elana at the counter, just as Tilly described. I nab the stool two down from my target. Apparently, I'm using spy jargon now. Whatever works to keep me motivated on this assignment and not think of kisses beneath a candied mistletoe. Elana glances over and smiles. She's probably ten years older than me and has excellent taste in handbags.

The barista takes my order, and once he walks away, I say. "It's freezing out, but I will forever order iced coffee."

"Me too." She lifts her drink in solidarity.

I don't expect to give an Oscar-worthy performance. My Christmas pageant era only taught me that I don't have the right facial structure to pull off wearing a foam star on my head, but I give it a go anyway. "Wait, are you Elana Keller?"

She smiles. "I am."

"I-I think we have a mutual friend." I intended to mention Tilly, but with a surge of boldness, I dive right in. "Your neighbor, I think. She lives on Bryan Lane." I make a show of putting my hand to my brow. "Man, my brain needs caffeine because I remembered your name, but hers isn't coming to me. She's older and is going through a really rough patch."

"You mean Adelaide?"

"Springfield?" My face drops.

"Yeah, that's her. She's my neighbor."

Looks like I wasn't fibbing after all. Adelaide Springfield *is* a mutual acquaintance. Though I had no idea she's the woman from Elana's Secret Santa letter.

Elana claims the stool beside mine as if we're instant friends. "I just feel so bad for her. Her husband got injured on the job, and his employer won't take responsibility. So now they have no income because she can't work either, since she's taking care of him." She shakes her head slowly, her bobbed hair sliding against her jaw. "I think she's becoming desperate for money."

"I've noticed that too." Mostly because she's been trying to con me out of thousands for several months. Now I understand why she's amped up her visits to The Memory Bank. But I didn't realize Adelaide had become a caregiver. My heart softens. While I was supporting Gran, I never had any financial setbacks, but I can imagine how that would add so much more pressure to the caregiving role.

"I wish I could help her," I say with all the concern I feel, hoping that Elana takes the bait.

"Me too. I wrote to that community thing they have every year. The Secret Santa. I'm hoping they will help her. I think she might be slipping into debt. It's awful during any time of the year, but especially tough during the holiday season, you know?"

I'm about to respond, but the very topic of our conversation is scurrying past the Brewtiful Grounds window, carrying a large box.

I know exactly where she's going.

CHAPTER 26

AFTER A RUSHED GOODBYE TO ELANA, I race toward The Memory Bank. Tilly is fabulous, but she's not mentally ready for an Adelaide encounter. The older woman's load is cumbersome, slowing her steps and giving me a chance to catch up to her.

"Oh!" Adelaide squeaks as I reach for the handle at the same time as her. "I thought you were inside."

"My friend's covering for me. Here, let me help you with that." I prop open the door with my foot, and to my surprise, Adelaide lets me take the large cardboard box off her hands.

"Be careful with it." Her panicky voice follows me inside.

Tilly's behind the counter, scrolling on her phone. She sees me and hops to her feet. "Success?" Her eyes are bright with anticipation, which makes my heart happy all over again that she's in on this secret.

I give a quick nod. "All because of you." I set the box on the counter and squeeze my friend in a hug. "Thanks, girl. I owe you."

"No." She pulls back and gives my shoulders a little shake. "You do *not* owe me. We look out for each other."

I smile and wave as she rushes back to work. I'm still

learning to accept help without feeling as if there are always strings attached. What's that old adage—"It's a marathon, not a sprint"? In real life, I hate both. But figuratively, I can see the value.

"Greta." Adelaide taps the side of the box, snapping me to the moment. "Santa has nothing on me."

"Oh really?" For the past several months, when Adelaide would sweep into the store, my main objective was to endure her scheming spiel and get her out as quickly as possible. I'd never taken the time to truly look at her or even get to know her. She's approached this counter at least once every two weeks, yet I had no idea her husband had been injured or that they were struggling. How many others cross my path who are fighting battles, suffering in silence, and I'm completely unaware? I'm sure I didn't always say the right words, but ... was I kind? Because kindness is a language we can all speak.

This new consciousness has me smiling at Adelaide. Her roots are outgrown, revealing more tinsel gray among the brown. The small creases fanning from the corner of her eyes and framing her mouth are the only other signs that time's catching up with her. But overall, the woman exudes energy. Which is impressive, considering what I discovered about her recent circumstances. I feel like I can understand her better.

"I thought of you the moment I set eyes on this." She tugs free a beach towel that served as a protective covering. With careful movements, she lifts a small trunk from the box. "This is the real deal."

My head rears slightly. "You didn't get this at Bowken's Flea Market." Because what I'm looking at is a Harrison & Co. New York cabin-sized steamer trunk that's at least a hundred years old.

"This was in my aunt's basement."

I run my hand over the floral embossed metal panels. The oak sides and lid seem in good condition. The key is attached to the latch by a velvet ribbon. I inspect the inside and note some cosmetic wear, but nothing out of the ordinary for a piece this old. "This is … a nice find."

"Well." She straightens with a gleam in her eye. "I believe it was once used by Calvin Coolidge."

I snort. "Adelaide, we were doing so good." I seriously doubt this trunk belonged to the former president, especially since the initials P.D.B. are painted in red on the top. "I can give you three hundred dollars for this."

Her jaw slacks at the sum, but then she counters, "Three fifty."

"Deal." I already have customers in mind who'd be interested. We fly through the paperwork, and I give Adelaide the cash.

Her gaze pins to the wad of twenties in her hand, and she softly whispers, "This should help some."

She didn't mean for me to hear. But I did, and this is the *in* I've been waiting for. "I'm sorry about what happened to your husband." I keep my tone gentle.

Her eyes snap to mine, and I expect her to clamp her carefully constructed mask into place, but instead, she lets it crack. "Thank you. It's been somewhat difficult."

I blink at her vulnerability but quickly recover. "Is there anything I can do?"

She pats my hand. "You're sweet, but unless you have an attorney in your back pocket or maybe a major news network to command, it's helpless. We can't get anyone to listen." The fire returns to her eyes as she relays the tragic accident that stole her husband's mobility. "Our lives are forever changed, but his employer won't take responsibility. The injustice of it all is enough to make you feel—"

"Hopeless? Like no one cares?"

"Yes, exactly." Her face softens. Then, as if her transparency hit its time limit, she squares her shoulders with a lift of her chin. "Well, I should be going."

"Oh, one more thing. Wait here." I hustle to my office and

grab one of my favorite books from the desk drawer. While in the back, the business line, which I left on the counter by my cell, rings. I return to the showroom, but don't get to it in time.

I hold out the book to Adelaide. "This is for you. Gran gave me this when I was first interested in antiques." Of course, my copy is upstairs, all marked up and highlighted. "It details what to look for when buying antiques. It breaks the information down into different categories, so it's easy to read. This will give you the knowledge to shop with confidence." And maybe stop trying to rip me off.

She takes the book from my hand, surprise marking her features. "Thank you."

"Merry Christmas, Adelaide."

I close the shop a few minutes early to catch Fletcher before he leaves for the day. Though I didn't have to worry because I find him in his office putting golf balls into a Sheetz cup.

"Things slow?" I ask with a knock.

He glances up and smiles. "Two Greta sightings in one day. Come in."

"I brought this for you." I hand him a paper with all of Adelaide's information. "The chosen one for this year's Silver Creek Secret Santa."

He props his putter against the wall and grins. "That wasn't so hard, was it?"

"A total breeze." Like catching a cool breeze in the Sahara.

He scans the page and raises a brow. "Adelaide Springfield? Really?"

I sit in the same chair I had when I came here almost a month ago. So much has changed. I've changed. "Adelaide's husband got injured on the job and isn't getting any support. Does your uncle still take on workers' comp cases?"

"He does."

"Good. I want to hire him to represent Adelaide's husband. I detailed everything." I nod at the paper. "I also emailed you a copy."

He lowers onto his plush seat and continues to read. "Says you will cover legal fees, offer debt relief, and you want to get her house modified." He lowers the page and looks at me. "Modified?"

"I want to make their entire home safe and accessible. I'm thinking of installing ramps, widening doorways for his wheelchair, and anything else that will help."

After a long second, he nods. "This will work."

"As for the media coverage, she's called the major news networks about what happened, and no one's gotten back with her."

"Leave it to me." He smiles and scribbles down something. "I can ensure they cover the story the way Adelaide wants and place an emphasis on the solution."

"The solution being sticking it to the former employer."

He laughs. "I'll do my best."

"I'm sure you will."

He leans back in his chair and studies me. "Your grandmother would be proud of you."

"Thank you." Though I think it's time for me to be proud of myself. For so long, I've been living for other people's approval. I'm through curating my behavior to gain acceptance. "Well, Fletcher, it's been … fun." It's been freeing. In searching for the recipient, it seems I've found myself along the way. Though it wasn't without its sacrifice. Leo and the Garrick. One won't return my calls, and the other won't return ever.

I stand to leave.

"I almost forgot." He rises to his feet. "Do you happen to be available Saturday night? It's the company Christmas party."

"I actually have plans." Mom and I are having a bake night. We have lofty aspirations of baking ten different kinds of cookies for a dessert exchange at the senior center. I'm not sure what the rest of my weekend looks like. I still haven't heard from Leo, but after Adelaide left, I called him. Voicemail again. So I shot off a text, thanking him for helping. I was polite, and I hated that the tone sounded suspiciously like a goodbye. If I can't get a happily ever after, maybe someone else can. "But if you need someone pretty awesome for a date, my friend Tilly has Saturday evening off."

He smirks. "Miss Ohio's second runner-up?"

Yep, he's her soulmate. "Something like that." I grab a pen from his desk, write her number on a sticky note, and place it in his hand. "If I don't see you before, Merry Christmas, Fletcher." With a smile, I return the pen to its home.

He glances down at the note, then to me. "Merry Christmas."

As I leave the office, I text my best friend.

GRETA

The Secret Santa mission is complete!!!

TILLY

Santa emoji and woman in red dress dancing emoji

GRETA

Also Fletcher Thomas might ask you on a date

TILLY

WHAT?!?!

CHAPTER 27

IT'S MONDAY NIGHT. The fifteenth.

At a quarter till seven, I pull into my usual parking spot behind The Memory Bank and … breathe. Being only ten days before Christmas, the park is packed, though the tightness in my chest has nothing to do with facing crowds, but facing Leo. That is, if he shows.

My phone's been silent all weekend. It's stupid of me to think he'll be waiting for me by the turtledoves display. I shouldn't expect to see his flirty grin or piercing eyes after I pushed him away. I'm usually too much, but my actions last week were over the top. So why am I clinging to this fragile hope? If I learned anything over these past months, it's that life is riddled with unknowns, but it's up to me to keep my heart open to something new. From being the Secret Santa to cultivating a relationship with my mom to discovering more about myself, I learned that I could face hard things even if it terrifies me.

The anniversary date of Gran's passing was a dark taunt in the alcoves of my mind all year, but I woke this morning determined to remember her legacy rather than dwell on my missing her. Yeah, the feelings were there—are here—but being the Secret

Santa has taught me to look outward, and I can see her in everything she loved. Today, I celebrated her life by making her favorite meals and spending time with Pap and Mom. Pap dug out old photo albums, and we revisited memories, Mom sharing a few I've never heard.

With that, I kill the engine, but somehow it feels like I'm turning the ignition to my dreams with the pedal to the floor. I have no clue what awaits me a hundred yards from here—most likely a Leo-less scene—but I'm stepping out anyway. Browsing those albums and looking back on Gran's full life inspired me to think ahead about my own goals and wants. I'd rather reflect on my days and be able to say more "I trieds" than "What-ifs." So tonight is me trying, me chasing the moment.

I make my way toward the park. Unlike last year, there's no snow blanketing the ground. It had all melted over the course of the week, but the cold temperatures remain. Is it really December in Ohio if you can't see your breath in puffy vapors? I slide my hands into my coat pockets and snake through the throng of people.

I've visited this place countless times during the holidays, but the lights seem brighter, and the air's scented with kettle corn and wonder. Children's squeals, the clop of hooves in the distance from a horse-drawn carriage, and the soft strains of "O Holy Night" floating through the speakers are this evening's soundtrack. I pass the North Pole Pavilion, complete with a grinning Santa Ned. He spots me through the window, and I lift my hand in greeting. I have a whole new appreciation for his role.

Fletcher called me this afternoon, telling me everything's in place for the Secret Santa recipient reveal on the news next week. The local news anchors plan on visiting the Springfield residence with one of those giant checks and the Silver Creek High School marching band, which will play carols. I guess Adelaide and her husband met and fell in love during band camp in tenth grade. How Fletcher unearthed that detail is beyond me, but I love that he went the extra mile to make the event more special. Plus, it proves that Fletcher Thomas is a bit of a romantic, something Tilly swears by. She accompanied him to his company Christmas dinner and, by the end of the evening, was half in love with the man.

I slow my steps.

This is it. One final curve brings me to the turtledoves, the park bench. The towering street clock reads seven sharp. With my pulse pounding, I ease through the foot traffic, bumping shoulders with someone and nearly tripping over a divot in the sidewalk. The crowd clears as if they can sense the importance of this moment.

I draw in the cold air and slide my eyes shut. The surrounding sounds shift and blend into a low hum. What happens in the next ten seconds could devastate me or … not. But I need to know the answer. Slowly I lift my lashes, my heart a wild cadence.

As the world comes into focus, so does Leo.

He came.

Leo stands by Gran and Pap's light display, wearing the same coat I mended last year.

I bite my bottom lip in response to the rising emotion. Though my hope remains as delicate as the snowflakes now swirling around me. We weren't supposed to get flurries tonight, but it seems this moment is filled with the unexpected. Though just because he showed up doesn't guarantee his feelings haven't dulled toward me. He could be here only to keep his promise, not wanting me to be alone on this pivotal day. Because he's that kind of guy.

I force my feet forward, my gaze transfixed on him. The second I'm in reach, he pulls me close, crushing me to his chest.

He breathes me in. "Man, I missed you."

"You made it," I say, almost in reassurance to myself that this is real. He is real.

He pulls back, eyes on my face as if memorizing every detail. "You thought I'd ghost you again?"

His incredulous tone, matched with the way his arms tighten around me, softens the rusted edges of my doubts. "When you don't answer my calls or texts, it causes a girl to wonder."

"I'm sorry." His left hand abandons its home on my waist to brush a snowflake from my cheek. His stubble is longer than usual, like he hasn't shaved in days, and my skin tingles with the urge to run a hand over his jaw. "I lost my phone somewhere in Berlin."

Surprise lifts my brows. "You went to Amish country?" Berlin is known for Ohio's largest Amish community. The town's rich culture and heritage mark it as a tourist attraction, especially during Christmastime. There's also a huge antique mall. Was … he looking for another Garrick? That's the only reason I could see him visiting. It's such a sweet gesture, but I would've told him I already checked with the antique dealers there.

"More like Berlin, Germany."

"What?" My shocked squeak is loud enough to attract a few glances. "As in—across the Atlantic, thousands of miles away—Berlin?"

He chuckles at my high-pitched inquiry. "That would be the one."

"Fletcher said you were out of town but neglected to say out of the country. Sheesh."

He toys with the edge of my coat's belt, as if he wants to reach for me again but is being patient. "It was a last-minute thing."

"I've got so many questions, but I've been rehearsing what I'm going to say, and it's starting to get hazy."

He cracks a smile—and oh I missed those dimples—but I can't get distracted.

"I'm sorry about Monday. You were right to be angry. I offered the set without thinking because it was a knee-jerk reaction. I've been impulsive like that all my life, feeling as if I had to give up things to keep the rest of the world happy. I promised you I'd do all I could to get you the Vallerton, though I went about it the wrong way." I meet his soft gaze. "It's a brutal lesson to learn, but I think I'm better for it."

He sweeps up my gloved hands in his bare ones. "I wasn't angry at you. I didn't want you to give up something you loved. That set is special to you."

I nod. "It was."

"After you dropped me off at the station, I let Chief Todd know I was leaving town and drove back to Sugarvale. I remembered what you said about that other antique store."

"Alice's Emporium?" I mentioned to Leo at the hotel that we should visit her place, though I hadn't realized he was paying that much attention. I should've known better.

He nods. "I returned to see if she had a Garrick, but the shop was closed. Alice passed away two years ago."

"Oh, I'm sorry to hear that." She was a lot like Midge but with a softer approach to life.

"Around that time, my mom called, and I explained to her about the sets. Turns out, she knows a lot of people who are into antiques. Is it a rich people's hobby or something?"

I laugh. "Well, antiques do get expensive."

"Anyway." He shrugs. "She has a friend in Berlin who's downsizing her collections. So, I bought you something." He tugs me toward the bench, and I spot a box, my heart billowing with hope. His slow grin builds as he watches me. "Open it."

With shaky hands, I lift the flaps. "Cinnamon bears?" Several packages of my favorite childhood candy fill the box. "Um, Leo, you didn't need to go to foreign lands for these. They have them at Walmart."

He steps closer with a chuckle. "Look underneath."

After I pull the bags of bears out and set them on the bench, I see another box inside. I work free the lid and spot it immediately. "A Garrick! You found a Garrick!" My eyes sting as I pore over the distinct figures. The antiquarian in me wants to inspect each piece to ensure the set's legit, but that can wait. What can't wait is me launching into Leo's arms. "Thank you."

His hands settle on my back, and he brushes his lips to my temple. "That's *your* Garrick, Greta."

"What? How?" I rear back so fast I nearly knock Leo's jaw. I make up for it by pressing a quick kiss to it. "My Garrick traveled abroad?"

"Long story short. My mom's friend had a set that I flew over and got. Then I came back to the States this morning and went to New Castle."

"And that is?"

"In Pennsylvania. Where Candace and Sal Whitman live."

My jaw drops. "How'd you know—"

"When you were talking with Candace Whitman in the ladies' room, her husband was trying to sell me office equipment. He only came to SugarFest because he heard a rumor that Mrs. Langston needed new copiers. I couldn't escape the conversation without his card."

Ah, that's why—when we were standing outside the hotel— Sal looked pointedly at Leo and told him, *"Think about what I said."* I'd thought it was odd then, but now it makes sense.

"This afternoon, I convinced them to trade the Garrick I found with the Garrick you gave. Plus, I've got a state-of-the-art printer arriving Friday, so there's that."

I laugh even as a tear slides down my cheek. "No one has ever done something like this for me." I'm still wrapping my brain around it. All week I thought he refused my calls and texts, yet he was tracking down a nativity set. "That was a lot of trouble to go through." Especially since he lost his phone. I'd be terrified to be in a foreign place without having all that's familiar at my fingertips.

He brushes away the tear and gathers me close again. "I remembered what you said." His voice is soothing as he strokes my hair. "When a man's in love, he'd do all he could to make her world right again."

His words are like a slow drip into my heart, steadily filling my soul until my entire being is affected by that single sentence. Leo crossed oceans to fix the problem I created. He recovered the treasure I stupidly gave up. But most importantly, he's in love with me. Could anything be equal to that? I wind my arms around his neck. "I can't even say how much that means."

He drops a kiss on my lips. "Looks like we're even because I can't say how much you mean to me."

I press against him, my insides ready to explode with happiness. "Now that you brought this set, you have another one to deliver. It seems we're both playing Santa this Christmas." That sweet widow will be overjoyed.

"The Vallerton." He smiles. "I plan on going tomorrow night. Would you like to meet her?"

"I would." The wind picks up, but I can hardly feel it. I'm cocooned in the surrealness of it all. "And to think this started by my skewering you with an elf." I skim my gloved fingers over my stitchwork on his coat. It's strange to think how little things, small decisions, can accumulate, changing the direction of your life. And sometimes, those moments that seem to tear apart your soul can rebuild your vision. I didn't see how much I abandoned myself until Leo challenged me to chase what I want. Which reminds me. "I have something for you too." I disentangle from his embrace and reach into my pocket. My gift seems silly compared to the enormity of his, but it's time for me to be brave. "I promised you I'd fill this out."

His brows lift as I hand him the folded paper. The confusion in his gaze clears as he takes in his own handwriting—*Greta's Christmas Wishlist*—at the top of the page. Over a week ago, we sat in his living room, and Leo insisted on knowing what I wanted.

I wrote two words:

Leo Mathis

His eyes warm as he points to his name. "You mean this?"

"I do." I step closer. "You told me it's okay to speak up for what I want." I skim my lips over the corner of his mouth. "And I want you."

Fire burns in his gaze, and I want nothing more than to be warmed by his touch. "Likewise, Greta Carlton." He pulls me to him and kisses me in the glow of twinkling lights.

EPILOGUE

LEO'S GOING to ask me to marry him. A girl can sense this kind of thing. Or maybe it's just cold, hard facts. The reasons for my suspicion are as follows: A ring of mine disappeared a few weeks ago, only to turn up in the same place a day later. A subtle yet effective way to get my ring size. This morning, when exchanging gifts, Leo said he's held one back for the "right time." After Christmas dinner with Mom and Pap, Leo suggested I dress warmly because he's taking me somewhere special outdoors. And that special place *must* be the turtledoves display, where Gran and Pap got engaged over sixty years ago.

Now it's my turn.

How perfect would it be to seal our love at that very spot?!

Which is why, when Leo guides me past the bend leading to our park bench, my steps falter. I'm rubbernecking like crazy, but he's not catching the hint. I squeeze his hand. "I thought we were visiting the turtledoves."

His gaze meets mine, and I realize *he* knows *I* know. By the handsome curl to his lips, he's not exactly bothered that I'm onto him. Instead, he wraps an arm around my back and lowers his head. "That's their moment." He points to the street clock where the turtledoves are nestled nearby. "Let's go get ours."

A surge of love swells in my chest, and I vow to follow those dimples anywhere. At this point, I don't care if he drops to one knee next to the porta-johns where Josie hijacked the light display two years ago. Okay, I might mind a little.

I glance around, taking in the sights and sounds of the season. Last Christmas everything spun by in a haze, but this year, I purposed to live in the present. Leo and Tilly helped me with this year's Secret Santa project, and we were able to select a recipient quickly this time. Just like last year, I didn't watch the big reveal on the news. For some reason, it didn't feel right, like it's almost transactional gifting if I saw their emotional response. As I've learned to receive help with no strings attached, I want to freely give without reciprocation of any kind.

I shake off my deep thoughts in time to realize we're close to the opening of … Killer Hill.

My grin breaks free, and we quicken our steps, which turns into a full-blown race. Leo hooks me by the waist, so I don't reach the crest of the hill before he does. My laugh spills into the snow-laden air.

He hauls me back against his chest and his lips brush my ear. "Do you trust me?"

"Yes." I'm breathless, and it has nothing to do with my recent sprint.

"Good," he says, slipping his hands over my eyes. "I'll guide you."

"If you dare push me down the hill, Leo Mathis, I will tell the old men you want to be a Maverick."

He tightens his hold, and I can feel his huff of laughter against my neck. "That's low." He may talk tough, but Leo loves those guys as much as I do.

Gently, he leads me along and removes his touch.

That's when I see it.

At the bottom of Killer Hill is a winter wonderland. Leo

decorated the surrounding evergreens with twinkle lights and lanterns. I squint and am able to make out a tarp on the ground. Oh my gosh. "A winter picnic!"

"Yeah, I was told once that hot chocolate after sledding is a must."

I open my mouth, but Leo seems to anticipate my question because he moves to one of the trees where he propped a sled. But not just any sled. "You fixed it."

Leo holds out the vintage piece I salvaged for my parade float. It's completely restored. He replaced the mangled rail and stained the wooden slats. He sets it on the edge of the hill and grins at me. "You're the only girl I'll ever share a sled with."

The one-sled trope. It's a thing now.

I lift on my toes and kiss him.

After several delicious minutes, he rests his forehead against mine. "I was going to wait until we got to the bottom of the hill, but I'm kind of nervous it will fall out of my pocket. I think"—he reaches into his coat pocket and lowers onto one knee, despite the four inches of snow—"that this will be safer on your finger." He peers up at me and opens a black velvet box.

My hand flies to my mouth at the platinum solitaire diamond.

"Greta Carlton, I love your beautiful heart, your clever mind, and the way you look at me in my firefighter gear."

I snort, but I'm also crying, so it comes out more like a gurgle.

Leo doesn't seem to notice because he continues, his own eyes shining. "I want to be the one who wakes up beside you every morning, to hear your addictive laugh, to be the man who makes you happy." He sets the ring box on his knee and gently removes the glove from my shaking hand. "I love you, Greta the Gatekeeper of my Heart. Will you marry me?"

"I love you too." Tears streaming down my face, I set my fingers into his. "Yes."

He matches my wide grin and slips on the ring. He launches to his feet, ignoring his snow-crusted pant leg, and takes me in his arms. I hold onto his shoulders, kissing him with all the love I feel. Who would've thought two years ago, dressed in a Mrs. Claus costume, I'd be standing in the same place? And yet, I'm not. I mean, physically, yes, but I'm not the approval-addicted, backward girl any longer. Through the support of those around me, I've grown and I'm just getting started.

Leo skims his lips across my cheek. "What do you say, future Mrs. Mathis?" He straightens the sled and pats the wooden slats. "Are you ready for this run?" The tone of his voice makes me think he means more than a jaunt on the sled. He's asking about the long run, with him.

"More than ready."

AUTHOR'S NOTES

NO raisins were harmed in the making of this book. Personally, I like them. My husband? Not so much. He sides with Greta in believing raisins are just grapes that gave up on life and decided to ruin people's taste buds in bitter revenge. Now that THAT is out of the way …

Thank you for reading *About Last Christmas*! This story began as a fun project solely for my enjoyment. I let my imagination run wild with all the things I adore about the holiday season, sprinkling in tidbits inspired by true life. For example, Killer Hill is a real place in my childhood hometown. I personally have raced down its slope at night and lived to share the story.

As for the Mavericks, there are hints of truth behind the fictional golden guys as well. I have older relatives who take their card-playing as serious as a courtroom cross-examination— every shuffle is sacred, every deal is do-or-die, and heaven help you if you table talk during a hand. Add my dear family with some *Return to Me* vibes, and the Mavericks were born. I hope they made you smile.

In addition to wanting to capture the wonder of the season, I also wrote this story as a love letter to Main Streets across America. Growing up, my family owned an auto parts store in the heart of a small town. I have wonderful memories of buying a bag of peach rings from the 5&10, ordering a cherry vanilla ice cream cone from Campbell's Cafe, and getting a frosted sugar cookie from Kretchmar's Bakery. Clearly, my memories revolve around food, but I've made my peace with it. Currently, I live less than a mile from a main street in a rural Ohio town, which is so utterly charming that it was named in the Top 25 Hallmark Christmas Towns Index. My little town has a famed street clock and hosts a yearly Christmas parade. Like Greta, I love the whimsical feeling of strolling down Main Street during the holidays. No matter what time of year you read this book, I hope the story fills you with joy, laughter, and the thrill of finding love in unexpected places.

ABOUT THE AUTHOR

Rachel Scott McDaniel is an award-winning author who writes historical and contemporary romance with heart, mystery, and humor. When she's not dreaming up happily-ever-afters, you can find her chasing adventures in Ohio with her husband and two amazing kids. Rachel loves hiking trails almost as much as plot twists and is always on the hunt for the next great story ... or snack. Connect with her at www.RachelScottMcDaniel.com or on your favorite social media platform!